FLORIAN

Also by Felix Salten

Bambi
Bambi's Children
Renni the Rescuer
A Forest World
The Hound of Florence
The City Jungle
Fifteen Rabbits

FLORIAN

The Emperor's Stallion

BAMBI'S CLASSIC ANIMAL TALES

FELIX SALTEN

Translated by ERICH POSSELT and
MICHEL KRAIKE

Aladdin

New York London Toronto Sydney New Delhi

ALADDIN

An imprint of Simon & Schuster Children's Publishing Division
1230 Avenue of the Americas, New York, New York 10020
This Aladdin paperback edition June 2015
Text copyright © 1933 by Paul Zsolnay Verlag; copyright
renewed © 1961 by Anna Katharina Wyler-Salten
English language translation copyright © 1934 by Bobbs-Merrill; copyright
renewed © 1962 by Anna Katharina Wyler-Salten, Erich Posselt, and Michael Kraike
Originally published in German in 1933 by
Paul Zsolnay Verlag as *Florian Das Pferd des Kaisers*
Cover illustration copyright © 2015 by Richard Cowdrey
Also available in an Aladdin hardcover edition.
All rights reserved, including the right of reproduction
in whole or in part in any form.
ALADDIN is a trademark of Simon & Schuster, Inc.,
and related logo is a registered trademark of Simon & Schuster, Inc.
For information about special discounts for bulk purchases,
please contact Simon & Schuster Special Sales at
1-866-506-1949 or business@simonandschuster.com.
The Simon & Schuster Speakers Bureau can bring authors
to your live event. For more information or to book an event
contact the Simon & Schuster Speakers Bureau at
1-866-248-3049 or visit our website at www.simonspeakers.com.
Cover design by Karin Paprocki
Interior design by Hilary Zarycky
The text of this book was set in Yana.
Manufactured in the United States of America 0515 OFF
2 4 6 8 10 9 7 5 3 1
Library of Congress Control Number 2014953798
ISBN 978-1-4424-8758-1 (hc)
ISBN 978-1-4424-8757-4 (pbk)
ISBN 978-1-4424-8759-8 (eBook)

FLORIAN

Chapter One

"YES, MY SWEET SIEBELE, YOU ARE very brave . . . very brave. And it wasn't so bad after all, was it? . . . There . . . good Siebele . . . brave . . . brave."

The milk-white mare listened attentively, her small delicate ears pointed. Her dark Juno-eyes watched the face of the stableboy as if she understood every word. Her name really was Sibyl; it was very distinctly lettered on the outside of her stall. But the youth entrusted with her care had called her "Siebele" from the very first. He could not do otherwise. If he tried to pronounce the name correctly before a superior, his tongue was sure to stumble over the hurdle of the foreign *y* and grow rigid due to his unconscious awe of the aristocratic sounding word, "Sibyl."

"He is beautiful, your little son. . . . You don't know yet how beautiful, Siebele," he murmured. "A true prince . . . as it had to be."

The mare shuddered a little, bowed her head and wiggled her ears. She sensed the kindness in the human voice, sensed that she was being praised, and was pleased.

Only three short hours ago Sibyl had given birth to the colt, the young man attending her. There had been no need of outside help, for all had gone quickly and smoothly. Now the tiny foal lay quivering in the warm straw at the feet of the mother, looking rather helpless. But the lad, glad that the difficult hour had passed so easily, was thrilled by the sight of the pitiful little creature. For three years he had watched over Sibyl. He had grown inseparable from the high-born mare. Every now and then he talked to her as he was doing now. His hand caressed her gracefully curved neck and bathed in the living warmth of her skin which gleamed and felt like silk. His knobby peasant brow pressed against her smooth forehead. And thus standing awhile, Sibyl contentedly permitted his hand to roam along her mane from poll to withers.

"You were fine, Siebele . . . you were brave. Brave Siebele . . . good Siebele."

Sibyl recovered from her first exhaustion rapidly. She knew her child needed rest; and she herself, under the spell of the soothing words, the quieting pressure of the friendly hand, the man's familiar scent, began to feel a comfortable drowsiness creep over her.

The morning sun shimmered in the stable. All the other stalls were empty, their occupants already out browsing and gamboling over the meadows of Lipizza.

"Well, Anton!" a voice sounded from the door.

The youth came to attention. *"Herr Rittmeister!"*

The officer approached. "Is it true, then?" he asked.

"Yes, sir," Anton replied, "a healthy colt."

Captain von Neustift hurried toward the stall. "By

jove," he said laughingly as he bent over, "excellent!" He rubbed his hands together. "Excellent. And what a handsome little fellow."

He attempted to enter the box but Anton stepped in his way. "Please, *Herr Rittmeister*, not yet ... Siebele will get restless."

"When did it happen?" the captain wanted to know.

"At two this morning."

"And nobody present?"

"With your permission, *Herr Rittmeister*, nobody but me."

"But you should have called the stud-master. Didn't you know that?"

"Yes, *Herr Rittmeister*." Anton smiled proudly. "But everything went so well. . . . So what for? Let the officers sleep. An hour ago I sent Franz over to fetch the stud-master and the doctor. They haven't come yet."

Sibyl turned her head and fixed her large dark eyes on the two men trustingly. Instantly Anton was at her side. "It's all right, Siebele," he soothed her. "Nobody is going to do anything to you. Nor to Florian. You're both nice horses ... very nice."

His hand glided up along her shoulder and back, over the sleek and shining white pelt through which her skin shone pink. Every time he touched this big, pungent, powerful body he felt, in the thrill of the contact, an intoxicating affinity with its dormant strength, as if he shared it with the animal; and felt, too, indistinctly but none the less rapturously, all the enchantment of equine existence. He had known the joy of husbandry in the growth and flowering of the creature entrusted to his care, a joy that had to do with motherly feelings and the mysteries of creation. Anton knew nothing of all this, of course, nor did he attempt to know. He loved Sibyl, admired her. Yet he could not have explained this, even if someone had asked him. He rubbed his hand lightly against the damp velvet of Sibyl's upper lip. "*Herr Rittmeister* ... if you please ... isn't he pretty, our Florian?" And Anton pointed to the shivering foal in the straw.

Captain von Neustift grinned. "Yes ... a fine little fellow. But—why on earth Florian?"

"I humbly report, *Herr Rittmeister* ... today is the fourth of May. ... And if you please ... the fourth of May is the day of Saint Florian."

"Oh, I see. . . . That's why."

"Yes, sir . . . that's why."

The broad, kind peasant face took on a trace of stubbornness.

"My dear Anton," said the captain, and in his voice, despite its friendliness, still lay the vast gulf between the nobleman-officer and the humble stableboy, "my dear Anton, that won't help you any. The stud-master doesn't care a rap about your calendar saints."

Anton grew rigid with fright.

"No," von Neustift proceeded, "the stud-master will give him an entirely different name. I'm afraid you'll be out of luck."

"But his name's got to be Florian!" Anton's stubbornness showed in the growl of his voice, showed in the contraction of his brows over his light blue eyes. "He's got to . . . if you please, sir," he repeated. "Florian. . . . Nothing else."

"You tell that to the stud-master." Neustift smiled. "Go ahead, tell him . . . if you've got the courage."

It was Anton's turn to smile. "Not I, *Herr Rittmeister*,"

he answered. "I haven't got the courage." He winked slyly at Neustift. "But somebody else is going to tell him. . . ."

The captain approached Sibyl who received him with a haughty upraised head. "Don't be foolish, Anton. . . . I wouldn't think of making any suggestions."

"And why not?" Anton insisted.

"There, Sibyl," Neustift whispered to the mare. "There, Sibyl, be nice. I simply want to congratulate you." He ran his fingers through her mane, patted her neck in a comradely manner, stroked her broad beautiful breast. "Fine work, Sibyl. A male foal, fine work."

"Why not?" Anton pressed.

Von Neustift turned around to him. They stood very close to each other. "Because it's none of my business . . . don't you understand, Anton?"

But Anton contradicted him. "It is your business . . . for sure . . . because . . . because . . ." he broke off, stammering.

"I am really curious to know why," von Neustift rejoined, continuing to fondle Sibyl. He, too, could not resist touching the magnificent body.

"Because you are the first one to see Florian," Anton explained. "Because you were the first one to come to Florian." And so saying, he again put his hand on Sibyl, stroking her croup.

Here in the cramped quarters of the box, close to the upstanding mare, close to each other, enveloped in the pungent odor of horses which both the captain and the peasant loved—here the difference in the station of the two well-nigh disappeared. Neustift lost his masterful air, and Anton, as though sensing that, became bolder.

"Will you do me the favor, *Herr Rittmeister?*" he blurted out, and lowered his voice. "I would be so grateful to you . . . please say a good word for Florian. . . . It's got to be his name, *Herr Rittmeister.* . . . I believe in signs . . . and so do you."

"Oho!" Neustift laughed shortly.

Anton insisted: "Surely you believe in them. Aren't you of the cavalry . . . a Dragoon? . . . as I was a Dragoon? He is born on Saint Florian's day, and an officer of the Dragoons is the first one to visit him. . . . He's got to be called Florian ... otherwise it won't turn out right for him ... and it's got to go right with him ... it's got to. ... Just look at him!"

They both bent over the colt snuggling in the straw. Sibyl craned her neck, eying the two, and snorted briefly. Anton, finding her ram's-nose and big dark eyes so close to him that her breath moistened his cheek, whispered: "Yes, yes, Siebele, your son is beautiful ... you just be quiet, we won't harm him."

Sibyl nodded her proud head, as if to indicate her assent.

Both Neustift and Anton had bent their knees slightly like men who are about to sit down, and rested their hands on their thighs.

As often before, when spending his furlough at his small estate in southern Styria, Neustift had come to look over the nearby stud-farm in Lipizza.

He worshiped horses. The extraordinary care they received here gave him keen pleasure. And the picture the animals made on the vast open meadows or between the trees—tableaux in flux—thrilled him. The grace of their movements, the heroic gestures of their gallop, the carefreeness of their humor, the gentleness of their instincts rejuvenated his spirits.

Anton had been born to humble peasants in Styria. His father owned a horse and three cows; chickens and geese, too, and a meager parcel of land. Peasant children didn't learn much in school: reading, writing, arithmetic, and of course, the catechism. Everything they knew—and that wasn't as little as it might seem—life and labor taught them. And life, grim and hard and unrelenting, started early for the peasant. Even as a small boy of eight, Anton had been busy in the fields and in the stable. He made friends with the cows, staying up whole nights to help them when they calved, and they trusted and obeyed him. If a calf was sold away from its mother, or if, in the course of the years, one of the cows had to follow the butcher, Anton would stand at the fence of his father's farm for an hour or two and stare into the blue sky, and afterward go back to his work quite resignedly . . . save that he didn't sing on days like that. However, eventually he became scarcely conscious of the faint sadness which was sure to overcome him on those occasions. He accepted the natural course of events against which it was useless to struggle or rail or cry, and didn't give in to sentimental notions; in fact, he never had. any. He had loved the old worked-out jade, Hansl, a brown bony Wallachian beast, like a true friend, a fellow worker and a chum. Saddleless he had ridden Hansl, seated on the somewhat curved-in back, and intuitively at first, and more definitely later on, had learned to understand the breathing of the big steaming body between his legs, learned to read every movement of the horse's neck and head and ears, learned to inter- pret every sign the animal gave him, no matter how imperceptible. At first he had held on to the shaggy mane, but he had soon learned to ride sitting upright. He had instinctively discovered how to guide the horse and change its pace by the pressure of his legs, by the knocking of his heels against its belly. And thus he had guided Hansl with neither reins nor bridle.

This came in handy as a subsidiary education when he went to serve his three obligatory years with the

Dragoons. Not only did he know horses intimately; he belonged to them as completely as anybody belongs to his life's work. He led an exemplary life; didn't drink, didn't run after girls too much, avoided quarrels, was even-tempered, cheerful and willing. While he was in the Army, his father, a widower, had married again; with Anton gone for at least three years the old man had been alone and in need of help, and a wife was cheaper in the long run than a farmhand or a servant girl. Anton did not particularly long for home. He owed to the commander of his regiment his job as a stable-hand on the stud-farm in Lipizza. "I doubt that you could find a better man in the entire Army," the colonel had written to the head of Lipizza after Anton had served his time. "Corporal Anton Pointner is cracked about horses, and as honest and industrious a man as you can find." The colonel's praise had got Anton the job over many applicants.

He had come to Lipizza as fatedly as a pious soul finds its way into Heaven. He had already passed three years among the aristocratic animals, sharing their sylvan existence with all his heart, so that there was no room in it for anything else.

Neustift straightened out, smoothed the blouse of his uniform and smiled. "All right, Anton. The little one shall be called Florian." He patted Sibyl's neck. "Don't say any more . . ." he added. "Of course the name does not fit the son of Berengar and Sibyl at all . . . but all right . . . say no more. I'll do what I can."

Anton was silent. Not even a "Thank you" escaped his lips. His face shining, he stood at attention, and raised his hand to his temple in salute. And this said all and more than he could have expressed in mere words.

From far away, wafting softly through the air and yet clearly audible, came the solemn strains of the national anthem. A military band was playing. *"Gott erhalte, Gott beschütze. . . ."*

Neustift stiffened. "That's his Imperial Highness," he said. "He is inspecting the troops."

But Anton had eyes only for Florian. He thought: Just as they play the Emperor's hymn the rascal lifts his head for the first time. . . . A good sign.

Florian had indeed raised his small fawn-like head, somewhat befuddled and still trembling. The thin neck shook, uncertain of this first movement. The long narrow face was piteously unfinished, and just because of that was as touching as the face of a baby. The eyes had as yet taken in too little light and were without luster. As they looked vacantly around, helpless surprise welled up in their dark pools, a surprise that quivered through the body which, recently flung from its accustomed warm dark home into the cool void of existence, was still shaken by the mystery of its transition.

Stretching her neck, Sibyl neighed melodiously, the sound mingling with the closing strains of the anthem.

"Signs . . ." Anton thought. But he remained silent.

Chapter Two

THE KARST PLATEAU OF LIPIZZA LAY sweltering under the summer sky. On the meadows the horses moved about, leisurely nuzzling at the parched grass, and every now and then the sound of their cropping could be heard. They sought out the thick shade of the old chestnut trees, threw themselves down and rubbed their backs and their loins against the cool soil. The mares and their young were kept separate from the stallions. But the two- and three-year-olds, here still considered foals, stayed with their mothers. From time to time the high gay whinnying of one of the males broke the stillness of the landscape; challenging, longing, vibrating with life. At that, several mares wiggled their ears coyly, while others began to gallop around; but most of them, in sheer animal comfort, rolled over and stretched even more comfortably than before, as if they had heard nothing, although the challenging cry deepened the voluptuous leisure in which they basked. Sometimes a male foal would give answer in his high young treble, when the neighing sounded. But his mother would act as if she hadn't noticed that one of her sons had been impudent. Or else, she might raise her head and glare disapprovingly at the innocent offender.

Neustift walked through the meadows beside a young girl, walked among the trees and the horses. Anton followed them. Suddenly the captain turned around and asked: "Where is Florian? I can't seem to pick him out among all these youngsters. Where is he?"

"Why, *Herr Rittmeister*," Anton replied, "right in front of you."

A snow-white colt, his spindly legs spread far apart, stood awkwardly to one side, seemingly wrapped in deep thought.

"*Herr Rittmeister* should recognize him by his mother," Anton made bold to add with hardly concealed reproach.

"Yes, if I saw Sibyl, I certainly should–" Neustift didn't finish the sentence for Anton interrupted him eagerly:

"Here! She is right in front of you!"

Sibyl lay on her back, her hindlegs drawn close to her body and her forefeet stretching toward the sky.

"Well," Neustift teased, "in this undignified position she hardly looks like herself. No wonder I didn't recognize her."

Anton would not brook any slight to his favorite, "Whatever position she is in . . . she is always like herself. Siebele," he called, "Siebele, come here."

In one unbroken motion of incomparable grace, Sibyl rose to her legs.

"Come, come," he summoned her.

Slowly she came over.

Now Florian awoke from his reverie, startled by the sudden appearance of his mother. Stumbling and swaying, he too came up close. It seemed each second as if he would change his course, as if distracting ideas or utter aimlessness were setting him off in another direction at every step. But all he wanted was to get close to his mother, and there he got after all.

The girl laughed aloud.

The sound made Florian stop short; he spread his forelegs far apart, then inanely jumped aside. He hopped into the air on all fours and much higher than was necessary. As a matter of fact the whole attempt at flight was not necessary, for neither the girl nor the officer had made any move toward him.

Calming down, the skinny little colt again stumbled close to his mother and the human beings standing by her side. In some hilarious fashion—from his spare frame, from the disproportion of his limbs, from his narrow ram-nosed head and the play of his childlike features—he appeared to be play-acting without knowing how amusing his comedy was. He seemed at once

sillier than the silliest being on earth, and shrewder and
cannier than anyone could guess.

"A clown," the girl said and laughed again.

"Just like all healthy foals," Neustift told her.

Anton felt obliged to break into a song of praise in
order to elicit admiration for his ward. "Oh, yes . . . this
Florian," he began modestly, "among a thousand foals
you pick him out . . . because . . . there is not another one
like him . . . not one."

He already saw the growing beauty of Florian from
his as yet undeveloped fine points, and already accepted
as accomplished what was still in the making. In this his
experience helped him; his devotion and his love.

"A clown," the girl repeated, and it was not clear
whether she meant Florian, or Anton, or both of them.

Anton was silent.

On his open palm Neustift held out a piece of
sugar for Sibyl. She sniffed at it and took it. The sugar
crunched between her teeth. A moment later, with ears
tilted forward and head lowered to Neustift's hand, she
asked for more.

The young girl offered a piece of sugar to Florian.

Curious, he stretched his muzzle far out, sniffed at the hand, brushed the lump into the grass, made a jump, and nestled by his mother.

"He doesn't understand yet," Anton excused him. "He is still sucking."

"Oh!" The girl was disappointed and a little ashamed of herself.

Neustift caught Florian and put his arm across his back. Florian tried to free himself but a light pressure of the man's arm was sufficient to quiet him, and he yielded. Sibyl pressed close to the captain, the better to see.

"Do you notice, Countess," Neustift said, "how patient and friendly these Lipizza horses are?"

"Really," the girl agreed, "born courtiers."

"Quite so," Neustift answered with a broad smile. "These Lipizza horses belong to the Emperor. They have that faith and trust which his Majesty has a right to demand . . . and they are far less egotistic than most other courtiers. They are neither intrigants nor snobs. Incidentally, look here. . . ." He forced open Florian's mouth. "Do you see these tiny milk teeth? Only when they get sharp at the edges and hurt the mother, does she stop suckling him."

He released Florian who, stumbling and lurching, began to chase around the group in a narrow circle.

"Florian," Anton called. "Florian!" But Florian didn't listen, wouldn't listen. In his erratic course it looked as if he would have to take a tumble. But nothing of the sort happened. He was simply jubilant. In silent rapture Anton watched Florian celebrate his regained freedom.

"These Lipizza horses teethe much more slowly than others," Neustift went on explaining to the girl. "Everything happens more slowly with them. Mother Nature goes very circumspectly about her task of forming a completely masterful creature."

As Sibyl kept on nosing at his hands and his pockets, the captain gave the girl a lump of sugar. "Here, Countess, you give that to Sibyl."

Sibyl accepted the tidbit daintily and the girl rubbed her palm dry. "Strange," she said, blushing, "it felt as soft and tender . . . as a kiss." Again she blushed.

Neustift did not seek her eyes and did not answer, and thus they strolled away.

On top of a hillock the girl stopped and looked to the four winds. "Ah," she cried, her arms spread wide. "Ah, beautiful! Beautiful!" And after a moment's hesitation, added: "And all these wonderful horses... like a fairyland!" She fell silent for a moment. "Has it been here long?"

"What?"

"Well, all this. Lipizza."

Neustift swept an arc with his raised hand. "For centuries, Countess, for centuries."

"Is that a fact... or do you just imagine so?"

"Oh, well... I know a few things...."

"Have you studied the subject?"

"Not really studied... I just know.... After all, I am a horseman."

The girl eyed him with an approving glance. "Tell me what you know," she said. It sounded like an order.

From the sea a cooling breeze rolled in, caressing the Plain of Lipizza and tempering the brooding heat of the fiery sun.

Florian stood directly in front of the girl and looked at her as at a miracle. "Clown!" She smiled and, turning, stood face to face with Sibyl who had followed them. "What rare soulful eyes," the girl remarked. "Eyes of love," she added half-involuntarily.

The captain fixed her with a look. "Do you know the eyes of love?"

With averted gaze she whispered: "No . . . but this is the way I imagine them to be . . . so dark . . . so full of kindness, full of boundless understanding. . . ." Suddenly she could say no more. She turned crimson.

There was a pause. The girl stroked Sibyl's smooth neck.

"My eyes, too," Neustift ventured humbly, "are the eyes of love when I look at you, Elizabeth. . . ." He stopped.

With a pressure so light as to make contact only with the down of her lips, Sibyl accepted a piece of sugar from the girl's palm.

"Like a kiss," Neustift said softly and went on: "I would like to know what brought that simile to your mind, Elizabeth. . . . It's right . . . the comparison is perfect. . . ."

Elizabeth stroked Sibyl. "How delicate . . . how fine." Then abruptly she asked in a matter-of-fact tone: "Full-blooded, of course?"

And with equal matter-of-factness Neustift informed her: "Full-blood is difficult to claim. Two hundred years ago these Spaniards were crossed with Neapolitans, and later on with Arabs. Half-blood, to be quite exact—but of the noblest."

"Spaniards? Why do you call these Lipizzans Spaniards?"

Neustift collected his thoughts. He walked over to Florian and tapped his breast and loins. "This little fellow is of older and nobler lineage than either of us. Even if we added our families together, plus the dynasty, it wouldn't be enough, by far. . . ."

Surprised and intrigued Elizabeth came and stood opposite him on the other side of the colt. Florian held his peace, permitted them both to stroke him, and sniffed at his mother who had joined the group, standing crosswise. "Why, that would be . . . that would be thousands of years." Elizabeth's voice sounded doubtful. "Thousands of years . . . isn't that slightly exaggerated?"

"Oh, no," Neustift returned. "Our cats, that came down to us from ancient Egypt, are thousands of years old, too."

"Cats . . ." Elizabeth shrugged her shoulders. "Cats."

"Well, to be sure," he smiled, "these horses are a far more interesting race than cats. . . . Why, Hannibal rode across the Alps on the back of one of them . . . just think of it!"

Which set Elizabeth off laughing. "Hannibal . . . on a Lipizzan! You're joking."

"At that time they were Spanish stock," Neustift said, again serious. "Or else from the northern rim of Africa."

Still Elizabeth laughed incredulously. "Who could make such a claim?"

"Just look at some antique reliefs or old equestrian statues," he retorted, "and then look at that animal." He pointed at Sibyl who stood silhouetted against the sky. He became enthusiastic. "That's exactly what the horses were like then . . . exactly! They had this same magnificent figure, the same heroic pathos in their posture, the same dreamlike rhythm of movement, even that gentle decline from forehead to ram's-nose—"

"Really?" Elizabeth interrupted him. "And surely her marvelous eyes . . ."

"Surely!" Neustift spoke on, his words pouring forth unrestrainedly due to his enthusiasm: "I am convinced I'm right about Hannibal's horses, I really believe they are the ancestors of these. Are you conscious of the fact, Elizabeth, that so many things—almost everything beautiful and lofty that we moderns possess—have come to us from the Mediterranean? God and the gods, art and poetry, and . . . and . . ."

"And horses," Elizabeth interposed and smiled once more.

"Yes, horses, too . . . these horses," Neustift said emphatically. He patted Sibyl on her croup. "Is there anything more beautiful than a horse? And in all the equine world anything comparable to these Lipizzans? Not for me. For me, Elizabeth, a horse is one of God's truly noble creatures. Excuse me . . . I am only a horse-man."

Elizabeth passed him. "Only a horseman," she said. "Only!" And drawing Sibyl's head down she pressed a kiss on her nose. "There . . . my sweet. For me, too, you belong to the noble things of this world; for me, too . . . even if I am but a bad horsewoman."

"Why, Countess," Neustift protested, "you ride excellently."

"Thanks for the compliment."

Anton, who had come shuffling up and remained standing a few steps removed, ventured to remark: "And how well the countess can drive . . . it is simply marvelous." He could not suppress the desire to air this opinion.

Elizabeth nodded amiably. "Thank you, too." Anton rocked in embarrassment. She turned to Neustift. "I am really very glad that we drove over. I have never been in Lipizza before. Strange . . . because it isn't very far from where we live."

"Yes, you had to wait until someone like myself came

into your house," Neustift said. "I planned to talk you into this visit the moment your parents invited me."

"And Lipizza?" Elizabeth asked again. "You said a while ago that the stud-farm has existed for a long time."

"A very, very long time."

"Tell me more!"

He hesitated.

"Tell me. . . . What are you thinking about?"

"Primarily," Neustift said softly, "of you. Only of you, Elizabeth. You have asked me, and therefore I dare speak. Of your copper-brown hair, of your lovely brown eyes, of your little proud nose, of the brave curve of your lips, of . . ."

"Stop," she checked him. "Stop!"

". . . of your whole beautiful self. . . ."

"Don't." Elizabeth, too, was whispering. "Not here, please. . . ." And in her natural voice she went on. "You wanted to tell me some more about Lipizza. . . ." From the corner of her eyes she glanced at Anton who was following them. But Anton paid but scant attention to human beings, ever. Right now he was preoccupied with Florian and Sibyl.

"Oh, yes, Lipizza," Neustift acceded, his voice trembling slightly as he struggled for an easy conversational tone. "There is little to be said, really, Countess . . . if I want to be brief, that is. Archduke Karl founded all this. . . ." He waved his arm in an encompassing gesture.

"He of the battle of Aspern, who conquered Napoleon?"

Neustift suppressed a faint smile. "No, no, this was an archduke who lived in the sixteenth century. The father of the Styrian Ferdinand. . . ."

"The Styrian Ferdinand? And who was he?"

"He? He was the Holy Roman Emperor during whose reign the Thirty Years' War was fought."

"I see . . . and why?"

"A religious war . . . Catholics against Protestants . . . the Styrian Ferdinand was a pious Catholic. He said that he would rather rule over a graveyard than over heretics."

"Oh, I am so ashamed . . . I know so little." Elizabeth's girlish voice grew sad.

Neustift took her arm, which she suffered without a word. "You are wonderful as you are," he said, his mouth close to her ear. And then, his lips pursing: "I hate educated people."

Elizabeth released her arm. "You, Neustift?" she evinced surprise. "A scholar like you?"

He laughed a quick bitter laugh. "I . . . a scholar? I know just about as much as an Austrian should know to understand what Austria is. . . ."

"At home you will tell me . . . will you . . . about the Styrian Ferdinand?" Elizabeth begged.

"Gladly, gladly," Neustift replied in quickening syllables. "And about Matthias . . . and about Rudolf II, who shared a room in the Hradschin, his castle in Prague, with lions and eagles. . . ."

"The same room?"

"Yes. He was the incarnate, the mysterious Majesty! We know hardly anything about the overpowering personalities among the Hapsburgs. Since 1866 history has falsified much in connection with these matters." Neustift now spoke heatedly. "This Rudolf, this glorious figure . . . he was really the first art collector. He felt the aura . . . the spiritual essence . . . which emanated from a painting, a statue, a goldsmith's piece. Since Maximilian, that ill-starred genius, he was the first to understand these things. And he loved horses. Do you know . . . after he was crowned Emperor he never sat in a saddle again; but he came to his stables every day to enjoy the sight of his noble chargers and to pet them. . . ."

"We ought to go home," Elizabeth suddenly suggested. She was highly animated. "We could sit and talk . . . and . . ." She said no more.

"We shall be together . . . always!" Neustift could hardly contain his joy.

Elizabeth helped him. "So this is Lipizza," she said. "Lipizza . . . and centuries old . . . ?" She turned completely around, slowly, pivoting on her heel.

"Well." He laughed. "It is almost four hundred years old . . . which isn't so terribly much, after all."

"For human beings, plenty . . . and for these noble four-footed beings, too. . . ."

Straight through the swarm of horses they sauntered

slowly toward the exit-gate. Intentionally Elizabeth pressed between the closest crowded mares each time they encountered a small cluster. "Ho!" she cried, "step aside." Or: "Go away, child," soothingly, in a friendly tone. She knew it was necessary to talk to the animals in order not to startle them. Of course, she did not know that a Lipizzan rarely shies.

Neustift paced behind her or beside her, just as it happened. He whistled softly—cavalry signals.

Sibyl and Florian followed the pair as if the visit had been meant for them alone and it was their agreeable duty to see the guests out. Anton did not leave his wards.

Continuing on their way, Elizabeth and Neustift caressed a horse here, slapped some beautifully rounded hindquarter there, stroked a broad, healthy chest, or a proudly curved neck, the satiny down of a young filly's pelt . . . and were themselves quietly and searchingly inspected by deep dark eyes and velvety nostrils.

They were in the middle of the herd, completely hemmed in, breathing deeply of the salt-laden air

wafted over the meadows from the sea and of the
pinching odor of these big strong forms. Out here in
the open the animal odor contained something refreshing, something warm, frank, innocent. Milk-white
horses there were, iron-grays, others whose snowy
flanks seemed flecks of clouds; here a pearl-gray color
appeared in irregular but always delicate designs on
back or breast and loins or legs. Most of them were
white of mane, with long bushy tails like rich plumes.
Sometimes it was an ivory-tinted white, sometimes the
white of moon-spun gossamer.

"Honestly," Elizabeth said, awed, "here one is among
the noblest . . . one might very well become timid and
feel like an upstart."

"Why . . . Countess!" Neustift smiled. "We human
beings have had something to do with preserving their
nobility. True, they don't know it . . . but we shouldn't forget it . . . although"—and he waited until Sibyl edged up
and he could stroke her back—"a feeling of humbleness . . .
yes, of humbleness . . . never quite leaves me when I am
among blooded horses. . . ." He faced Elizabeth. "Even if

it be nothing else than some sort of genuflection before Nature for the generous gratitude with which she rewards us for our endeavors."

"*Au revoir,*" Elizabeth almost sang, such was the joy in her voice, "*au revoir* . . . very soon, Lipizza."

Somebody softly touched her shoulder. "Oh, Sibyl," she breathed in ecstasy, "I certainly would have said good-bye to you . . . you don't need to remind me. I know what is proper."

Again she held out a lump of sugar. "There . . . as a farewell gift . . . and I won't ever forget the kiss of your lips." There was more between the white horse and Elizabeth than the lump of sugar: The joy of existence, the willing deliverance to Fate which unites every living thing. But neither the girl nor the horse knew it. They knew only that they liked each other.

"*Au revoir,* Sibyl."

Florian began his grotesque foal's dance. He galloped about his mother, about Elizabeth and Neustift, while Anton cried: "Florian!" shouted, "Florian! Florian!"

Florian wouldn't listen.

"Let him be," Elizabeth begged Anton. "I have always been against forcing little children to say good-bye."

Long after they had gone, Anton stood there, pressing Florian's soft little head against his chest, stroking him with both hands over neck and shoulders, and murmuring into his ear: "Was that nice? Now you are all hot, all hot you are . . . and you wouldn't come when I called you. Is that nice? You know it isn't. But you won't do that again, will you? You want to be a good little horse. Don't you, Florian? The very nicest little horse"—he released him—"for you are already the most beautiful one anyway."

Enraptured he watched how the fumbling colt, on his stiff little legs, approached his mother who appeared to be waiting; watched the innocent, graceful poses Florian adopted while he pulled thirstily at the teat.

Chapter Three

ONE DAY BOSCO CAME.

Bosco was a fox terrier barely two months old. His mother's name was Maya; she lived in Lipizza, was owned by Herr Voggenberger, spent her time in the stable with the stallions and had been married to her stable-fellow, the handsome fox terrier, Jackie. A litter of five had constituted the first blessed event of this halcyon marriage: five round, stumbling, struggling, squirming, lively fox terriers. Voggenberger insisted on leaving Maya only three; five were too much for poor Maya. He had been on the point of drowning two of them, had even a large pail of water ready, when Anton arrived. "Give me one," he begged, "I've wanted a dog for a long time." Herr Voggenberger had given him the tiny blind ball which stretched out four silly paws and devotedly but without success sucked Anton's finger when he put it in its mouth. Voggenberger, noticing that, had remarked: "If he remains alive, his name will be Bosco." Anton was satisfied. "All right . . . for all I care, Bosco. Thank you very much."

Whereupon Voggenberger had grabbed the other puppy and prepared to stick its head into the pail. Anton couldn't endure any form of cruelty.

"Wait a while, Herr Voggenberger," he had stammered timidly.

Voggenberger was not cruel by nature. He had not enjoyed the prospect of killing even one of the young brood. He only wanted to make things easier for Maya. "What do you want me to wait for?" he asked. "How long do you want me to wait?"

"Well, till tomorrow," Anton replied. "At most till the day after tomorrow. There is that game warden, Woinovich, down in the village." He hesitated for a moment.

"Well, and—?" Voggenberger had demanded.

"His cat has lost all her kittens except one . . . he could put this little one with the mother cat. . . ." Anton's face shone.

"All right," Voggenberger said. On his palm he had carried the little bundle of fluff from the kitchen into the stable, to Maya. Anton had hidden Bosco under his coat and accompanied Voggenberger, who said on the way: "I'll call your attention to the fact, Pointner, that this last one is a female . . . if she lives, her name is Faline. Don't forget."

Thus Anton had saved the lives of the two puppies. For the matter with Game Warden Woinovich and his cat was easily arranged.

Anton had carried little Bosco to his room. There he had procured a milk bottle with a rubber nipple and thus replaced the mother. The tiny fellow, soon over his blindness, grew fast and pleased Anton no end. By day as well as by night Anton let him sleep in his bed. Sometimes he carried him around sheltered between his shirt and his coat; he liked to feel the warmth of the restive little body against his own, knew when Bosco slept there peacefully, and laughed when he curiously stuck his head out from under and gnawed at Anton's hands or anything else within reach of his needle-sharp teeth.

By and by Bosco had begun to wriggle so, in his place between Anton's shirt and coat, that he had to be scolded. But one day when Anton was wandering through the enclosure of the stallions he had seen Herr Voggenberger's Maya playing with her offspring among the horses. Grabbing hold of one of the puppies, he had, with a feeling tantamount to motherly pride, established the fact that Bosco was a little bigger and that his distended little milk-belly was fuller and smoother.

Later, outside with Sibyl and Florian, the frisky little dog had once more begun to struggle, and Anton had to open the two lower buttons of his coat. Bosco fell to the ground, rolled over and suddenly, to his own consternation, found himself standing on his own legs; slowly and with growing curiosity he raised his head and began to inspect the world.

Thus did Bosco appear among the Lipizzans.

It was a mild November day. In from the sea came a faint sirocco, and the sun, although pale, was warm and pleasant.

Bosco blinked and sneezed, and his expressive face seemed to say: "What shall I do now?" Like any other creature, particularly a very young one, when confronted with a realm of infinite possibilities, he could not reach a decision.

Suddenly Florian, who stood near where Bosco had fallen, gave a jump. He had been startled by Bosco's sudden appearance because heretofore he had seen dogs only from afar, or else been too young to notice them at close range. So from sheer surprise he jumped with stiff legs into the air. Bosco greeted this spectacle with one shrill yelp. It sounded like a child soprano emitting a shout of joy.

Florian and Bosco stared at each other.

Bosco's eyes beheld a gigantic creature, a monster, a fabulous something. Yet he was not afraid for a single moment. He felt curiosity, nothing but curiosity.

Before Florian, on the other hand, stood an incongruous, energetic little ball—all white, with two black spots around the eyes, and a forehead and ears separated by a thin white line running from the top of his head down to the pink nose.

Neither of them—neither Bosco nor Florian—knew he himself was white. Nor cared.

It was strange, however, that at sight of the little creature Florian felt a slight aversion and for the first time in his life a sensation akin to fear.

Just then Bosco ceased to consider what to do first. He rushed at Florian, yelping and yowling playfully.

Florian turned tail and ran.

Bosco chased after him, and Anton's "Florian! Bosco!" did not do a bit of good. Neither paid any attention. They dashed across the meadow. Little Bosco, burdened by his full belly, was far in the rear. He still wasn't used to running fast.

But Florian quickly tired. He noticed that he had outdistanced his fearsome pursuer; from his gallop he fell into a trot, from the trot into a leisurely saunter, and soon he came to a halt beside Sibyl. Anton approached just as Bosco arrived quite out of breath. With the proverbial stubbornness of the terrier, Bosco rushed at Florian's hindlegs and was about to bite into one of them, without malice, just for fun, when Florian, who apparently did not think highly of such harlequinade, shot both his hindlegs so high that, looked at from the front, with his neck and head bent, he seemed to execute a formal bow.

Bosco soared into the air. The hooves hadn't hurt him, but the spring of Florian's legs sent him gracefully up and away in a high curve. He rolled over a few times in flight, turned a few somersaults after coming to earth, and when he had caught his breath broke into a pitiful whining interspersed with short angry barks. His tail between his legs and his back arched, he finally got up but remained at a respectful distance.

This stormy and not altogether painless experience of Bosco's produced excellent results. He never again—really, never again—dared rush at a horse's legs, or even snap at them.

Florian was angry, and, with his ears laid back against his head, he clung to his mother's side.

Anton felt that the time had come to make peace between the two youngsters.

He called to the flabbergasted, inconsolable Bosco, who hesitantly and shyly crawled near. Anton had to meet him halfway, whereupon Bosco rolled over on his back. That meant: "Do with me what you please." It spelled at once a complete surrender of his own will and boundless trust.

Anton lifted him up and carried him over to the colt. "There," he said, holding Bosco in front of Florian's nose. "There . . . why aren't you nice to each other . . . there." More he didn't know.

Florian recognized his puny foe and was still huffy, an attitude he indicated by ears laid back. He didn't seem the least bit kind, or intelligent . . . only slightly malevolent. This upset Anton. Malevolence—that did not go with Florian at all; it couldn't and mustn't.

Meanwhile Bosco had struggled up in Anton's arm and was audibly sniffing at Florian's muzzle, becoming visibly gayer and affectionate.

Florian was tickled. He blew his breath at his tiny flatterer and brought his ears up again. The great dark eyes were questioning and full of expectation.

Anton grinned with joy. That was better. Ever since he had come to work here at the stud-farm he had never seen a Lipizzan either angry or malevolent or pugnacious—not to speak of his Florian who, in Anton's eyes, was the most beautiful, most faultless Lipizzan that ever grew toward a glorious destiny.

Bosco began to wash Florian's nose with his quick little red tongue. It looked like a passionate declaration of love, an ecstatic explosion of friendship. Only the very young can love thus, innocently, can follow an impulse with such complete abandon. Florian plainly enjoyed it, for he bent his head and allowed Bosco to plant moist kisses on his nose and forehead.

"That's enough," Anton said, his calm restored, and set Bosco down.

The terrier scurried around Florian with an expression of rapture in the gaze he cast up at his big newly won friend, singing for him in the highest pitch tiny love songs that ended abruptly and then started again in hasty, uneven little stanzas.

"Now I go," Anton cogitated, "I've got to go, I've got work to do. Bosco!" he called, ambling away. "Bosco!"

Once, twice, Bosco chased after him, ran around him and darted back to Florian.

Again Anton called, whistled, shouted and whistled again. Bosco could not tear himself away from his friend. The two played all kinds of games, some that had a serious background and were slow-paced, and others so gay and active that they verged on madness.

When Anton had left and ordered the little dog to come along, Bosco had said to Florian approximately: "Excuse me . . . I've got to obey."

And Florian's answer had been something like this: "Too bad . . . too bad."

That had torn Bosco's heart between Anton and Florian. He chased away, rushed back, ran away a second time, came back again and intimated to Florian: "Here I am."

And it may be taken for granted Florian answered: "That's nice of you. I am very pleased."

On Bosco's second return he was all out of breath. He stretched out in front of Florian's legs and let his tongue dangle from his open snout.

"Bosco!" came the sound from afar.

Bosco listened and closed his mouth. A sigh, indicating: "Oh, I am so tired." A second one, meaning: "Oh, I would much rather stay with you."

Florian bent down and snorted: "Why don't you, my friend?"

Sibyl trotted over, bent her head and heartened the terrier with a stare that implied as much as: "You just stay with us."

The two horses, mother and son, stood side by side, their heads bent down to the little fellow who lay there and flicked the grass with his tail. Bosco peered up into the dark shining eyes, first into Sibyl's and then into Florian's, and waited.

All at once he sprang up. He had rested long enough. "What do you think?" asked his posture, betraying coiled speed and good humor.

Florian raised his head sharply. His ears wiggled and his closed lips assumed a gay and curious expression. Sibyl raised her head.

Like mad Bosco whirled round on his axis, danced for the audience of two. A sign from Florian must have told him: "I am with you." A sign from Sibyl: "All right."

He gave everything he had: breath, legs, heart and brain. He darted away as if shot from a pistol . . . a white, longish projectile streaking across the meadow.

Florian followed him rather nonchalantly, as if it were but a small matter to catch up, should he so desire.

Sibyl came after them only to supervise their play, to keep an eye on Florian. She purposely stayed somewhat in the background, adapted her stride to Florian's. It was obvious that she could easily have shown quite a different speed, but she partook in the game with the controlled energy of a staid grown-up; she wanted to spare her child.

For a while it amused Florian to keep little Bosco in front of him. Then the desire to overtake him awoke in his breast. He fell into a trot... in vain. He forced a still faster pace ... in vain. He began to pant.

Sibyl heard that. Lengthening her stride she came abreast of him, forged ahead and thrust herself in his path. His legs dug into the turf, but momentum carried him along until he bumped into his mother's hard stifle-joint and fell to sucking.

What a cooling draught. . . .

Cuddling against his mother's body he felt her pulse-beat on his lips. His own quickened pulse hammered in his face, neck and temples.

When the rhythmic double beat of the hooves behind him broke off, Bosco halted in his tracks and looked around, his first sense of triumph changing to perplexity at the disappearance of his two companions. Sniffing, he raised his nose to the air and smelled the scent of many, many horses, yet recognized Sibyl's scent among all the rest, and easily sifted out Florian's. In a beeline he went bobbing over to where they were.

He stood for a few seconds in the shadow of the mother and son, reverently watching the scene which had temporarily ended the game. He had no memory of his own mother, none of stretching out voluptuously to be nourished from her body. His first blind days were too far away in the haze of infancy, completely forgotten, and Anton's bottle did not offer any salient points of comparison. But being of the very best pedigree, a fox terrier through whose veins coursed canine blue-blood handed down to him from prized ancestors, he had finely sensitized instincts and rare understanding. Well-mannered, he looked on at mother and son, and never for a tiny second thought of disturbing them. Quietly he slunk into the grass and lay down opposite the two horses. His tongue lolled from his mouth and by its staccato lapping betrayed how strenuously his lungs and heart were working. Nevertheless he laughed at them: "Wasn't that grand fun?" His shining terrier-eyes said distinctly: "How wonderful to be with you."

Over from the domain of the stallions came loud passionate neighs.

Bosco pointed his ears. He liked the world.

Sibyl rolled in the grass, rubbed her back and displayed the sweeping lines of her belly as she lazily beat the air with her four hooves. She rubbed her cheeks against the grass, in sheer comfort, urging Florian to be gay.

He was glad to oblige. He performed mad contortions in the grass, cut funny capers with his legs, rolled on his side and drummed against his mother's high back with his small hooves.

Bosco was intensely interested. He stood up, unable to lie, carried away by the sight of mother and son enjoying each other. He was tremendously exhilarated . . . and amused by each of them and by himself. These two exalted creatures he constantly looked up to, whose faces always swung so high above him, had shrunk almost to his own dimensions. He frolicked in front of Sibyl and Florian, then jumped over them; and jumping over such mighty beings gave him as much subconscious satisfaction as the welcome intimacy it engendered. Sometimes his paws grazed Sibyl's neck, and once Florian's crest. He jubilated, he yipped incessantly, he created a Lilliputian bedlam in contrast to the vast silent contentment of the two horses. And judging from their attitude, his noisy behavior seemed less disturbing than complementary to their mute serenity.

When Anton returned, after a few hours, he found the triumvirate peacefully resting.

Bosco greeted him stormily, wagging his tail, spinning round and round, leaping up to his master again and again. Sibyl simply looked at the man with large dark eyes shining as if in meditation. And Florian stretched, bent his neck far back, and showed in this fashion how good he felt.

Chapter Four

FTER CLOUD-HIDDEN DAYS, AFTER
raging storms, a thin crust of snow covered the meadows of Lipizza. From horizon to horizon blue skies, and a pallid
sun that gave weak warmth but still spread good cheer.
Crystal clear and motionless hung the air.

All the horses roamed around in the open, trotted,
galloped, sauntered over the snow which is so rare
in this region; and the white animals on the white
ground made it appear that Nature had arranged a

costume fête for the sake of the human carnival.

In crisscrossing tracks the horses wrote the screed of their hooves into the melting snow. Some of them sucked up soft snow through half-closed lips, the cold sending their heads up with a powerful heave and making them snort loudly and gallop aimlessly. Not one of them tried to throw himself down, to stretch or to roll. The snowy coverlet scintillated in the light of the sun but did not invite recumbent rest.

Bosco and three or four other terriers, however, were soon on intimate terms with the snow, gamboling and scampering about like children coming home from school to whom snow is an invitation to frolic.

Bosco exchanged brief courtesies with his kinsmen, did not care that there might be close relatives among them. He did not engage any of them in lengthy conversation. He did whatever good form among fox terriers dictated, as briefly as possible, and thereafter devoted all his time and attention to Florian.

Florian was apparently unable to get along without Bosco. He stood motionless and waited whenever

Bosco strayed farther afield than usual. Sibyl, too, stood and waited. At last Bosco came. Already from afar he called to them: "Here I am. Here!" He leaped up to them, always in front, always so that they could see him. He might have been wanting to bite their noses. But that wasn't true at all; he remembered well being catapulted through space by Florian's legs!

He frisked around Florian, ran on ahead, rolled in the snow, jumped up again and shook vigorously from his body a rain of tiny drops. Hither and yon he darted, and every once in a while Florian had to come to a jarring stop to avoid stepping on the roly-poly terrier in the snow. At such times Florian turned a sharp angle and made off in another direction followed by Sibyl, so that Bosco had hardly time enough to rise and shake off the wet clinging snow, in order to catch up.

Bosco had grown considerably; he was about half again the size he had been when he first met Florian. He was riper, and despite all the earmarks of youth his slender figure approximated the proportions of the grown terrier, the sturdy smooth figure which betrayed carefreeness, grace and reckless courage. No longer did a fat little milk-belly distort his waistline; for now he drank very little milk and when he did, lapped it up out of a saucer, baring his sharp almost full-grown teeth.

Bosco slept with Sibyl and Florian in their box. They had arranged that among them. To accomplish this, a trifling breach of faith had been necessary, a breach which Bosco had lightheartedly committed against Anton. He loved Anton, recognized in him his master, and without hesitation would have sacrificed his life for him. Yet he was closer to Florian; they were closer to each other than man and beast could ever be.

In the beginning Bosco still had to fall back on his cunning and his intrepid terrier stubbornness.

The first time he sneaked away from Anton in the commissary Anton searched high and low for him: out by the hurdles, in the house, at his comrade's. He whistled and shouted; but Bosco, who heard distinctly, refused to budge from his place next to Florian in the straw. Anton was desperate until somebody suggested that he take a look in the stable. Bosco pretended to be fast asleep. Anton lifted him tenderly and carried him to his room.

The second time, Bosco escaped from Anton's bed shortly before it was time to retire. Anton promptly missed him and fetched him back.

So Bosco made a practice of slinking out of bed during the night; and in the morning Anton, finding him curled up at the foot of the bedstead, thought it must have been too hot for the dog and suspected nothing.

Then one morning Anton did not find him there. He had got away during the night and joined Florian. Bosco had waited until Anton was fast asleep; he knew just when Anton had reached the depth of his deep slumber and would hear nothing short of a thunder-clap or a pistol-shot. And as Bosco could neither thun-der nor shoot, he had succeeded in slipping out.

This became his practice.

He would press his paw against the unlocked door, usually standing slightly ajar, and would push it open just enough to let his slender body through. In case the latch held, for a change, he by no means lost hope; it only required a little more cunning. He would climb up on the chair that stood by the door and shove against the latch until it gave—he knew when by the short metallic click. He would remain utterly still for a while, not daring to breathe, and listen for any sound from Anton's bed. If nothing stirred, he would then steal out on cautious pads and make straight for the stable. Truth to say, his conscience would trouble him, but his craving for the company of Florian outweighed all else.

Snuggling up close against Florian's back, he was blissfully content. He slept in a profound repose. Often, waking before his comrade, he rested his chin on Florian's back; another day of happy activity would soon begin.

When Anton appeared in the morning, Bosco would greet him with a spasm of enthusiastic tail-wagging, his eyes popping from their sockets, his body convulsed by joyous yelps and barks. That was always a great scene. He feigned utter innocence; as if his making off in the night had been a natural thing which Anton understood and agreed to.

All Anton understood, however, was that Bosco had shamelessly deserted. He took Bosco's noisy greeting for a sort of regret, and was always consoled immediately and anxious on his part to calm Bosco. "You rascal," he whispered, "you sneak... well... well... that's all right." But Bosco did not rest until Anton stopped grooming the horses to come and catch hold of him, petted his back or rubbed his head, and said: "Nice Bosco... nice doggie." Then Bosco would sprint up and down the whole length of the stable once or twice, inordinately proud of that public testimonial. And Anton laughed and proceeded with his work.

Evening after evening Anton stubbornly carried Bosco to his room and laid him to sleep, thinking his will would prevail against the dog's seemingly inexplicable predilection. He had to carry him because Bosco refused to obey his order and come along voluntarily.

Once, just after Anton had picked up the terrier and walked toward the door, he heard light hoofbeats at his back. There stood Florian with a naïve face, his ears tilted forward and his large expressive eyes on Bosco.

Anton did not quite grasp what it all meant.

Florian edged nearer and stretched his neck. His nose touched Bosco's as the little dog struggled up in Anton's arms. It was as though the two were kissing each other good night. Or else, as if Florian were asking Bosco, "Please stay," and Bosco answering, "I can't, don't you see?"

Anton bent low and set Bosco on the floor.

Whereupon Florian swung around and sauntered back to his stall where Sibyl stood watching. He walked slowly, and Bosco, with wagging tail, walked slowly beside him.

Anton followed them with his eyes until they disappeared in the stall. So Florian wanted his friend with him. That much he suddenly understood. There was nothing to be done about it. "All right with me," he thought, and went to bed alone.

Chapter Five

LIPIZZANS TAKE LONGER TO ARRIVE at maturity than other horses.

Florian grew slowly. A year after his birth he still had the physical attributes and the mannerisms of the foal. Younger than he, Bosco was already running around, grown-up, gay, intelligent, and attached to Florian with an unwavering loyalty. They had to be always together. Each grew restless when out of the other's sight, even if for only a few brief minutes.

Florian still clung to his mother although he was

almost as big as she; he had yet to show the least sign of independence. Bosco, on the other hand, had learned, knew life, was absolutely self-reliant and considerably cleverer than his big playmate. In spite of that, or perhaps just because of it, Bosco admired Florian, admired his mother, admired all the great, white, majestic beings living here. Within him there was a bond of sympathy which somehow united him with these gentle quiet giants; a bond wrought by the realization that all, all of them, belonged to mighty Man, whom Bosco adulated as Man does his God. Bosco's lot was a happier one than Man's. He could see his god, smell him, hear him. From the hands of his god he received caresses, from his mouth kindly words; and besides that, Bosco had an especially good god, one who never beat him and never seriously scolded. Anton could not maltreat any living thing. He understood animals too well, was too close to them.

Oftentimes, when Sibyl was harnessed and put before a light barouche to drive around the estate of Lipizza for a half hour or so, Florian ran alongside her, so close, so well attuned to her stride, he might have been harnessed with her. Bosco would dash ahead, whirl around dizzily, bark merrily at first, and soon fall silent—as if to prove that he could be as self-contained as his friends. As much as he might like to, at times, he never outstripped them by too far. He always maneuvered to stay near Florian, except once or twice to circle the carriage, and after a few introductory caprioles always settled into his dog's trot.

The reins were held by this or that stud-master, or by one of the higher officials of the stud-farm. The driver invariably held a whip in his hand but never lashed a horse. Such a thing did not happen at Lipizza. The horses did not need it. They were not allowed to be whipped, and were not whipped. This system had produced such extraordinary results that in the course of many generations it had become an unwritten but religiously observed law to be gentle with these gentle animals. And thus had been bred in the Lipizzan strain an inherited insight into the human will, an atavistic readiness to obey willingly and promptly. Thus the long whip flicked only lightly and softly, barely to be felt, over hindquarters, tickled back of the ears—and these signals were sufficient to change the tempo. A scarcely perceptible tug at the reins, or a sound from the lips of the driver, arrested the horse in its course. Never was an animal torn at the mouth. Soft and delicate from birth, so they remained, even after they were lodged in the Imperial Stables in Vienna.

Anton knew all that. Nevertheless it always gave him a mild shock to see Sibyl in her harness, driving off accompanied by Florian and Bosco. He would stare after them full of anguish, and be freed of the strange feeling only after he had unharnessed Sibyl, brushed her and Florian down, and fastened their blankets over them.

Time lazied by in a placid unbroken rhythm. Only by the passing of summer into winter, of long days into long nights, did the clock of eternity tell man that the earth once again completed her circular flight.

Florian finished the third year of his existence. Now he enjoyed his splendid full growth. And of the entire herd of horses at Lipizza he was the most beautiful. None of the others was as dazzling white as he. Not a false tinge anywhere mottled his perfect coat. He shone like silver, like milk, like freshly fallen snow, like moonlight. No comparison quite fitted. Florian shimmered as only Florian could. Already it was fabled in Lipizza that only once, and that already ten decades ago, had any of Florian's ancestors been as pure white.

Florian's body had the flawless symmetry of physique of all Lipizzans. He carried his neck in a proud regal curve, and his marvelous head, with its well-formed ears, its wonderful dark liquid eyes, enthralled everyone. The white of his head was shaded around the nostrils and lips a delicate rose-tinted gray which still preserved the undertone of white. Those nostrils and voluptuous lips–they really were voluptuous and suggested unstilled sensuality–were tempting under the touch.

Anton would stand in front of Florian and press those nostrils and lips with his palm, would fondle and stroke and rub; and Florian would accept it patiently for a while. As for Bosco, he would squat on his haunches and look on reverently. At length Florian would thrust his head up high, snort and glance at Anton half-apologetically:

"Don't be angry—but that's enough." Then Anton would slap the white back and say: "Don't be angry . . . Florian, you are quite right . . . that's really enough."

Florian would execute a few side steps, beat his flanks with his silvery white tail which he bore on a short handle like a flag, and shake his mane of spun ivory. Bosco would be already waiting, his snout raised in a mute query. After this slight pause—the equivalent of consideration for Anton—Florian would lope decorously across the meadow with Bosco playfully pacing him.

Florian danced when he walked, glided when he galloped. He seemed molded out of power, fire, grace and softness, was temperament and measured force.

This summer Captain von Neustift once again visited Lipizza. He was accompanied by his wife, Elizabeth, in appearance as much a girl as ever. They strolled across the rolling meadows in and out of clusters of horses.

Anton smiled when he saw them, stood at attention and saluted.

"Ah, Pointner!" Neustift stopped and glanced around.

"The Florian can't be very far away. Am I right? Where is he?"

"By your leave, *Herr Rittmeister*." Anton saluted again. "I am sure you can find him yourself."

Neustift's eyes roved. "I am to find him ... it isn't as easy as all that."

"Oh, yes: it is," Anton assured him, "very easy."

"There!" Elizabeth cried, and with her outstretched arm she pointed at the white stallion. "There he is! It must be!"

"Your Grace is right," Anton nodded, "that's him ... that's Florian." He turned around, waved, whistled and hallooed: "Florian ... Bosco ... Here, Florian!" And, again to the visitors: "Just a moment ... he'll be right here."

They did not have to wait long. Florian sauntered near. The two visitors paid no attention to the terrier who ran ahead of him; they fell silent in sheer admiration as if a prince were approaching.

Like a creature of light Florian stood before them, almost majestically innocent, bewitching in his beauty and in his serene confidence.

Neustift whispered: "Have you a piece of sugar?"

"Yes!" replied Elizabeth with bated breath. As if awakened from a dream, she rummaged through her pocketbook and then proffered the lump on her palm. Florian took it with careful lips.

Elizabeth smiled: "He kisses it away." She, too, spoke in a whisper: "You really can't describe it as anything else . . . he kisses it right out of my palm."

They were both a little embarrassed in the presence of this innocent young animal.

"Do you remember, child . . . ?" Neustift asked.

Elizabeth countered with another question: "Could anyone forget?"

"That was the day of our betrothal," Neustift said, and stroked Florian.

"How strange," Elizabeth mused, "that we have not been here once since then. . . . It seems ungrateful."

"Ungrateful!" her husband protested. "Oh, no. There was our marriage . . . our honeymoon . . . the garrison in Galicia . . . You can't always do just as you wish. . . . This has really been our first chance."

In the meantime Florian had come a step closer and sniffed at Elizabeth's hands and then at her pocketbook. His breath was warm mist.

"He wants more. Just look at the beggar," she exclaimed. She was pleased, and her pleasure rose out of a subconscious feeling of youth and health.

Hastily she found another lump and offered it, and while Florian accepted it with gentle courtliness, she said to Neustift: "How big he has grown! . . . and how handsome. . . ." she added.

Florian stared into her face expectantly, pleadingly, and yet with a certain proud air; a mien so expressive, so spiritual, so noble, that it was impossible to withstand.

"He's coming along, Pointer," Neustift said approvingly. "He's coming along . . . He will be the pride of the Spanish Riding School."

Anton agreed gloomily: "That's true, *Herr Rittmeister* . . . There's nothing to be done about it . . . I hate to think of the day when Florian's got to leave here."

Chapter Six

GRIM REALITY SENT ITS ADVANCE messengers masquerading in festive garb. Anton alone did not share the high spirits of his comrades and of the officials of the stud-farm; the director, the stable-master, the veterinary and all the rest of them.

When Anton took Florian over to the smithy, that day, for his first set of shoes, Florian seemed quite happy. This event and its consequences excited him, intensified his self-assurance and his love of life. To Anton he was just like a child going to be confirmed by the bishop. With a group of other three-year-olds Florian stood in the smithy. Bosco lay on the ground at his feet, his dangling tongue feverish with curiosity, and studied first Florian, then Anton, and in turn all the horses and the men around him, his gaze coming to rest on the roaring open fire of the forge.

Anton held Florian lightly by his mane and was the only sad one there. He had to force a smile when the other stableboys called out compliments and praise to Florian. He was accustomed to that. All the other horses wore traces to which their halters were attached. Some champed nervously at their bits, flecks of foam dripping down; for they had only just been broken to the bridle.

"Naturally," one of the men said, "Florian is still free . . . still has nothing on his head or in his mouth." There was no trace of admiration in his voice.

Curtly and arrogantly Anton replied: "He doesn't need anything."

"That's what I said," the other one confirmed. "He's still free."

One of the smiths came up. "And what the devil is this?" he asked uncouthly. "How are we to hold the nag?"

"This isn't a nag," Anton retorted. "Don't be afraid . . . he'll hold still, all right."

"Afraid?" the smith growled. "Who's afraid?"

Anton took one of Florian's legs by the fetlock. "There . . . look at that," he said, bragging. And indeed Florian permitted Anton to do with his leg as he pleased; he was as docile as a little dog learning to give his paw. "Try the size," Anton ordered the smith. "You don't need big ones anyway . . . he has such a small hoof," he felt obliged to add. And he cautioned: "Light and thin irons. They are his first ones."

The smith growled: "I see that, stupid."

But Anton decided not to hear the insult. He wanted to be on friendly terms with the man who gave Florian his first shoes. Obediently Florian lifted one leg after the other. He felt Anton's fingers spanning his ankles. Each blow of the hammer coming down on his small yellow hoof, sent his head higher, arched his neck more proudly.

"Watch out, he'll buck in a minute," one of the lads laughed.

"And bolt," another one yelled.

"Like hell he will!" Anton barked without straightening up or releasing Florian's leg. "He's an angel," he whispered into the smith's ear, "there's never been one like him."

The smith laughed. "I know him." And he hammered on.

At first Bosco had barked at the sight of the smith hitting his comrade with a hammer, and had been scolded by Anton. Now he looked on attentively, his ears pointed, his head cocking now to this, now to the other, side. He followed the two men around from one leg to the next, and stood close up, as if he had to supervise the goings-on.

At last the task was done. Florian had his shoes.

"Jesus, he is glad," Anton said to the smith, who patted Florian's hindquarters, leaving traces of his sooty fingers on the white rump.

"He has every reason to he," the smith rejoined.

Anton did not quite catch the meaning of his words but didn't bother to think about them.

"Let's go," he addressed Florian and walked ahead.

With Bosco in his wake, Florian followed Anton, picking his way right through the crowd of foals waiting around. When he passed Nausicaa he threw up his head and whinnied longingly.

Nausicaa answered. She was a young mare, well built, with a beautiful white head and rosy nostrils. But her body was white only at the neck, loins and middle. The rest of her was a cloudy gray that grew darker down her legs; just as if she wore pearl-gray leggings.

"Come, Florian, come," Anton adjured. And Florian did not tarry.

The turf sounded different under his hooves. He noticed this, and sensing an added importance in himself, moved about in something of a trance.

He was habitually self-controlled. That was in his blood. And so now he did not run wild, nor did he neigh indecorously again. He enjoyed his exalted mood quietly, for himself. Only in the springiness of his gait, in the lofty poise of his head, in the fire that flashed from his eyes, was it noticeable.

With no other filly was he on such friendly terms as with Nausicaa. He had romped and rolled around in the grass with her while their mothers stood by. He had raced with her, with her alone, among all the fillies. They understood each other perfectly, had become inseparable and in all innocence agreed never to part. When Florian greeted Nausicaa in the smithy he had no idea that there was such a thing as leave-taking, as separation.

Anton walked on before him. Bosco was as frolicsome and diverting as ever. But they did not go back to where his mother, Sibyl, was. Unaware, Florian had forever left the home of his childhood. He joined the young stallions, separated from the mothers, parted from the young mares. He entered a strange stable and received a stall of his own. Bosco stayed with him. So did Anton, who had managed to have himself transferred.

The new home, too, wore a holiday air. His longing

for his mother Florian felt only dimly, although the longing for Nausicaa—that was sharper. He did not know what was behind his desire, and what beyond. . . . However, there was but scant time left to brood.

One day the stud-master came and forced a cold iron chain between Florian's teeth. Anton put the traces on his head, thin leather strips that lay flush against forehead and cheeks. Florian suffered it, there being no instinct of protest within him. Down through count-less ancestors had come his willingness to subject him-self to the will of Man. His instinct knew that his days of service had begun. And so, on this hallowed occasion, he stood pawing the ground with one hoof, champing to accustom himself to the bit which rested on his tongue. Bubbles of foam formed at the mouth-corners. He scattered them around in big white blobs when he shook his head. A slight pressure in his mouth, at the corners . . . Florian understood the order and obeyed.

Anton threw a light harness across his back. Like a belt the broad leather encircled his chest. Next he was carefully shoved backward a few steps and found himself between two poles, the thill of a light carriage. He waited impatiently. It did not take long, but each second dropped deliberately, heavily into eternity. He pawed the ground more vigorously, the foam fell in larger specks from his lips, and his ears moved incessantly.

Anton patted his neck, talked soothingly. Florian felt nothing, heard nothing. Everything in him, each nerve and fiber, waited for a sign. He was held fast, that much he knew definitely because of the bit between his teeth and the belt on his chest by which the cart was hitched to him. In his mounting impatience he attempted a step.

"*Psst,*" he heard from behind and felt a gentle tug at his mouth.

Florian stood motionless.

"*Tssk!*" The bit grew lax in his mouth.

Florian rushed forward. Gallop! Cleaving in twain the surge of joy which had suddenly befallen him came the voice of his master. "Whoa!" And once again he felt the pressure against his lips. It had all happened in three or four seconds. He understood instantly, and obeyed the order without hesitation, altering his pace to a comfortable trot.

He had never felt so good. The trappings on him did not hamper his running, gave him a sensation of ordered freedom too complicated for him to unravel but delightful notwithstanding. He was conscious of the hand of the driver, the turning of the wheels. The burden of the cart, which was hardly a burden at all, thrilled him. In one burst of gladness he reveled in his youth and in the power of his limbs. With loud snorts he drove the air from his lungs. Drops of foam fell right and left. His flanks grew moist, and sweat purled down his back and neck. Occasionally his gleaming eyes laughed down to Bosco who ran ahead of him and who only by strenuous exertions was keeping up the brisk pace.

Florian enjoyed his debut in a world his ancestors had peopled in the service of men as trusted chargers in battle and attack, as saviors in peril and flight, as skilled and untiring companions at jousts and falconry, and on hunts and overland journeys; as carriers of messages, and as the pride of processions and parades. His heritage flamed within him. He served; he became a carrier, executant of a divine and adored will.

Florian was happy.

A half hour later the carriage rolled to a halt before the stable.

"This Florian is perfect!" the stud-master cried, throwing the reins to Anton and jumping down from the dashboard. "It's unbelievable!"

"Isn't he?" Anton smiled happily, bending down to unbuckle the harness.

"I have never seen anything like it! He runs as if he had carried harness for God knows how long. He knows everything himself, the least hint is sufficient. . . ."

"Yes, that's Florian," Anton agreed gravely.

"He doesn't even try a gallop anymore . . . just trots . . . a beautiful, steady trot . . . he rolls along like a billiard ball. . . . Unbelievable!"

Florian, led by Anton, stepped from the thill. "Yes," Anton reiterated, "that's Florian!"

He threw a blanket over the steaming stallion and

began to unharness him. As he removed the traces and the bit, Florian shook his head vehemently with relief.

"Let him keep the bit," the stud-master suggested. "So he'll get used to it."

With his bare hand Anton brushed the lather from Florian's heaving chest. "Oh, no . . . if you please, sir . . . he doesn't need to get used to anything . . . not him . . . he just knows everything."

Bosco lay, utterly exhausted, where he had sunk down to rest, but his pointed ears kept him apprised of any developments. He had ample time to recuperate. Anton had brush and currycomb ready, and now stripped the blanket from his charge's back and began to groom him.

Chapter Seven

CAPTAIN VON NEUSTIFT CAME again on a visit, this time alone.

"Where is her Grace, the countess?" Anton asked.

"She is in bed," Neustift answered, and laughed when Anton showed concern. "Oh, no, my dear Pointner. Not sick! No, on the contrary! Yes, just think of it, we have a son, a very small son, a tiny mite of a son. Leopold Ferdinand Rainer Maria! Just a wee bit of flesh and already Leopold Ferdinand Rainer Maria ... he is really cute."

Anton stammered congratulations.

"Perhaps this is to be an important occasion for you, too." The captain stood with his arms akimbo. "Do you know what brings me here today? I want to buy Florian . . . if I can get him."

Anton shook his head. "Florian you will not get, *Herr Rittmeister*," he said with finality.

"Don't be silly, Anton, I've got to get him. My wife wants Florian . . . do you understand, Anton? Well . . ."

Anton repeated. "I don't believe . . ."

Neustift laid his hand on the peasant's shoulder. "And you are to come along. You and Florian, together. What do you say to that?"

But Anton insisted. He laughed as he said for a third time: "I don't believe . . ."

At that Neustift grew impatient. "Why quarrel? Fetch him and hitch him to the carriage."

"The carriage . . . ?"

"Yes. Today I am permitted to drive. What do you know about that?"

Anton whistled and Bosco rushed up, stood with head tilted, questioning.

"Go fetch Florian!" Anton demanded.

Bosco fled, and after a short while Florian came at a light canter with Bosco bounding all around him.

The stable-master came over, and when Anton had put the harness on Florian, stepped into the carriage with Neustift. The captain took the reins. "You will be surprised, *Herr Rittmeister—*" That much Anton heard and then they were off.

Naturally Bosco went along. Anton remained alone. He stared after the disappearing carriage, rubbed his chin and thought: "He won't get Florian. . . . No, they couldn't be so stupid as to give him away."

The cart came back, and with scarcely any slowing down, Florian stopped and stood like a statue.

"Marvelous!" was Neustift's verdict, climbing down. "It's absolutely incredible! He knows everything by instinct. Why, a child could drive him."

Smiling contentedly, Anton busied himself with the harness, and overheard fragments of the conversation between Neustift and the stable-master.

". . . not up to me, you know that. . . . But I am afraid there isn't a chance. You see . . ."

"... willing to pay any price ... whatever you ask ... I'll pay and ..."

"Not a chance. You'd better find another ..."

"I want Florian."

"... another one gladly. Anyone you like. Florian is not for sale."

Anton led his charge into the stable. Like a conqueror Florian stepped after him.

When Anton came out again the captain had gone.

Chapter Eight

SEVERAL GENTLEMEN OF THE IMPERIAL Court arrived in Lipizza. Their first inquiries were after Florian. And being the first name they mentioned, Florian was the first stallion they saw. He was thoroughly gone over and then tested in harness.

One of the gentlemen read from the stud-book: ". . . son of Berengar out of Sibyl."

Another, lost in admiration, who was apparently the highest in rank, asked: "Four years old . . . isn't he?"

"Yes, your Excellency," the one who had read Florian's

family tree answered. "Born on May 4, 1901. . . . Exactly four years and one month old."

Anton stood sadly by. Nobody took notice of a stableboy.

Suspiciously Bosco ran to and fro, as if he sensed something ominous.

"He really trots marvelously," the slender gray-haired important gentleman declared. "He won't need a great deal of training to make him ready for the carriage of his Majesty."

"Forgive me, your Excellency," another ventured to say. He was smaller than the one he addressed, very slim, and had a smooth face and a brown complexion which turned almost violet at the neck.

". . . But this Florian is really too valuable for that."

"Is that so?" said the tall one not without some irony. "Too good for the service of his Majesty? Interesting . . . very interesting."

The brown face grew a shade darker. "We are all in the service of his Majesty, your Excellency, men and horses. . . ."

The other wrinkled his brow, stroked his short gray

mustache, and murmured: "Thank you for your information . . . but there is a difference, I think."

"That's just what I meant!" The dark brown face
did not lose its strict self-control, yet underneath there
had been an explosion at those words. "My God! I was
thinking of driving, your Excellency, nothing else. And
a carriage is a carriage, after all."

His Excellency straightened up. "The carriage in
which his Majesty the Emperor . . ."

"That is immaterial to the horses," his adversary
interrupted him. "I beseech you, your Excellency, this
stallion here . . . for decades we haven't had anything
like it in the Riding School. No, your Excellency, even
if you are enraged at me now . . . I simply have to say
it . . . it is my duty . . . I beg of you, I entreat you, your
Excellency, don't deny this marvelously gifted animal
his God-given destiny. Someday we shall all be proud of
him." And as his Excellency was about to reply to that,
he added confidently: "Someday your Excellency will be
grateful to me for speaking so freely."

Florian stood with head held high. Bare of his

trappings, he seemed created for no other purpose than to inspire enthusiasm by his matchless beauty and majesty. Those who viewed him were thrilled, refreshed and stimulated.

Florian was not aware that this scene spelled goodbye to the home of his youth, farewell to childhood. Bosco squatted on his haunches with his head tilted and his ears stiffly pointed, attentively studying his beloved friend. Bosco had a presentiment, deep down in his little heart, of an impending change. And he was troubled.

Anton knew what all this meant. He stood a few paces aside, forgotten, hanging on every word that was spoken. Each word, while it sounded melodious to his ears, was like a dagger thrust in his breast. Lovingly his eyes swept over Florian. Yes, it was Florian being lauded and appreciated. And that was right. Yet that very appreciation was causing Anton to lose Florian. And he could not imagine what life without Florian would be.

Without Florian! Anton's eyes clouded. Had it only been possible for Captain von Neustift to buy Florian!

The captain would take him, Anton, along with Florian, and there need be no separation.

Florian pawed the ground. He lifted the slender, well-formed leg with consummate grace, held it gravely and hesitantly aloft, and then struck the ground.

The noble curve of the neck, the head so poised that the chin was pressed to the breast, made an incomparable picture of gentility and humbleness combined. Florian snorted loudly.

His Excellency, who had not answered the brown-faced man during a constrained pause, now said: "Upon my word . . . he is as beautiful as the horse of Colleone."

"Yes," the other one agreed. "That was a Lipizzan, too."

"Well," his Excellency modified, "not exactly a Lipizzan . . . but at least of a lineage which later came to Lipizza."

"It's all the same." The brown face beamed. "I call the Colleone a Lipizzan. And a rider's horse that was, too. One to bear a rider, not to drag a carriage. That's certain. Surely there's your answer."

Instead of replying, the courtier stepped over to Florian, took him by the nose-bone and pulled his head close. With his great luminous dark eyes Florian bored into the man. He was asking a question that merely lacked the spoken words. Nor did the courtier say one word. He straightened Florian's satiny forelock, straightened it as carefully as if this were of vital importance. Then he ran his fingers through the full white mane which lent the curved back its daring note. The expert hand patted the warm sleek shoulder, the broad breast.

"Very well, Ennsbauer." His Excellency at last came to a decision and moved away from Florian. "I don't want to quarrel with you. You are convinced Florian belongs to you."

"As sure as there's a God above, your Excellency," Ennsbauer cried, "he belongs in the Spanish School!"

"I repeat, I don't want to quarrel with you. On your responsibility, then, he won't be put in his Majesty's carriage. . . ."

"To any carriage . . . on my responsibility."

"Perhaps you are right."

"I am right." Ennsbauer spoke with fanatical conviction.

"All right." His Excellency brushed everything else aside. "I prefer to say you *may* be right. We both agree as to the extraordinary qualities of this horse. There is no difference of opinion on that score." Once more he turned to Florian, stroked his back and, his hand still resting on the stallion, concluded: "We'll talk about it in Vienna."

Chapter Nine

TOGETHER WITH EIGHT OTHER young horses Florian was taken to the station to start on the journey to Vienna.

In all, there were five stallions and four mares. A special train stood ready, one that made the trip overnight. Two, and in one case three, animals were confined to a boxcar. Florian remained in the company of another stallion.

A small troupe of stablemen had come down from Vienna to escort the animals to the capital.

The walk to the station, however, the entraining itself, and finally the farewell did not go so smoothly. Anton, Florian and Bosco were too closely bound to one another, Florian was too much a part of their lives for both Anton and Bosco, too much the hub of their existence, to make it simply a matter of tearing the three apart in order to separate the two from the one.

When they left the stud-farm, the misery began. At first only for Anton. For the young stallion and Bosco were as yet blissfully ignorant of what was in store for them. After the courtiers had departed, Bosco had calmed down completely. The Viennese stablemen did not bother him much. Sniffing, he had investigated them carefully and established the fact that they belonged to stables, horses and dogs. Thus he accepted the joint exodus as a novel and adventurous undertaking, scampered with short barks around the cavalcade or else trotted beside Florian and Anton, confirming his undying friendship with the incessant wagging of his tail.

Florian wore a loose headgear decorated around

the eyes with laurel twigs. So did the other horses. No bit had been clamped between his teeth. When the Viennese lad had insisted on it, Anton's answer had been short: "No need for that."

The fellow from Vienna, Wessely was his name, wanted to take the guide rope and lead Florian. But Anton was ahead of him, holding the halter loosely in his hand: "Let me." Then he gulped and became tongue-tied.

On the way Wessely started a conversation which ended before it really began, since Anton would not answer.

After a while Anton asked: "You . . . ?" He halted, and added falteringly: "Tell me . . . how is it in Vienna?"

The description of the Imperial Stables Wessely gave, he didn't hear. All his thoughts, his feelings circled constantly and entirely around one fact: "Now I still lead Florian . . . and tomorrow he is here no more . . . nor the day after . . . never again." This "never again" he simply could not fathom, the more since Florian, milk-white, dazzling, still walked at his elbow and whinnied every now and then. Deep down Anton knew that this striding, this dancing, this gliding was a going away . . . far away . . . forever. . . .

Anton examined the boxcar as a father examines his son's dormitory in a strange boarding school.

Wessely laughed. "It's just as clean here as in the stables in Vienna."

He didn't get a response. Anton was too sad, too depressed to find a word of praise for the cleanliness of the boxcar, the abundance of clean straw and oats and water. He stepped into the open door and said softly: "Come." And much to Wessely's surprise, Florian ran up the narrow gangplank. Bosco came along and stretched comfortably in the straw.

"What else do you want now?" Wessely asked.

Anton paid no heed. He held Florian in a close embrace. "Florian," he whispered, "my Florian . . . good-bye . . . good-bye." Again and again the same words: "Good-bye, Florian . . . good-bye."

"Get out of here!" Wessely cried in exasperation. "We're pulling out."

It came like a dagger thrust. To be torn from Florian! Anton paid no attention to Wessely; he looked once more at this beautiful soft creature whose white body seemed to fill the boxcar with light. "Well, Florian," he whispered without touching him, "don't forget me. Do you hear?"

The runway was withdrawn. With a loud metallic clatter of the coupling joints the car lurched. Anton jumped down.

"There's your dog," Wessely shouted, and flung Bosco out. Anton just managed to catch the yowling terrier. The train rolled faster and faster into the dusk of the landscape.

Anton visioned Florian's astonished face, the last helpless glance of surprise in the large dewy eyes.

Bosco whimpered forlornly. Anton could not quiet him. The terrier refused to budge and had to be carried away.

"Quiet, Bosco," Anton tried to console him on the way home. "There's nothing to be done about it." He pressed the dog against his chest, suffered him to lick his face pleadingly, helplessly, and felt like crying him-self. "Be sensible, Bosco. Gone is gone."

That night the stableman, Anton Pointner, sat in the inn for the first time. For the first time he drank, and drank heavily. Bosco lay on the bench by his side, his nozzle thrust between his master's knees. As often as he whimpered or yowled, Anton clutched his glass and downed a big draught.

Opposite him sat the stableman, Franz, and leered. The others sitting at the neighboring tables nodded encouragingly to Franz. Anton did not notice. He saw nobody and nothing around him. He kept on star-ing into his beer mug or into the thick smoke of the room. If his glass was empty he motioned the waiter to refill it.

"Why, there's Anton!" Franz exclaimed, feigning delighted surprise. "Anton . . . what a rare guest. Tell me, how did you get here?"

Silence.

"Why don't you say something? Aren't you going to bed?"

Silence.

"Look at the fellow—how he can drink! Like a fish. Well . . . I'd never have thought he could guzzle like that."

Silence.

"Well, sure, of course . . . he hears nothing and sees nothing. He's got to drown his sorrow over Florian. Florian's left him."

Anton leaned across and lifted his fist. Like a hammer it fell on his tormentor's head. Franz sagged. His chin hit the table.

"Shut up!" said Anton, gnashing his teeth.

Franz stumbled to his feet, rubbed his head and changed his seat. Nobody in the room said a word.

Chapter Ten

EARLY NEXT MORNING THE SPECIAL train drew into the Südbahnhof in Vienna. The nine horses were detrained. Wrapped in warm flannel blankets they stood ready. The night journey had shaken them up. This strange new world disturbed them, but they all remained tranquil and patient.

All, that is, except Florian. In a near frenzy he stamped, lashed his luxuriant tail, reared his head high, and neighed again and again.

He sought Anton. He waited for Bosco. In vain.

Abruptly he gave in, with the instinct of his breed for obedience at all times and in all circumstances. His heart was still with Anton, and he was wracked by longing for Bosco's diverting antics. But he permitted Wessely to lead him by the halter-cord, and submitted to the cold steely bit between his teeth.

The streets were still barely awake.

Stony streets between stony rows of houses were a novelty to Florian. Intently he looked from side to side, his nostrils telling him of the existence of many strange horses in this strange stony world; the innumerable other smells he caught he did not recognize.

A milk-wagon clattered by over the cobblestones. Two scrawny sorrels clop-clopped unrhythmically, pulling it.

Relatives! Florian had an impulse to greet them with a loud neigh. But they looked too shabby. Their eyes were hidden behind black leather blinders. Plodding along so mechanically, they seemed of a different race to their noble kinsman.

Florian snorted and began to curvet.

Slowly, puffing and panting, two heavy Pinzgauers passed dragging a mountainous load of brick. They stepped deliberately and heavily, putting one foot down before the other. Sparks shot from under their shoes.

Florian flicked his ears and settled down to a leisurely gait.

At a light smooth trot, cabs rolled by. It was pleasant to hear the even hoofbeats come closer, thunder by and die away in the distance. Fiacres!

Here and there trees and bushes rustled and nodded in small grassy areas. But to Florian's mild surprise and dismay nobody noticed them or visited them. When they crossed the Ring, he was tremendously bewildered by the spectacle of long red carriages, strung together in twos and threes, which ran by without horses to pull them, all by themselves!

They wended their way through a narrow street which, farther on, nestled close to a wide open square; and came into the shadow of a squat archway, making through a door into a small court. The scent of horses, fresh and pungent, the smell of straw, hay, oats, pinched their nostrils. They were at their goal.

Florian had all the time expected to find Anton awaiting him there, expected Bosco to rush at him with a hymn of joy. Neither Anton nor Bosco was there.

Led into his stall, combed down and brushed by Wessely, Florian ate scarcely a mouthful of oats, took a few hasty sips of water from the brown marble trough, turned away from the crib, pressed his head against the grating which closed him in, looked and listened to every side, wiggled his ears at every footfall he heard.

Anton . . . Bosco . . . Where are you? The open spaces . . . the free and easy play . . . the couch of warm grass . . . the caressing, warming sun . . . where is all that? Where? But above and before all else; Anton and the little dog!

Gone, overnight!

Chapter Eleven

IN THE SPANISH RIDING SCHOOL THEY are working the young stallions. The Emperor's equerry, that Excellency who came to Lipizza to make his selections, watches the proceedings. With him are Captain von Neustift and his wife, Elizabeth.

The riding master, Ennsbauer, takes one horse after another on the longe.

But Florian is not present.

"What do you say about Florian, your Excellency?" Elizabeth presses the question.

The equerry brushes his hand nervously over his short gray mustache. "We'll see . . . Perhaps he'll come around. . . ."

"Perhaps!" Elizabeth cries, almost offended.

"Yes. Perhaps."

This agitates the countess. "Something must have happened to Florian. I cannot understand it."

"It's quite a puzzle to me, too," his Excellency replies. "Obviously something has happened to him. But what?" He shrugs his shoulders. "Nobody knows."

Neustift joins in the conversation. "My wife wanted very much to have Florian . . . very much. It was almost an obsession with her. I was ready to pay any price for him . . ."

"Too bad," says the equerry. "Too bad, Countess, that you did not get the horse. Now he is *of course* not for sale. I'd rather see him die. Too bad."

Sadly Elizabeth replies: "A puzzle. Quite a puzzle."

Neustift adds: "Florian was the nicest foal of the whole lot. Handsome. And in splendid condition."

"He is losing his beauty," the older man reveals, "and

from day to day he is in poorer condition. I fear the famous Florian is going to be a bitter disappointment. Isn't that so, Ennsbauer?"

Ennsbauer nods and calls back: "A colossal disappointment."

"May we see him?" asks Neustift.

"Why, certainly."

The three walk over to the stable.

Florian stands forlornly in his stall.

"He has lost weight," Neustift observes, shocked.

"Naturally," Wessely speaks up, disgruntled. "He is off his feed."

"Sick?" Elizabeth inquires anxiously.

"Not at all." Wessely stops his work, losing his temper altogether. "Absolutely healthy, the vet says."

Elizabeth opens the door. "Florian," she calls, "Florian!"

The stallion, who has stood in his corner with bowed head, slowly cranes his neck and peers around.

"Come here to me . . . come," Elizabeth beckons.

Florian takes a few steps toward her. His once

luminous eyes are dull and wear a sorrowful, blurred expression. He sniffs at the young woman, then at Neustift, and snorts.

"Not really," Neustift says. "He recognizes us."

From Elizabeth's palm Florian kisses away a piece of sugar. She strokes his nose and his upper lip.

"Poor Florian," she whispers, "you would have had things nicer with us. We wanted to take Anton, too. . . ."

Florian's ears tilt forward.

"Anton," the captain repeats, "Anton and Bosco."

Florian thrusts his head up, his ears play, his dark eyes dart forth joyous glints of light.

"Anton and Bosco . . . Anton and Bosco . . . Anton and Bosco . . ." Neustift and Elizabeth pronounce the names together, speaking softly in chorus. And Florian livens up, more and more.

Triumphantly Elizabeth turns to the equerry. "That's it! He is lonely, our Florian."

And the equerry answers with an indulgent smile: "If that's all it is, it can easily be cured."

As they are leaving the stable, Florian attempts to

follow them, and has to be shoved back into his stall.

"How touching!" Neustift philosophizes. "Too bad such an animal cannot speak."

"He has spoken, our Florian," his wife corrects him. "He has spoken quite clearly."

Chapter Twelve

IN A FEW DAYS ANTON ARRIVED.

When he received orders to proceed at once to the Spanish Riding School in Vienna, Anton was not surprised. It struck him as no more than natural that Florian should send for him. Whatever Florian wanted had to happen. Nothing in the world could be simpler.

Anton packed his belongings. He told Bosco that they were leaving together to go to Florian, and would have sworn that Bosco understood.

During the train ride he sat bolt upright and didn't shut an eye all night long. For the first few hours the dog sat upright by his side, but in the end he curled up comfortably on the hard wooden seat and slept until morning. Anton tenderly laid his arm across the terrier's neck, his hand resting on the lean flank.

In Vienna, Anton, his bundle on his shoulder, and accompanied by his dog, marched stolidly from the station to the Spanish Riding School. It was the first time in his life that he found himself in the great, rich, beautiful capital; yet he paid no attention. He had to ask his way, stopped a few passersby to get information. But in reality he virtually guessed where he had to go.

A battalion of infantry, parading back from the Prater, barred his passage along the Schwarzenbergplatz. He waited without growing impatient, and instead of watching the soldiers on their musical way, he stood transfixed, staring up at the bronze horse of the monument that dominated the square. "He is far more beautiful," he said to Bosco. The terrier did not disagree.

When at length he was able to proceed, he said

repeatedly, "Quiet . . . wait . . . we'll be there in no time. Not so fast." Once he even bent down and spoke to the terrier: "Don't be in such a hurry. Haven't we stood it for two months? We'll stand it another half hour."

Bosco could not repress his nervous impatience and became more unruly from minute to minute. His tongue hung out of his gaping mouth. He panted, tugged at the leash Anton had been forced to put on him. His master could not tell whether it was the trundling tram-cars along the boulevards that put the dog in such a feverish state, or the knowledge of the imminent reunion, or both.

Beyond the narrow Augustinerstrasse the Josephsplatz spread its monumental expanse. Anton showed no interest. He did not waste a glance on the statue of Joseph II which rose austerely in the center of the square. He knew when he got there: this is the Imperial Palace. And he felt certain that the three mighty facades his eyes beheld comprised all the home the Emperor had.

Who can say what impelled Anton to open the small door of the massive portal under the archway?

Was it because Bosco had caught the beloved scent and begun to leap against this door? Or could it have been that Anton himself had detected the scent? In any event, the porter upon being questioned directed him toward the stable, and Anton murmured: "At last."

He crossed the courtyard with unhurrying steps. He merely held the leash shorter. Bosco was not to get to Florian a second sooner than he. At the entrance to the stable stood Wessely with a group of other stablemen. He greeted Anton affably and started right in. "Now we'll see whether things improve with Florian."

"Are things bad with him, then?" Anton asked gravely.

Bosco yowled his fretful eagerness and for his pains received so hard a jerk at the leash that he nearly fell over. "Quiet!"

"Are things bad with him?" Anton repeated.

"Rotten!" cried Wessely, and asked the other men to bear witness. "He refuses to eat or work. Isn't that so?"

Herr Ennsbauer, the riding master, emerged from the stable. Anton stood at attention and gave his name as well as his destination.

"A good thing you came, Pointner," Ennsbauer remarked. "This is the last thing we are going to try with him." And noting Anton's dubious expression, he added: "Yes, the last thing. If this goes wrong"—he shrugged his shoulders—"well, then, we can't do a thing with the beast."

Without another word Anton passed Ennsbauer by and entered the half-dark stable. He did not see that all the others followed him. In a moment he came to the ell where, stretching away to both sides, were the compartments of the horses.

"Right," came from somebody behind him.

But Anton went no farther.

"Florian," he called. "Florian!" And Bosco broke into a jubilant baying.

Hooves suddenly beat against a wooden partition.

Anton did not stir from the spot, but he released the dog.

Wessely rushed down the corridor and swung wide the door behind which the hooves thundered. Florian broke out, almost knocking the man down. Bosco leaped high in the air, again and again, like a rubber ball, shrieking.

There stood the white stallion, looking hoary, as he used to when still a knock-kneed foal, his forelegs slightly apart. His bushy tail lashed the air excitedly, his neck bent downward, his head near the terrier on the ground. Bosco hopped about, whimpered as if saying: "So long to be separated," then exulted again shrilly: "At last I am with you!"

Florian, with rapid, gasping movements of his lips, softly touched the nose, the forehead, the back of his little comrade.

Anton, still rooted to the spot, said quietly: "And I, Florian?"

As if struck with a whip, Florian threw up his head. Step by step he came closer, his beautiful ears pointed. The dark soulful eyes blazed in the sun of recognition. He came up so close to Anton that he pushed him gently backward with his nose, pushed him against the wall and covered him with facial caresses, until Anton, who had rapturously accepted it all, raised his hand to the rose-tinted muzzle and whispered: "Enough."

From that hour on Florian was changed, was

what he had been before, the courtly and obedient Lipizzan, displaying no sorrow or ill-will. He began to feed again, hungrily, his body rounded out once more, and once more the silky bloom came over that sleek white skin.

Ennsbauer was plainly flabbergasted when he took him on the longe. "What an uncanny animal!"

"Countess," he later told Elizabeth, "as fine a horse as Florian we have never had in my time at the Riding School. Not one!"

Elizabeth and her husband came often. And just as often she came alone or with her little son. Neustift had been promoted to the rank of major and was the Emperor's adjutant. They both watched Florian on the longe, stood with Ennsbauer and observed how Florian guessed the slightest wish, the faintest command; how smoothly he changed pace, from walk to trot, from trot to gallop—short gallop or long gallop, as was desired—and how he halted on the instant and stood motionless as stone.

Shaking his head, Ennsbauer marveled: "No correction

is ever necessary. He does everything perfectly, by instinct."

Elizabeth responded with a smile: "And in the beginning how different it was."

"My God!" Ennsbauer sighed happily. "In the beginning I almost despaired. He balked and sulked and didn't want to do anything."

"... Until my wife recognized what he really wanted," Neustift concluded.

Ennsbauer wagged his head again. "Yes... strange as it may seem..."

In a serious vein, Elizabeth now said: "Just think how much soul an animal like that has. And how much loyalty."

Whereupon Neustift added: "And to think how quietly, how patiently, such an animal endures everything... loneliness, misunderstanding, longing."

"Yes," Ennsbauer concurred, "you wouldn't believe it possible."

Florian walked around in a circle, taking short paces at first, then longer strides. His milk-white powerful body in some devious manner reminded his observers of beautiful naked human beings, and this subconscious memory only augmented the impression of stark beauty, of the perfect harmony of youth, force and fettle, that he made. He snorted and his foam scattered in large flecks to the ground. He had a peculiarly graceful way of nodding his slightly tilted head while running, as if with these movements he was beating time to an inner music audible to himself alone.

Elizabeth and Neustift were thrilled. Their little son stared at Florian for a long time and then cried: "Mumsy, he sings . . . only we can't hear it."

Chapter Thirteen

ANTON SLOWLY ACCOMMODATED himself to his new surroundings. Of the city of Vienna he still knew next to nothing, for he stuck stubbornly to his stable, hung around even on his day off, roamed no farther than the courtyard which, surrounded by the high buildings of the old castle, was a universe in itself. At least it was Anton's. He never dreamed of taking a walk. The outside, the overwhelming, voluptuous, elegant city and its gay scintillating life, held no attraction or lure for him. Within the walls of the gigantic Hofburg he lived his life. There stood Florian behind the grating of his stall; there lay his terrier, Bosco. That was all and enough. Now and then a short conversation with a comrade. Anton was close-lipped and, as is frequently the case among those who devote themselves to the care of animals, extremely shy, almost timid.

At first the stable in all its glory filled Anton with a feeling of awe. The ornate brass-studded wood of the grilled doors and the expensive appointments of the stalls aroused his admiration. Here each horse had its own wide crib, and inlaid in the crib itself a water trough of red marble into which fresh water poured from the faucet. An elaborate leather harness, incrusted with the gilded Imperial crown and in some cases even Franz Joseph's initials, hung in front of every stall. There were fine, warm flannel blankets bordered with leather, accoutered with buckles, and the finest grooming utensils, brushes and currycombs. Bandages there were to soothe eyes pricked by straw, soft leather muzzles to prevent the animals from licking the salve from raw wounds.

Anton came to love the place. The high smooth walls curved concavely toward the ceiling and above every compartment was a beautifully modeled horse's head. How many generations these heads had looked down upon, didn't occur to Anton. He knew nothing of Karl VI, the founder of the Spanish Riding School. As a matter of fact he knew nothing about such things The Imperial Palace had stood for ever and aye, just as the Hapsburgs had ruled Austria for ever and aye. That had always been so and would always be so. That was that. Anton wasted no thought on the hazy future or on the unknown past. For him, as for Florian, only the present existed.

To reach the Riding School, the street leading underneath the archway had to be crossed. Anton regarded this street as something profane, something encroaching, and sometimes he wondered why the Emperor permitted all the people to walk and drive to and fro underneath his home.

When Anton entered the Riding School for the first time he stopped short in the entrance and put his hand to his mouth so that nobody should hear the soft exclamation which escaped his lips: "Jesus Mary!" Deeply moved, as in church, he stared and stared at this cathedral of the art of riding.

The wide hall was incredibly high, reaching to the very roof. The pale, ivory tone of the walls, the white arabesques of the balcony encircling it, the pilastered gallery above it, the curve of the faceted ceiling, the decorations of the balustrades, the two rows of windows, the grandiloquent escutcheon held triumphantly by genii high above the Court box, the larger than life-size portrait of Karl VI on the end wall—Anton could never quite take it all in, for his eyes invariably blurred. He grew bewildered before the majestic pathos which these figures and emblems declaimed in their stony impressive language of postures and designs.

The greatest event of his whole life occurred when he was granted permission to be present during the riding of the High School. Those gentlemen whom he had hitherto seen only in civilian garb wore brown frock coats with gold buttons, white stag-leather breeches taut about their thighs, and high patent-leather boots. They had on white gloves, white perukes with stiff white curls and a black silk riband tied about the queue, and two-cornered cocked hats.

The horses, on the other hand, were sparingly though richly bedecked. A narrow, gold-encrusted leather belt ran across each animal's breast, with a glittering little round gold shield or brooch dangling from it.

Anton observed how horses and riders entered the arena which they called the *Kobel.* The riders swung their hats low before the portrait of Karl VI.

The riding began.

Anton laughed. The noiseless, helpless grin that sat on his face made him appear more of a simpleton than usual. Only the ecstatic light in his eyes revealed that he was at this moment beside himself, completely self-effaced but assuredly not stupid. He was overwhelmed. Here before his eyes were presented the highest accomplishments of horsemanship. He saw the almost fabulous unity of horse and rider, recognized the invisible harmony uniting beast and man, the stream of will which poured itself forth like molten steel and mingled with a surging desire to love and to serve. He heard the silent language of human nerves speaking to expectant, listening equine nerves. Anton was figuratively swept off his feet, dazed. He had never fancied such things as this could be; he had paid little heed whenever the High School had been mentioned in the stable, never tried to picture what it was like.

Now everything was clear to him. He understood at last the reason for the stud-farm at Lipizza, understood the motive behind the sybaritic luxury of the stable appointments, understood the majestic grandeur of the great luminous hall where the white stallions from Lipizza performed their wondrous dance.

Those fanatical aspirations which Anton had had for Florian, up to that time, had been rather vague and in themselves devoid of any tangible goal. Now in a flash they became very definite. He moved around like one drunk, stood beside Florian and held his head in his arms while he whispered into the trembling ears: "You can do it, Florian. You can do better . . . much better than the others."

Chapter Fourteen

ENNSBAUER ASSISTED THE ACTRESS, Gabriele Menzinger, out of her coupé. He had been awaiting her at the portal of the Riding School on the Josephsplatz. When the light carriage drove up, drawn by two huge Russian horses, he had stepped forward and offered her his arm.

"*Grüss' dich, Gabi,*" he murmured.

And she answered melodiously, "Leopold," and nothing more.

For months these two had been having an affair.

Nobody knew anything definite, but all Vienna guessed, prattled and tattled, lifted eyebrows, shrugged shoulders, smiled and let things go on as they might.

Gabriele Menzinger was the reigning favorite of the Viennese stage. No other woman appearing before the public dared to measure herself with Menzinger. Even old theatergoers, gentlemen and ladies who still revered the memory of Geistinger, Gallmeyer, and Wolter, admitted that Gabriele Menzinger was incomparable. Princes and artizans, officers and bankers, all without distinction fell into a turmoil of erotic desire when discussing her. And they discussed her continually. When this young woman appeared on the stage, her face framed in coppery hair, her eyes seeming to say: "Come, my beloved," her mouth formed as if ready to kiss, her lusciously graceful figure freely outlined or shrouded in costumes—then all men who watched her were gripped by fierce longing.

Her voice, too, voluptuously throaty and laden now with the soft accents of her emotional ecstasy and now with the shrill wrath that was like a whiplash on raw nerves—her voice ever and again aroused tumults of the blood. From the first row in the orchestra to the farthest row in the gallery all were set ablaze by this voice.

But Gabriele Menzinger's movements, her gestures of surrender, of resistance, of coquetry, of sentimentality, constituted a strange mixture of girlish chastity and a harlot's abandon, of aristocratic aloofness and of crass vulgarity, of the knowledge of every vice and of touching innocence. No man could withstand her witchery. Everyone, the prince in his loge and the apprentice standing in the rear, felt convinced; one hour alone with this woman and she would be his. The women, without exception, the young misses as well as the dowagers, the staid wives and the bachelor girls, the noble ladies and the salesgirls, the virtuous and the cocottes, adulated her, maligned her and tried to fathom the secret of her terrific allure.

Gabriele Menzinger had had many amours. Many more had been imputed to her. She had lovers who for years took regal care of her and either knew nothing of one another or pretended they didn't. In between were episodes with young artists and officers and millionaires' sons, who ruined themselves over her. For the Menzinger's demands, her craving for luxury, were beyond bounds. Her palace in the Ambassadors' quarter, her castle in Moravia, her wealth, had become legend. The Shah of Persia, on the occasion of a visit to Vienna, had seen her, asked her to come to Marienbad, and made her a gift of twenty diamonds of rare size and luster. She had thereafter worn the necklace as proudly as one wears a high order.

As a past master in the art of love she was esteemed above all of her sex. During one of Eleonora Duse's guest appearances Gabriele went on the stage, devoutly kissed the hand of the great *artiste,* and received in return a kiss on the forehead from this queen of the theater. The scene had been described graphically in every newspaper. The Viennese remembered that in Gabriele Menzinger they had not only a hetæra of genius but also a great histrionic artist; and her fame grew.

About Leopold Ennsbauer the papers were silent. Never did a word about him leak out in print, never was he exposed before the public. Despite that, he was one of the most famous figures of the monarchy. He enjoyed a unique and exclusive fame. At Court, among the nobility, in the Cavalry regiments of the Army, with the regular patrons of the racetrack in the Freudenau, the square-built Ennsbauer cut the ideal figure of a horseman. His close-shaven, dark brown face carried the stamp of an unfathomable and courageous will-power. He was habitually very quiet, so that some were inclined to think him phlegmatic; but his Buddha-face that was like chiseled bronze attracted women and caused picaresque tales to be told of his stormy temper. He sat a horse as no one else could, and was without a peer with rein and stirrup; everyone conceded this. He broke in the horses for Emperor Franz Joseph himself. And he was the only one who dared contradict the Heir Apparent without having to fear bodily injury or other dire consequences.

Ennsbauer had had countless adventures with ladies of the Court. Nobody ever talked of *them*! His reticence, his tact, his absolute trustworthiness offered no opportunity. Furthermore, the scandalmongers feared this man whose solitary existence was somehow forbidding.

He met Gabriele Menzinger one day when she visited the Riding School in the company of a tall handsome officer of the Imperial Bodyguard. He was aware of her existence, of course, and had occasionally seen her pictures in the illustrated journals. But he had never attended the theater, and what had nothing to do with horses held absolutely no interest for him. The Menzinger in turn had no idea that a man like Ennsbauer lived, that in his own world he was as famous as she in hers. In short order she dismissed her officer of the Guards. She fell in love with Ennsbauer. Madly. Fell in love with the nonchalant way he treated her, with the fiery storm of his embraces. Fell in love with his acceptance of her as a woman and his complete indifference to her artistry. Her success meant nothing to him; he never even wanted to hear of it.

Through her alone, because she was forever in the spotlight, news of their relationship leaked out and started a flood of gossip. And, ironically enough, only in this fashion did the name Ennsbauer come to the attention of the newspapers. Still, they remained silent. Ennsbauer wisely surrounded his life with a wall of silence.

Now, then, he approached the two big Russian blacks harnessed to her carriage. "Rather nice," he murmured while he patted one of them on the neck. To Gabriele, who started toward him, he said briefly: "Go inside."

She obeyed, slipped hastily into the dark vestibule.

Like somebody totally disinterested Ennsbauer casually followed her. He glanced around. A few carriages waited on the Josephsplatz. He knew every livery and its owner.

In the vestibule he overtook the actress. She pressed his arm. "So you like my horses?"

He disengaged his arm. "New?"

"Today. How *do* you like them?"

"I told you . . . rather nice."

She flared up. "Rather nice! They are divine! Wonderful! The finest coach team in Vienna."

"For all I care," he growled.

Meekly she asked: "And how are things with him, with Florian?"

Ennsbauer at once grew animated. "Today I try him," he said. "Today I shall take him between the stanchions!"

Gabriele produced dramatic astonishment. She halted in her tracks. "Today? Today? My God! Isn't that entirely too soon? For heaven's sake, don't be rash, Leopold."

He walked past her. She ran after him.

"Rash?" he echoed, so quietly he might have been saying it to himself. "Am I rash?"

"No, no, no!" she apologized. "I am only talking. But today? After such a short time? Florian is hardly through with the longe. . . ."

Ennsbauer cut her short. "That's something you know nothing about! Why do you cluck about things that are beyond you?"

"Why . . ." she threw in, her voice high-pitched. She knew how to make this man talk.

"I know exactly what I am doing," he declared.

"Florian can do anything. Yes! He isn't like any other horse. I have never come across a fellow like him."

They had reached a glass door. Ennsbauer veered to the boy standing guard and made a gesture with his hand which meant:

"Show her the way."

Gabriele had to follow the boy, had to follow him to the gallery. Ennsbauer wouldn't permit her to use the balcony. Members of the Court were to be present today. They might arrive at any moment, unexpectedly. Ennsbauer had no idea what impression the famous *artiste* might make on the various countesses, princesses and ladies-in-waiting. In any case, he took every precaution to avoid creating a sensation or even attracting undue attention.

"Good luck," Gabriele whispered to him as she disappeared.

He did not bother to answer her. Quietly he opened a small side door and let himself into the arena.

Down from the low balcony came loud careless voices. The equerry was ensconced there, along with a cavalry commander, Major von Neustift and his wife, several young officers and a group of young women. They felt quite at home.

Only the equerry acknowledged Ennsbauer's curt bow officially. Neustift raised his fingers to his vizor, while Elizabeth nodded and smiled.

Anton led Florian into the hall. In the presence of Ennsbauer he did not dare walk ahead of Florian to demonstrate how Florian would follow him unled. The people in the balcony did not exist for Anton.

Florian wore a saddle and complete harness. From the balcony came cries of admiration.

"Wonderful creature!"

"Faultless!"

"Not a speck on him."

"What is his name?" a girl inquired.

The equerry informed her: "Florian, Princess."

The girl laughed, whereupon the others began to giggle also.

"How amusing!" another girl exclaimed mirthfully. "Florian—how droll."

"Quite so," ventured the equerry. "I have never learned how he acquired that strange name."

Gaily the girls called down: "Florian! Oh, Florian!"

Florian pricked up his ears, raised high his head and neighed. It was as melodious as a song.

"He answers!" The girls laughed more. "How courteous."

Elizabeth turned and addressed them. "Florian is an old friend of ours."

"Not really?"

"How nice."

In the meantime Anton had removed the two leather belts that lay like reins on the saddle. Florian now stood between the two upright posts in the middle of the arena, the "pillars." Anton fastened the two belts, left and right, to rings on the posts so that it was impossible for the horse to move forward or backward.

"Princess," the equerry explained, "these are the rudiments, the first basic rules. Here the horse must learn the Spanish stride."

The princess tried to put on a thoughtful mien. "Is that very difficult?"

"To be sure. Most difficult."

She put her fingers on her lips. "Oh, dear, then he is sure to be beaten."

The officers and some of the ladies laughed aloud at that. The equerry smiled. "Oh, no, Princess. The horses are never beaten. To use the whip would be a grave mistake. That would ruin them forever."

The princess breathed deeply. "Thank God for that." She turned to the other girls to defend herself. "How should I have known? This is the first time I've been in Vienna. And"—this to Elizabeth—"at the Sacrè Coeur in Paris there was nobody to tell me."

"Attention!" Neustift cried. "Attention!"

They looked down.

Florian's head was drawn in by a double white belt. His powerful neck rose in a stiff curve from the shoulders. His posture was an expression of replete pride.

The ladies went on with their chatter almost immediately, for the princess in her youthful vivacity felt like talking of her plans. "We'll stay in Vienna only a few weeks."

"For the wardrobe?"

"Yes. I've got to have a few clothes. The others we shall order after Christmas when we return."

"Where are you going from here?"

"Oh, first to Zistavety, and then to Mezohaza for the hunts."

"And later?"

"I am telling you. Then we shall return and I shall be presented at Court. And then we have our ball. . . ."

"Are you happy?"

"Very happy . . . and yet I am afraid . . ."

"Afraid? Why afraid?"

The conversation was interrupted by Neustift's loud outcry: "Marvelous! Marvelous!"

All the officers had leaped to their feet, leaned across the balustrade and fixed intent eyes on the scene in the arena.

The chattering of the girls ceased. The officers in subdued whispers expressed appreciation, admiration, astonishment.

"Unbelievable!"

"*Sapristi!*"

"This animal hasn't an equal on earth!"

"If you told anyone about this you would be called a liar."

"Quite right. You've got to see it to believe it."

"Why, why," the princess exclaimed, pointing down, "this man does have a whip . . . your Excellency!"

The equerry reassured her. "He uses that only to give the horse signals . . . only for that."

Ennsbauer had approached the stanchions, patted Florian's neck, then touched his upper lip with his palm. A quick inspection of the harness, of the body belts, and then he accepted the whip Anton held ready for him, waiting until Anton disappeared.

Anton joined the other stablemen standing outside the wooden enclosure and peeped across the high rim. His heart pounded.

Florian stood motionless. He was inwardly aquiver. His heart beat a violent tattoo, but he had himself under control. He concentrated and gradually submerged everything but his curiosity and his instinctive willingness to respond to the master. His beautiful dark eyes shone. His ears showed listening expectancy. His whole body listened, waited.

He had an impulse to neigh but thought better of it. He would have liked to snort but his instinct commanded him not to disturb the fluid seconds of waiting. His nostrils opened wide, exposed their rosy interiors, contracted and opened again.

Then the whip touched his left forefoot. Very softly. Like a falling leaf. Florian promptly lifted his leg. Involuntarily he also lifted his right hindleg. He did that slowly. Ceremoniously. He made no attempt whatever to walk forward, did not cause the slightest strain on the belts that fettered him to the posts. He set his hooves down on the exact spot he had raised them from.

Before the whip could graze the other leg, Florian had duplicated the performance. He stepped—not to take himself anywhere but merely to make the gestures. Festive, pathetic, declamatory gestures.

The light touch of the whip, the touch as a breath, comparable to the fluttering wing of a passing butterfly, had been enough for Florian. His nerves and his

instincts had guessed what his blood carried as latent
knowledge. All his ancestors and their training slum-
bering in his breast, in his brain, awoke at the flick of
the whip. Age-old tradition, spanning many centuries,
struggled forth in Florian as something akin to genius,
making it easy for him to fulfill his destiny, a destiny his
forebears had again and again fulfilled down the ages.

Within him to a great degree that happened which
happens in its purest form in all selected species of
thoroughbred animals. Racehorses, the offspring of
victors, inherit the craving for the race. And hounds,
still unschooled, come into the field for the first time
and prove after the first shot and the first pheasant has
dropped, that they know all that is expected of them,
instinctively, with but few last-minute instructions.

"Ennsbauer," the equerry called down.

Ennsbauer softly said: *"Pssst."*

Florian stood still.

"Your Excellency?"

"How often has this stallion been between the stanchions?"

"Never before."

"Is that a fact?"

"Why, your Excellency," Elizabeth burst in, almost wild with enthusiasm, "just remember other horses, after such a short time, are still on the longe!"

Ennsbauer offered no reply, but lowered the whip and once again Florian swung into his syncopated striding. While in action the whip touched the inner side of his fore- and hindlegs. Florian understood. Ever slower, ever more ceremoniously he lifted his legs. The play of his muscles and of each individual joint was visible from shoulder to croup. He was an animate statue. In each of his movements was silent music.

The young ladies began to applaud and the officers followed suit. The thin ripple of applause floated down into the arena.

"He *piaffes* like a thoroughly trained School horse."

"What does that mean—to *piaffe*?" the princess asked curiously.

"What you see there," Elizabeth explained. "That striding is called *piaffing*."

"I'd like to know what young ladies of today really learn at school," Neustift whispered to his wife and chuckled.

Florian accompanied his exercises with a rhythmic waving of his head.

"He has an incredible sense of rhythm," Elizabeth commented.

The equerry agreed with her. "It is really hard to believe how musical some horses are."

"This one in particular!" cried Elizabeth.

And Neustift added: "He loves his work, our Florian."

Again Ennsbauer made the sound, "*Pssst,*" thinking: "Enough for today." He was highly gratified. "That went rather well. Only I can't stand so many spectators."

He saluted the ladies and officers in the balcony with a brief bow.

The equerry leaned over the balustrade and shouted down: "You were right, my dear Ennsbauer." And when the riding master eyed him questioningly, he added: "In Lipizza, don't you remember?"

Ennsbauer bowed once more. In silence.

As they left, the equerry told the others: "I wanted the stallion for the carriage of his Majesty, but . . ."

The riding master motioned Anton to free Florian from the posts and lead him back to his stall.

Florian snorted and neighed metallically, musically, full of the indestructible joy of life.

In the dark corridor Florian answered Anton's caresses by pushing nose and forehead against his shoulder, a gesture denoting satisfaction. Florian knew he had achieved a triumph.

When they crossed the street under the archway and stepped into the light of the outer court, Anton saw that Florian's eyes were full of laughter.

Anton, too, laughed soundlessly.

The Josephsplatz lay empty. The carriages had disappeared. Only Gabriele Menzinger's coupé still stood there.

Ennsbauer stepped from the doorway and peered around, outwardly indifferent. Nobody about to spy on them. Only in the street along the far side of the square did the life of the capital pulsate; there flocks of passersby were on the move, but none took any notice of the solitary vehicle. Ennsbauer slipped into the carriage and hid in a corner.

"Bravo," Gabriele gurred. "It was thrilling!"

"What do you know about it?" he mumbled. Then he slipped an arm about her waist and said: "I'd dare to ride the *Hohe Schule* on Florian today."

Chapter Fifteen

NEUSTIFT HAD BEEN ON ADJU-
tant's duty for weeks. Today he had
been chosen to accompany the
Emperor on his ride from Schönbrunn,
where Franz Joseph was residing, to the Imperial Palace.

From the summer castle to the Imperial Palace was
not a great distance. On the few occasions, however,
that Neustift had ridden with the Emperor, the way
had seemed interminable. Sitting at the left hand of the
monarch he had to be careful to keep his figure in the

background as much as possible and yet keep his eyes peeled. Regicide, however far-fetched, was an omnipresent possibility. This called for quickness of mind, called for greater tenseness than any other service in the immediate orbit of the Emperor.

Personal contact, for Neustift as for everyone else, dissolved all the current Franz Joseph legends and heroic schoolbook tales, and made him conscious of the man Franz Joseph, Emperor though he was.

His exalted status Franz Joseph never forgot, and it remained indelibly stamped on the consciousness of everyone surrounding him. Rarely, indeed, only at exceptional and fleeting moments, did others perceive in the august person of this Emperor the human being. Always he was a solitary, majestic, towering figure. Unworldly, he was at the same time wise; shrewd, and yet narrow; almost pedantically conscientious, and withal irresistibly masterful. Possessing the dry sardonic wit of the Hapsburgs, he was nevertheless close-lipped, almost bashfully reticent. But there were times when he could be crushingly direct and candid. This princely man could hide his emotions, unless it be that jealousy occasionally shone through the veneer. His outbursts of rage were dreaded as death or the clutching hand of fate is dreaded. And more than others, the members of the Imperial family quailed before him. He was supreme and sovereign, with power over life and death, over imprisonment, exile and liberty, for the archduke as for the peasant; and he was accountable to no one.

In his personal service he consumed an enormous amount of human material drawn from the ranks of the diplomats and the military. Without ado he discarded anyone who threatened to become popular, banished whosoever challenged his carefully guarded popularity. In spite of this arrant faithlessness he yet preserved lifelong fealty toward certain individuals.

His character cannot be portrayed in a few words. It is wrong to say: "He was good"; wrong to claim: "He was wicked"; wrong to insist: "He was untrustworthy, irascible, vindictive"—just as it is erroneous to think: "He was without suspicion, open and condescending."

Whoever makes such claims is equally right and wrong. That he was unapproachable is all that could be claimed truthfully and incontrovertibly. Unapproachable, and a true gentleman, he was the embodiment of meticulousness in the performance of duty; exact, reliable and punctual in his work and in his associations. His style of living was Spartan in its simplicity, although he loved the finest, the most cultivated in luxury.

Neustift, of course, did not dare address the Emperor. On their few previous drives together Franz Joseph had maintained a stony silence. Today he came out of his study in high spirits, and had his valet brings him a cigar. Ketterer, the first valet, on handing him the cigar ventured to remark: "Your Majesty should not smoke in the open carriage."

The Emperor laughed: "And why not?"

Ketterer held firm. "Your Majesty has already smoked one cigar today. . . ."

"Well," replied the Emperor good-humoredly, "perhaps you are right," and returned the cigar.

With a deep obeisance Ketterer said: "I am right, your Majesty."

Still laughing, the aged monarch walked down the stairs and stepped into his carriage. His *chasseur* spread a blanket over the Emperor's and his adjutant's knees, and hopped up on the box.

When the heads of the two white Lipizzans came into view on the terrace, the foot guard leaped to attention.

Three times came the barked: "Present arms!"

Drums beat the general march. The company presented arms. The commanding officer saluted with his saber and the flag was lowered while the light elegant carriage, its gilded spokes glinting, rolled through the portal.

The Emperor saluted and as usual scanned each soldier in passing; another sign of high good humor.

"Too bad," he murmured. "I should have liked to smoke." And smiling wearily, he said: "He is an old tyrant, this Ketterer...."

Neustift sat erect, immobile. An answer was neither desired nor possible; he smiled uncompromisingly.

The carriage, already signaled from Schönbrunn and

easily identified by the white plume on the *chasseur's* hat and by the livery of the State coachman, rolled along the center of the broad avenue. In perfect step the two white horses trotted along, nodding their proud heads. They did not slacken their pace for street-crossings or anything else. Every vehicle on the road ahead of them had been waved aside. Traffic laws did not exist for the Imperial carriage.

Again the Emperor spoke, the while he repeatedly raised his right hand in gracious acknowledgment of the bowing throngs.

"Bertingen was telling me yesterday about a stallion Ennsbauer is breaking in ... marvelous things. ..."

Bertingen was the equerry, General Count Bertingen.

"Wait a minute. . . . What was the name of the beast—?"

"At Your Majesty's service . . . perhaps Florian?" Neustift suggested in a low voice.

"Yes, that's it. Florian," Franz Joseph said, brightening. "Queer name for a horse from Lipizza, Florian. ... But how do you know?"

Neustift hastened to explain: "Son of Berengar out of Sibyl—"

"Never mind that," the Emperor interrupted. "But how did you guess Bertingen was talking about this . . . this comical Florian?"

"Your Majesty, there is no horse like—"

The Emperor cut in again. "According to Bertingen it is something unheard of. . . . Unless Bertingen exaggerates. . . ."

Emboldened, Neustift said: "With your Majesty's permission, his Excellency Count Bertingen did not exaggerate. Florian is the handsomest and most gifted horse in decades."

"Really?" Franz Joseph turned his still handsome old face to his informant. A face that was a silver sheen. The white mustache and the white sideburns framed the reddish brown cheeks and the steely blue eyes. At this moment Neustift loved his Emperor fiercely. "Really? You grow quite excited. . . ."

"Forgive me, your Majesty."

"Well," the Emperor went on amiably, "I am glad to

hear it. At last a star performer who won't embarrass us."

Obediently Neustift laughed at the *bon mot*.

After a while the Emperor began once more. "Bertingen begged me to come to the Riding School ... to watch this fabulous animal. He has really tormented me with this matter."

Silence.

The carriage crossed Mariahilferstrasse.

Neustift thought of a story his father had told him long ago. In the year 1866, after the defeat at Königgrätz, Franz Joseph had to avoid Mariahilferstrasse and go to Schönbrunn by a roundabout way, because the widows and mothers of the fallen soldiers had been lying in wait for him, shouting: "Our husbands! Our sons!" Franz Joseph had then been as unloved and unadmired as any man in the shadow of defeat. And today! How seldom has success been his lot, thought Neustift; and he could not repress an inward surge of veneration for the man who sat by his side. His long life was in itself a measure of achievement: his unbroken power of existence! Fate had bloodily torn his son from him, and laid out his wife under a murderer's dagger thrust. But Franz Joseph sat on his throne. He, inaccessible to man, seemed inaccessible to Fate. It was this that inspired the veneration of the masses and the devotion of his servitors, that tore the hats from the people's heads and caused them to break into *vivas* whenever they caught sight of the white-bearded old man as he drove trustingly through their ranks.

Insignificant as the conversation with the Emperor had been, it left Neustift shaken to his depths. He thought: "My grandfather was cabinet minister when Franz Joseph began his reign; my father was then a cadet—and he died a field-marshal. And here sit I, beside this self-same monarch, a major, his adjutant!"

This was the *only* Emperor! Any other Emperor was unthinkable, any other Emperor could not be.

The carriage swerved toward the Ring.

"Perhaps I shall really visit the Riding School someday," the Emperor mused aloud. "You make me curious, you and Bertingen."

Neustift bowed.

The Emperor chatted on. "I haven't visited the Lipizzans for a long time." He sighed briefly. "Oh, lord, how long ago that is."

Just then they passed through the outer Palace gate. The shouts of the Guard, the roll of the drums—it all sounded hushed in the great wide square.

Franz Joseph faced around and his glance rested on the two bronze horsemen, then wandered to the clean blue sky, the trees in the public park, the overshadowing roof of the Parliament and the marble frieze of the Court Theater.

Neustift did not move his head. He saw these things only with his mind's eye, and reflected: "All that has come during his reign, has begun with him and through him, and has grown."

To the salutes, the drums and the shouts of the watch, the carriage rolled into the courtyard, described a graceful curve around the monument of Emperor Franz, and stopped directly in front of the Michael wing.

While the horses pawed the ground, their hooves resounding from the vaulted ceiling, the Emperor stepped from the carriage and in a casual matter-of-fact tone commanded: "You will remind me when all is ready."

Neustift understood that his Emperor referred to the Spanish Riding School and the completed education of Florian. He followed Franz Joseph up the stairs past the motionless guards.

Chapter Sixteen

T HE DAY SOON CAME.

Ennsbauer had been notified of the Imperial disposition and became more assiduous than ever.

Florian was also afire with ambition, as if aware of what was to follow.

The equerry came often, and from day to day his amazement grew.

"Bravo, Ennsbauer!" he praised. "This will be your masterpiece."

Ennsbauer thanked him mutely. He refused to give his superior the satisfaction of showing his pleasure. You could never tell. One fine morning Florian might forget all that he had learned and slip back into the beginner's stage. It was possible for the horse to get the colic or to suffer some other mishap that would incapacitate him for days and possibly weeks. Everything was possible. And Ennsbauer had a superstitious fear of every eventuality; he believed only in the good fortune of the moment.

Once he rebuked Anton because of Bosco.

"Since when has the dog been sleeping in Florian's stall?"

"Always."

"This must stop! Do you hear me?" he roared.

"Merciful God!" said Anton, on the verge of tears, "then we'll have our cross to bear with Florian."

"Nonsense!" the riding master thundered. "Our cross? Why our cross?"

Bosco sat on his haunches, his head cocked, and listened to the two men. Florian stood at his bin, complacently grinding oat kernels between his teeth.

"Get out of here!" Ennsbauer shouted. "Git!" and aimed a kick at Bosco which the terrier evaded as he fled down the corridor.

Like a shot Florian veered around, let the oats in his mouth fall into the straw, and stalked out of the stall.

"Whoa!" cried Ennsbauer, holding him back.

Over his shoulder Florian stretched his head and searched for Bosco who came up wagging his tail.

"You see for yourself, *Herr Oberreiter,*" Anton managed to say, half timidly, half triumphantly. "They are friends . . . and such friends have never been. . . ."

"Shut up!" Ennsbauer scowled.

Anton had to defend his beloved comrades. "They've been together ever since they were little, in Lipizza. They mustn't be separated. There's nothing to be done about it. You remember, *Herr Oberreiter,* how sad Florian was at first? Without Bosco. . . ."

Ennsbauer checked him: "All right."

He looked at Florian who had dropped his head to watch the mercurial Bosco; they acted like long parted friends just reunited. He knew these attachments of the stable, knew the moods of horses, knew how stubbornly they clung to preferences and habits. He did not deem it wise to upset Florian right now at any price.

"All right," he said in a more conciliatory tone, and on the way out he cautioned Anton: "Watch out that the dog doesn't run away."

"I'll watch him all right," Anton laughed, placated. "And Bosco won't run away either. Not he!"

But Ennsbauer didn't hear a word.

A few weeks later the equerry reported: "The other stallions are not ready yet. But Florian can be introduced at any time."

The equerry did not dream of reporting this to the Emperor. Neustift had received the command, consequently Neustift had to make the report. This was the procedure; to deviate was to risk an Imperial frown. Neustift, then, reported to the Emperor.

Franz Joseph mentioned the trifling matter to his chief adjutant, Count Paar, saying: "Perhaps Bertingen remembers that he begged me. . . ."

Count Paar notified the equerry at once. Forthwith Count Bertingen made inquiry of the secretariat of the Cabinet as to whether it would be possible to see the Emperor.

Franz Joseph, who had been expecting the request, received him immediately and set a date for his visit to the Riding School.

There was little time left, scarcely half a week.

The Emperor had expressed a wish that there be present "a very intimate gathering," but had granted permission to have the announcement transmitted to the archdukes.

Elaborate preparations were set on foot. In the chancelleries of the Imperial Palace, in the depots where the furniture and gobelins were stored, unnecessary excitement reigned; for the preliminaries ran smoothly and excitement only disturbed the well-oiled mechanism. Although haste was imperative, it was not difficult to observe the traditional formalities.

In the stable, under the lid of iron self-control clamped down by Ennsbauer, nervousness seethed like water boiling in a kettle. Count Bertingen never left. The master of ceremonies appeared from time to time. High functionaries strutted about giving the impression of actually functioning.

Ennsbauer put Florian through all his paces. Everything went smoothly. That did not allay the high-strung riding master's morbid fears. In the saddle, in oneness with Florian, he found calm. The stallion seemed to anticipate everything, translated hardly perceptible tactile and vocal signs into immediate action. At every phase he proved himself ready, capable of merging his identity with his rider's so well that he even corrected Ennsbauer when the latter seemed about to err or to miss a given tempo by a hairsbreadth. Then it was that Ennsbauer guided Florian into an even pace and patted him gratefully on the neck.

Before long Anton took charge of Florian and went into the stable with him. On the way they exchanged all kinds of pleasantries. Anton, to be sure, was on edge. The universal nervous suspense had contaminated even his stolid nerves. At last he was to see—the Emperor! But since the Emperor came really to see Florian, Anton's curiosity was overshadowed by stage fright.

Of Emperor Franz Joseph I this peasant had a supernatural idea. A flea, if it can think, must have such an idea of man. Anton had overheard the talk of the courtiers and listened to the tales told by coachmen who came over from the Mews to visit the Spanish Riding School. He had heard it said that there was a Hungarian general, Knight of the Order of Maria Theresia, a hero universally acclaimed for his bravery, who, every time he had to come before the Emperor, quaked from head to foot and lost his power of speech. Once someone mentioned the Emperor's brother, Archduke Ludwig Victor, who had been permanently banished to Castle Klesheim and could, only rarely and with the Emperor's special sanction, drive over to neighboring Salzburg. Those engaged in the conversation had stopped and said no more about this delicate subject.

At the very thought of the Emperor Anton froze with fear and awe, as a sinner must before a wrathy god. To him the wrath of the Emperor was an elemental force; none could withstand it. It was a far-reaching, annihilating force to which everyone was inexorably delivered. Thus Anton was astonished at the pride and ease of the courtiers who, to his lights, lived in perpetual danger. It began to dawn on him how lucky one was to be "in the Emperor's grace," a phrase which had hitherto told him nothing.

While Ennsbauer rehearsed with Florian, work in the Riding School had to be suspended. He would not suffer the noise made by the carrying in of laurel and palm trees, nor permit them to go on decorating the balcony with purple drapes and bunting.

"The horse must not be disturbed."

Could he have had his way, the courtiers and their ladies would also have been eliminated from the Riding School, or at least forbidden to do more than whisper. This, of course, he dare not propose. Thus he often rode angrily, bitterly, and saw to it that society kept away from Florian when visiting the stables. Even Elizabeth had to refrain from seeing Florian.

"Please, Countess," he entreated her, thereby making

her his ally, "Florian must under no circumstances be made restive. Please speak a word in his behalf."

Elizabeth interceded with everyone as Ennsbauer had asked her to.

As for Florian himself, he remained free from nervousness and stage fright. Emperor Franz Joseph meant nothing to him. He knew nothing of the man and hadn't the remotest idea of the fabulously magnificent Court and the difference in rank among human beings. He did not so much as guess that he belonged to the Imperial house, that for centuries his ancestors had led select existences at the behest of the Hapsburg monarchs, no less. No instinct apprised him of the fact that he was the property of the Emperor of Austria. In his own mind he belonged to Anton and Bosco, his beloved companions, and his ambition was to subjugate himself to the will of his rider.

In the very heart of the gay variegated life about him, Florian remained a fragment of Nature. Molded by the intelligence of man to superfine service, and dependent upon human hands as one can be dependent only upon a supreme and ofttimes enigmatic fate, Florian had all the disarming naïveté and the simple unwavering trust of gentle, serving creatures.

He made mischief with Anton whose manner, whose hand and whose scent were dear to him. Anton played on him and he on Anton the same pranks over and over. When Anton removed his harness, Florian would bury his downy nose in his friend's neck and snort faintly. He would nudge his shoulder as he was leaving the stall. He would drum against the woodwork of his stall with his hooves to call him. And if Anton came to groom him he would retreat with feigned displeasure; then Anton would stop and murmur: "Well, do you want to or don't you?" And Florian would come forward and touch Anton's hands with his lips. "Here I am," his clear innocent eyes would say; and ever anew Anton would be deeply moved.

Bosco, the untiringly attentive and ever gay Bosco, who was ready for mischief at any time, accompanied every prank with a short bark. Not loud, not a real bark; rather subdued merriment. Florian often amused himself with Bosco. As soon as they were alone together they played; always the same game. Bosco would run to and fro between Florian's legs, spring upward and with his black cold nose touch Florian's breast and lips. Suddenly Florian would lie down. Bosco, informed beforehand of this intention, would squeeze himself into a corner and wait until the heavy body of the white horse rested on the straw. Then he would sniff him all over. Carefully. Seriously. From forehead down to stomach. At last he would crawl under Florian's chin and nestle against his neck. And so they would sleep for a few hours.

Chapter Seventeen

AN EIGHTEENTH-CENTURY FAN-
fare sounded through the wide hall as
the Emperor stepped into the Court Box
at the Riding School. Above the box was
the escutcheon held aloft by genii and martial emblems.
Behind it had been placed the bugle-sextet, musicians
from the orchestra of the opera.

Purple velvet hangings covered the balcony and
enlivened the hall with their luminous tints. Few people
occupied the balcony; officers, ladies, chamberlains of

the archdukes present, ladies-in-waiting, and the wives of various Court officials.

In the Court Box five archdukes sat waiting, the Heir Apparent, Franz Ferdinand, in their midst. He had "decided" to come without his wife. In other words, the House Ministry had once again answered the request which he stubbornly made before every function, by refusing to grant his wife admittance to the Court Box. Defiant, he came alone. He did not acknowledge the greeting of the equerry and showed the Imperial princes an unfriendly countenance. "Blessings, blessings, blessings!" he said in rapid succession while his right hand described the sign of the cross in the air. That precluded the necessity of shaking hands.

He blandly refused to notice the Archduke Friedrich and his wife. A hearty friendship had once existed between him and them. Since his marriage to Countess Chotek, however, Friedrich and Isabella were his enemies. Franz Ferdinand feared the short plump Isabella for her sharp tongue. Whenever somebody informed him of a pointed remark she had made, he went into paroxysms of rage and swore to avenge himself, later, when he should be Emperor.

The old Archduke Rainer addressed him informally: "How are your wife and children, Franz?"

Franz Ferdinand shot a suspicious glance at him but could detect no hidden malice in this question, simply the uncalculating kindness of old age. He also scanned the faces of the others, his eyes glittering with ill-concealed wrath. All of them acted as if they had heard nothing. He smiled and replied:

"Thank you!" He spoke with demonstrative loudness. "My Sophie is very well, and the children also. The fact is, we are very happy."

He glared at everyone of them, noticed that Isabella smiled mockingly, her look saying, "Believe it who will," and bit his lips.

Then the fanfare.

Franz Joseph entered. After their obeisances the princes remained silent. The archduchesses rose from their deep curtsies.

A brief "Good morning" from the Emperor was accompanied by a circular movement of his hand. The moment he sat down, a door in the opposite wall was thrown wide, and four horsemen rode into the arena. In a straight line they swept toward the Court Box and stopped at an appropriate distance. Simultaneously they doffed their two-cornered hats and swung them until their arms were horizontal. Then they wheeled and to the strains of the *Gypsy Baron* began their quadrille.

The circle and capers cut by the four horses were precisely alike, and gave the effect of music in the flowing rhythm of their execution. The regularity of the horses' strides, and the horsemanship of the four riders aroused the spectators to a gay pitch, no one could have said why; it was sheer rapture evoked by the beautiful, blooded animals and their artistry.

Everyone in the hall could ride, knew horseflesh, and enjoyed the spectacle with the relish of a connoisseur. Franz Joseph, too, was stimulated by it all, his brows contracted. His white-gloved right hand kept pushing up his thick white mustache.

Suddenly a voice close to him whispered: "How boring!"

The Emperor recognized the Heir Apparent. Turning his head, he said with some heat: "Whoever is bored ought to leave." His voice betrayed rising anger.

Franz Ferdinand mock-apologetically replied: "Forgive me, your Majesty. I didn't mean the quadrille."

With a negligent wave, his uncle commanded: "Be still."

Franz Ferdinand obeyed, remained sitting, and grinned covertly behind his thick black mustache. He had succeeded in ruffling the Emperor.

The quadrille was over, the horsemen had made their exit. The wooden door remained wide open.

Next seven mounted stallions entered and filed in front of the Court Box. Seven bicornes were removed from seven heads, swung to a horizontal position, and replaced.

Florian stood in the center. To his right stood three older stallions, thoroughly trained, and to his left three equally tested ones. He resembled a fiery youth among men. In a row of white steeds he stood out as the only *pure* white one. His snowy skin, unmarred by a single speck, called up memories of cloudless sunny days, of Nature's gracious gifts. His liquid dark eyes, from whose depths his very soul shone forth, sparkled with inner fire and energy and health. Ennsbauer sat in the saddle like a carved image. With his brown frock coat, his chiseled, reddish-brown features and his fixed mien, he seemed to have been poured in metal.

The Emperor had just remarked, "Ennsbauer uses no stirrups or spurs," when the sextet began to play.

The horses walked alongside the grayish-white wainscoting. Their tails were braided with gold, with gold also their waving manes. Pair by pair they were led through the steps of the High School; approached from the far side toward the middle, and went into their syncopated, cadenced stride.

The Emperor had no eyes for any but Florian. Him he watched, deeply engrossed. His connoisseur's eye tested the animal, tested the rider, and could find no flaw that might belie the unstinted praise he had heard showered on them. His right hand played with his mustache, slowly, not with the impatient flick that spelled disappointment over something.

Ennsbauer felt the Emperor's glance like a physical touch. He stiffened. He could hope for no advancement. Nor did he need to fear a fall. Now—in the saddle, under him this unexcelled stallion whose breathing he could feel between his legs and whose readiness and willingness to obey he could sense like some organic outpouring—now doubt and pessimism vanished. The calm, collected, resolute animal gave him calmness, collectedness, resolution.

At last he rode for the applause of the Emperor, of Franz Joseph himself, and by Imperial accolade for enduring fame. Now it was his turn. . . .

Away from the wall he guided Florian, into the center of the ring. An invisible sign, and Florian, as if waiting for it, fell into the Spanish step.

Gracefully and solemnly, he lifted his legs as though one with the rhythm of the music. He gave the impression of carrying his rider collectedly and slowly by his own free will and for his own enjoyment. Jealous of space, he placed one hoof directly in front of the other.

The old Archduke Rainer could not contain himself: "Never have I seen a horse *piaffe* like that!"

Ennsbauer wanted to lead Florian out of the Spanish step, to grant him a moment's respite before the next tour. But Florian insisted on prolonging it, and Ennsbauer submitted.

Florian strode as those horses strode who, centuries ago, triumphantly and conscious of the triumphant occasion, bore Caesars and conquerors into vanquished cities or in homecoming processions. The rigid curved neck, such as ancient sculptors modeled; the heavy short body that seemed to rock on the springs of his legs, the interplay of muscle and joint, together constituted a stately performance, one that amazed the more as it gradually compelled the recognition of its rising out of the will to perfect performance. Every single movement of Florian's revealed nobility, grace, significance and distinction all in one; and in each one of his poses he was the ideal model for a sculptor, the composite of all the equestrian statues of history.

The music continued and Florian, chin pressed against chest, deliberately bowed his head to the left, to the right.

"Do you remember," Elizabeth whispered to her

husband, "what our boy once said about Florian? He sings—only one does not hear it."

Ennsbauer also was thinking of the words of little Leopold von Neustift as he led Florian from the Spanish step directly into the *volte*. The delight with which Florian took the change, the effortless ease with which he glided into the short, sharply cadenced gallop, encouraged Ennsbauer to try the most precise and exacting form of the *volte*, the *redoppe*, and to follow that with the *pirouette*.

As though he intended to stamp a circle into the tanbark of the floor, Florian pivoted with his hindlegs fixed to the same place, giving the breathtaking impression of a horse in full gallop that could not bolt loose from the spot, nailed to the ground by a sorcerer or by inner compulsion.

And when, right afterward, with but a short gallop around, Florian rose into the *pesade*, his two forelegs high in the air and hindlegs bent low, and accomplished this difficult feat of balance twice, three times, as if it were child's play, he needed no more spurring on. Ennsbauer simply had to let him be, as he began to *courbette*, stiffly erect. His forelegs did not beat the air, now, but hung limply side by side, folded at the knee. Thus he carried his rider, hopped forward five times without stretching his hindlegs. In the eyes of the spectators Florian's execution of the *courbette* did not impress by its bravura, or by the conquest of body heaviness by careful dressure and rehearsal, but rather as an exuberant means of getting rid of a superabundance of controlled gigantic energy.

Another short canter around the ring was shortened by Florian's own impatience when he voluntarily fell into the Spanish step. He enjoyed the music, rocked with its rhythm. These men and women and their rank were nothing to him. Still, the presence of onlookers fired him from the very outset. He wanted to please, he had a sharp longing for applause, for admiration; his ambition, goaded on by the music, threw him into a state of intoxication; youth and fettle raced through his veins like a stream overflowing on a steep grade. Nothing was difficult any longer. With his rider and with all these human beings around him, he celebrated a feast. He did not feel the ground under his feet, the light burden on his back. Gliding, dancing with the melody, he could have flown had the gay strains asked for it.

On Florian's back as he hopped on his hindlegs once, twice, Ennsbauer sat stunned, amazed.

Following two successive *croupades,* a tremendous feat, Florian went into the Spanish step still again. Tense and at the same time visibly exuberant, proud and amused, his joyously shining eyes made light of his exertions. From the *ballotade* he thrust himself into the *capriole,* rose high in the air from the standing position, forelegs and hindlegs horizontal. He soared above the ground, his head high in jubilation. Conquering!

Frenetic applause burst out all over the hall, like many fans opening and shutting, like the rustle of stiff paper being torn.

Surrounded by the six other stallions Florian stepped before the Court Box, and while the riders swung their hats in unison, he bowed his proud head just once, conscious, it seemed, of the fact that the ovation was for him and giving gracious thanks in return.

Franz Joseph himself had given the signal for the applause by lightly clapping his hands together. Now he rose and turned to Archduke Rainer, who, as the most distant claimant to the Throne, sat farthest removed from him. Rainer was the oldest among all the archdukes, older even than the seventy-six-year-old Emperor himself. "Well, did you ever see anything like it?" Franz Joseph asked.

"Never!" Rainer answered.

"Well, then," said the Emperor, enunciating each word sharply, "I cannot understand how anyone could be bored by it."

Rainer tried to pacify him.

"Nobody could have said it bored him."

"Oh, yes," Franz Joseph shot back, the point in his words as sharp as a knife's tip. "Oh, yes!"

Franz Ferdinand stifled a yawn.

What ensued, four young stallions between the pillars and on the longe, did not interest the Emperor. He became impatient and made ready to leave.

"I can't stand any more," he explained to Isabella and Friedrich. "After Florian—impossible."

To the equerry, who appeared in the box, he said: "I have no more time . . . you know. . . ."

Count Bertingen ventured to remark: "Too bad . . .

Florian on the longe is really magnificent, your Majesty."

Franz Joseph's mettle was still high: "Quite. But I, too, am on the longe—of my duty."

The equerry bowed.

The Emperor smiled: "I thank you, my dear Bertingen. It was really beautiful. An unusual performance."

He stopped. "This is something for the King of England when he visits us." And in accents as sharp as before, while his laughing eyes took on a steely glint: "He won't be bored with it. . . . Not he."

He walked out.

Franz Ferdinand made a face, shook his head and murmured: "How mad he is. Marvelous!"

Everybody heard it. Even the Emperor might have heard it.

Franz Joseph stood in front of the open door and talked with the equerry. "Tell Ennsbauer that I am very pleased."

Then he departed, and the rest did likewise, since Bertingen announced that the final number on the program, Florian on the longe, had been canceled.

Count Bertingen sent for the riding master who arrived full of dour forebodings. But the equerry had good news.

"Congratulations, Ennsbauer!" he began, obviously aping the Emperor in tone and attitude, a rather necessary and unsubtle cliché in Court circles. "Congratulations! His Majesty has condescended to have me express to you his very highest satisfaction."

Ennsbauer bowed. His face remained unchanged, his mien as inscrutable as that of a statue. His eyes, however, shone.

"A great success, Ennsbauer," Count Bertingen went on. "The performance will be repeated on the occasion of the visit of his Majesty the King of England. Then you may show Florian on the longe also."

Chapter Eighteen

A FEW DAYS LATER FRANZ
Ferdinand came to the Riding School
accompanied by his wife. Count
Bertingen, who had been apprised of
the impending visit, was there.

Ennsbauer introduced Florian.

Franz Ferdinand, when not cramped by the presence
of Franz Joseph and not rankled by the ever aggravating sight of the Emperor, was quite a different man. Free
and easy, witty and obliging. He knew of the relationship

between Ennsbauer and Gabriele Menzinger. He condemned such illicit love, although nobody would have been able to explain his singular attitude nor whence it sprang; for as a bachelor Franz Ferdinand had been wild and unregenerate. But whether his attitude lay rooted in his gratitude to God for ridding him of tuberculosis, or in his love for Sophie whom he had finally won after embittered quarrels with Franz Joseph, or in the strictly moral viewpoint of the future ruler, nobody could say. Perhaps the three wells had united to form one stream sweeping everything unclean from the being of the Heir Apparent.

Today, however, the Successor to the Throne was in an affable mood.

"Well, you Casanova," he addressed Ennsbauer, "show the duchess the tricks of your wonder horse."

Ennsbauer's mien remained unchanged. He bowed and prepared to back away.

"Just a moment," the Prince Heir called. "First I shall have to present you to her Highness." He turned to his wife. "Permit me, Sopherl, to introduce the Don Juan of the Spanish Riding School."

He did not mention Ennsbauer's name. By the terms Casanova and Don Juan, he desired nothing more than to indicate to the riding master that he knew of his clandestine relations with Gabriele Menzinger and disapproved. Ennsbauer did not move a muscle of his face as he bowed before the Duchess Hohenberg, who greeted him with a friendly smile.

"I can't endure this person," Franz Ferdinand told the equerry while Ennsbauer was walking off but still within earshot.

"A remarkably capable man," the count replied.

In return he received one of those glances of abysmal hatred which could darken the eyes of the Heir Apparent almost into blackness.

"Don't talk nonsense, Bertingen, that's ridiculous. Because this person knows a little something about horses, you immediately laud him to the sky!"

The duchess awarded Bertingen that peculiar smile of hers with which she tried so frequently to overcome the harshness of her husband.

But Count Bertingen countered reservedly: "Gifts such as Ennsbauer's are extraordinary."

"I don't care," came the still angrier reply. "The liaisons of a stableman are even more extraordinary."

In a frigid tone Bertingen said: "Excuse me, your Imperial Highness, Ennsbauer was never a stableman. He is the Imperial riding master . . . and"—preventing Franz Ferdinand from interrupting him—"his liaisons are his private affair."

"Is that so?" the Successor to the Throne snorted. "Is that so? Not a stableman? I don't make such fine distinctions. For me, whoever has anything to do with horses is a stableman. Without exception. Do you understand?"

Bertingen shrugged his shoulders. "I understand," he replied ironically.

Threateningly the Archduke swept on: "Private affairs! Ha! A nice attitude that is! He will be the first to be thrown out, when . . . when I . . . In my service there are no liaisons!"

"Oh," Count Bertingen said in an innocent, almost jocular tone, "your Imperial Highness, until then . . ." He dragged his words. "Ennsbauer will long since have ceased having gallant affairs and will doubtless be pensioned." And just as the Heir Apparent turned a livid face on him, he added quite amiably: "Just remember, your Imperial Highness, that his Majesty the Emperor is only seventy-six."

"Oh, how beautiful!" thrilled the duchess at this moment. "Really, divine . . ."

Florian, ridden by Ennsbauer, had appeared in the arena and terminated the unpleasant scene.

"No, really, Franzi," the duchess gushed. "You really didn't say too much. A wonderful animal. I am enchanted."

Franz Ferdinand underwent a metamorphosis. "Do you like him, Sopherl?" he asked tenderly. "I knew you would."

Unaided by music, Florian impressed purely by the power of his own personality. He was musical enough, his body completely alive with harmony; his being vibrated so tensely with unspent power that the mere sight of him imbued his observer with high spirits. He rose into the *levade*, rose with bent hindlegs; his forefeet upraised he performed the *capriole*, the jump into the air from a standing position. He did this as if it were no effort at all, thrusting his hindlegs into a horizontal position parallel with the front legs as if his body were more buoyant than air. Then in the long Spanish trot he gave the impression of touching the ground only for fun. He glided. He wafted himself like some winged horse starting out to scale the heights of Olympus. Then he set one leg carefully across the other in cadenced paces until he appeared to be enjoying this exercise like a game.

The Archduke and his wife entered the arena. Count Bertingen followed them.

"Come here," Franz Ferdinand ordered.

Ennsbauer dismounted and dropped the reins.

Florian approached the group, slowly, with the friendliness of his kind which expects friendliness in return.

"Why didn't the ass remain in the saddle?" Franz Ferdinand shouted at Count Bertingen. "He heard me tell him to come here."

Ennsbauer remained where he was. Hat in hand.

Silent. But when Bertingen glanced toward him questioningly, he reluctantly said: "I thought it would
please their Imperial Highnesses if Florian came by
himself."

The Heir Apparent did not give him another glance.
To the equerry he growled: "These people shouldn't
think, they should obey. That's all I expect of them."

Meanwhile the duchess had taken Florian by the
reins, since the horse at the sound of harsh voices had
raised his head and begun to retreat. She held him by
his nose-bone, patted him and cooed in his ear. Florian
listened and moved his shapely ears, his great swimming eyes questioning. He exhaled in tiny snorts and
sniffed at her gown.

"Too bad," Countess Sophie said, "I haven't a lump
of sugar."

"Sugar!" Bertingen called. And Ennsbauer quickly
handed him a few pieces.

Franz Ferdinand came and stood very close to his
wife, and while Florian crunched the sweets patted him
on the neck. As if it was all settled, he said:

"What did I tell you, Sopherl? A horse for me! Absolutely made for me! Isn't that true?"

"Certainly, Franzi, just made for you."

The equerry said not a word.

"Well, Bertingen," the Archduke demanded, "why don't you say something?"

Bertingen shrugged his shoulders. "All I can do is obey."

"Quite right," the Archduke laughed. "But I want to know what you think about it?"

"Your Imperial Highness is the only one who has the right, upon his Majesty's orders, to take a horse from the Mews."

"Don't tell me things I already know." Franz Ferdinand had regained his good humor. He stroked Florian's neck and flanks. "I ask whether you agree with me."

"Provided," Bertingen assumed an innocent mien, "provided your Imperial Highness is not too heavy for Florian. . . ."

"Nonsense. Too heavy for such a strong beast!"

Bertingen protested: "Your Imperial Highness has ridden Irish horses till now."

Franz Ferdinand changed his tone: "Very well, then. Provided, as you say, Bertingen, I am not too heavy. Well and good." He addressed his wife: "But you . . . you, Sopherl, will make an excellent figure on this horse."

"–Oh, I?" The Duchess showed surprise. "I?" And then her head drooping in resignation: "They will never give me that horse, Franzi. . . . You know . . . not me."

"We'll see about that," her husband temporized, his stubbornness stirring again.

He took his leave coldly. Bertingen could still hear him telling his wife: "I'll see this through. I want to. You on that white stallion. Only when you ride him will he be complete. Like a fairy tale."

The visit of the Heir Apparent and his wife was excitedly discussed among the stablemen. Anton had listened behind the door of the arena and was horrified by Franz Ferdinand's intention. He worked up the courage later to ask Ennsbauer: "What will happen to me and Bosco . . . ?"

Ennsbauer informed him readily enough. It did him good to talk disparagingly of the Successor to the Throne who had offended him.

"Nothing will happen," he said with sarcasm. "Neither to you nor to the dog." He leaned down and for the first time stroked Bosco, much to the terrier's amazement. When he straightened up he added: "Nor will anything happen to Florian either. He stays where he is."

Anton's baffled expression launched the riding master into an almost obscene description of the Imperial ostracism against which Franz Ferdinand fought vainly. "He? The Emperor can't stand him. Maybe he can do something with the Army. Yes, something. But here, in the Imperial Palace? Not that much!" he snapped his fingers. "All he has to do is ask for something, and everybody will be more than happy to say 'no' to him."

He was right as usual.

The equerry reported Franz Ferdinand's visit to the first chamberlain and mentioned his request.

The first chamberlain laughed aloud. "I wouldn't

have thought our good Franz quite as naïve as all that. But... he must have been joking."

Franz Ferdinand was the last person to joke with the Imperial courtiers. He had been smitten with Florian, fallen victim to the *idée fixe* of winning this horse for his wife. He did not easily desist from his desires. . . . The first chamberlain was ordered to appear before the Heir Apparent in Castle Belvedere.

"Look here, my dear Prince," Franz Ferdinand addressed him, cajoling, "you really could do me the small favor.... It'd be the first one anyway. And this would be a favor which would oblige my wife very much."

The Prince remained unmoved. He pointed out that it wasn't up to him to grant favors, particularly not favors that were in contradiction to his line of duty.

"Why, I ask you!" the Archduke fumed, losing his patience rapidly. "You do your duty a little more punctiliously than is absolutely required of you." And before the prince could ask him whether this were possible, he cut him short. "I want a horse, a horse I happen to like.... Is that so much?"

The prince explained that Florian had been appointed to perform before King Edward.

"But later," Franz Ferdinand persisted, "when that's over?"

"I shall ask his Majesty for his decision," the prince declared.

"No!" cried the Prince Heir with mounting rage. "No, I don't want you to do that." Overcome by his temper, he broke out: "Just imagine for a moment that it is already my turn ... that might happen any day now ... and that it is my command—"

Icily the prince replied: "Then another—not I—will obey, your Imperial Highness!"

He was dismissed curtly.

Franz Ferdinand went straight to the Emperor to ask for Florian. It meant much to him, not only to get the horse, but once, just this one time, to enforce his will on the hated first chamberlain. At the time when he had decided to marry the Countess Chotek, he had implored the Emperor, the princes, the entire Court for their good offices. In vain. Since then, however, he nursed his bitter enmity. He understood the attitude of the Emperor. He understood the father who had lost his only son, the monarch who had seen his heir laid in the grave. Later, though, after Franz Ferdinand had recuperated from his lung affection, had returned, and had felt strength surging into his once sick body, he had come to regard himself as one chosen by God to lead the moribund realm of the Hapsburgs to new glory. He viewed Franz Joseph's reign with critical eyes. His crafty, alert mind disapproved of the chronic tendency of the monarch to give in. It was said that his marriage to the Czech countess had made Franz Ferdinand a foe of the Magyars and a friend of Slavism. Perhaps so. But his unbending iron will did not becloud his political foresight. He recognized instinctively that the dualistic construction of the realm, the twin personality of Austria-Hungary precluded any other national structure; that any abortive rearrangement would only threaten the very existence of the empire.

His impatience had grown from day to day, from year to year. Franz Joseph clung to life entirely too long to suit him. He said it at home, said it quite openly to courtiers, to politicians and friends. Naturally it reached Franz Joseph's ears. Both true and invented utterances were brought back to the Emperor. Franz Ferdinand's plan, formulated during this period of waiting, during these years of burning impatience to ascend the Throne, grew and developed to its minutest details. It provided the Czechs with state sovereignty and a coronation at Prague, the new form of monarchy to be a federation of states which would guarantee to all its nations equal rights. Franz Ferdinand entertained seriously the possibility of an alliance with Russia, dreamed of reestablishing the old alliance of three emperors and the reinstallation of the world-wide power of the Vatican. Hungary, of course, would resist to the last. He knew how jealously Hungary's politicians guarded the special privileges granted them by the compromise of 1867, and knew well how little love the Hungarians bore the Russians. The Magyars had not yet forgotten that Russian soldiers had crushed their successful revolution and forced them to lay down their arms at Vilagos.

Franz Ferdinand feverishly waited for the day of his succession. The alliance of Russia, Germany and Austria would be unassailable, or at least unconquerable; a realm reaching from the Atlantic Ocean to the Pacific which could scoff at any attempted blockade. Perpetual peace would be assured, and the Hapsburg dynasty would be secure for centuries to come.

For the sake of this vast dream he even accepted the friendship of the Protestant, Wilhelm II. Besides, Wilhelm had treated the Duchess von Hohenberg as the future Empress and thereby gained Franz Ferdinand's gratitude. True, in his eyes Wilhelm was a heretic and wore the Holy Roman Crown of Charlemagne—illegally. For half a thousand years it had rested on Hapsburg heads, and even now reposed, with all the other crown insignia, in the Imperial Palace at Vienna. Wilhelm wore it in name due to the breach of faith Friedrich II had started, and Bismarck, in another war against Austria, had finished. Franz Ferdinand cared little about the Germanic cause. Of first moment, to him, was the influence of the House of Hapsburg which had been thrust outside the purely German sphere of interest. He could do nothing against this historical development; he thought of the many nations the Hapsburgs had ruled at one time or another, and felt Slavic sympathies stirring in his heart. He always received Wilhelm II cordially. But each time Wilhelm departed he had his rooms fumigated of the desecrating presence of a Protestant and consecrated anew by a Catholic priest.

The Hungarians were not to disturb or interfere with his plans. He'd handle them.

There was a story told to Franz Joseph: One day, during maneuvers, the Heir Apparent had stood in Bruck on the River Leitha which divides Austria from Hungary, pointed across to the other bank, and exclaimed: "We'll have to conquer Hungary all over again."

The more pronounced Franz Ferdinand's hostility to the régime became, the more openly he admitted how fiercely he longed for the day when he would have the power to do away with the "old trash" of a misguided reign, the deeper grew Franz Joseph's resentment against his heir. He had never cared for his brother's children anyway, had always referred to them as the "Carl Ludwig brood." He realized, of course, how helpless he was before the future, which would begin only with his death; but as long as he lived he did all in his power to embitter the existence of Franz Ferdinand, did it with finesse and relish. The Duchess of Hohenberg had to appear at formal Court functions and take her place behind the youngest of the archduchesses. As a result, Franz Ferdinand, who was entitled to the first place directly behind the Emperor, had to make a display of joining his wife. The Emperor did not tamper with that. He left it to the first chamberlain, who could be sure at the slightest opportunity to make the Heir feel the continual pinpricks of Imperial disfavor and his complete divorcement from any influence. And the first chamberlain was always certain of Franz Joseph's approval. Often scenes between Franz Joseph and Franz Ferdinand were engendered in this fashion. An irritable, touchy atmosphere pervaded the Imperial household.

Today, however, Franz Ferdinand appeared as the

soft-spoken charming, obedient servant of his sovereign. He didn't want to be stubborn. What he wanted was to plead and to soften the Emperor by his abject subservience. Franz Joseph immediately read his intention, somewhat too stickily put on, and became the frostier for it.

The Heir Apparent pleaded, he practically begged, for Florian. Heavens, a horse, a single horse! What could that mean to the monarch? He, on the other hand, wanted it so badly and would truly be eternally grateful.

"If it is possible, gladly," Franz Joseph said this in such a friendly tone that the distance between him and the Heir widened immeasurably. "I shall talk to the prince about it."

The audience was over. There was nothing more to be done. Franz Ferdinand went away almost suffocating with rage. Florian would never be his.

Chapter Nineteen

KING EDWARD CAME TO VIENNA.
Major von Neustift was in the
Emperor's retinue when he received the
English ruler at the station. Franz Joseph
wore the uniform of a British marshal, the brilliant red
coat, the bronze helmet. He cut an unfamiliar figure.
If he wore anything but the uniform of an Austrian
general, which is in every Austrian's mind identified
with the Emperor, he invariably appeared foolishly
disguised.

Neustift witnessed a slight mishap at this reception which his memory retained forever after.

The moment for reporting to the Emperor that the train bearing the visiting sovereign was about to arrive, had been calculated to a nicety. It allowed the Emperor time to inspect the Guard of Honor, to hold a short *cercle* for the various officials, and to take his position on the small carpet leading to the gala car of the royal guest.

Thus it was. From the narrow side of the station, where the Court waiting room was located, the Emperor walked along the platform at the end of which, already half in the open, the Guard of Honor and the military band had been stationed; beside them the city commandant, the chancellor, the stadholder of Lower Austria, and the mayor.

In the van of the Emperor marched a master of ceremonies in a gold-braided uniform, white-plumed, two-cornered hat, white breeches and patent-leather boots, the gold-crested ceremonial baton in his white-gloved hand. Behind the Emperor came the adjutants.

The captain in charge of the Guard of Honor stood ready, his saber drawn, looking toward the approaching monarch. It was his duty to order the salute as soon as his Emperor reached a certain point. Instead, the captain simply stood and stared, totally unnerved by the sight of the sovereign whom he had never seen before at such close range. He stood there dumb, intimidated by a paralyzing impression of majesty, robbed of his senses.

Franz Joseph, who knew the precise distance prescribed, knew intuitively when the salute should have come. He took two additional halting steps, stopped, made an impatient gesture with his hand, and muttered angrily: "What's the matter?"

The city commandant strode to the fore and bawled "'Tention! Company. . . . Eyes right!" Drums rolled. The national anthem blared solemnly to the sky. The soldiers stood stiffly to attention.

The captain got hold of himself, saluted with his saber and stepped forward to make the prescribed report. But Franz Joseph did not listen, passed him by scornfully, and inspected the Guard of Honor, man by man, with stern and thorough gaze.

Major von Neustift recognized the unhappy captain. They had been cadets together. The son of bourgeois parents, a capable soldier, an honest man; he was now finished, his career cut short forever. And Neustift did not protest, even inwardly, could not see injustice in the man's automatic dismissal and immediate retirement on pension. An officer lacking presence of mind simply lacked the qualifications expected of any soldier.

Thus was a career broken in two by very awe of Franz Joseph. Even awe could turn to guilt.

Neufstift collected all sorts of experiences during his term as adjutant.

"It's the most taxing service of all," he told Elizabeth subsequently.

"But the most interesting, too."

"Certainly. And not without its dangers. Present and future."

"Danger? Present danger, that I understand," Elizabeth conceded. "With an Emperor like Franz Joseph you must be always on the alert, isn't that so? Always in control of your nerves, your memory, and your tact, too . . . and sharpen them. . . ."

"I must be a mind reader," Neustift pursued. "I must forget I am a gentleman, and at the same time never forget it—else I become a lackey."

Elizabeth smiled: "That doesn't worry me, my dear."

"Well, it isn't so simple," he said thoughtfully. "You need patience, patience and still more patience.

"How incongruous the whole thing is: He who is always and under all circumstances right—to him nothing can ever happen. While the other fellow—myself, for instance—to him anything, even the worst, can happen."

Elizabeth laid her hand on his shoulder. "What silly ideas!" She shook her head. "His Majesty! Don't forget—that is no empty phrase."

"I dare say!" Neustift exclaimed. "Especially with him. Majesty such as his is unmatched on earth." After a few moments of silence, he concluded hastily: "But it breeds austerity. . . . For months, since that time in the carriage—you remember—when we talked about Florian . . . not a single word! In the course of my duties, yes, one or two syllables, an order–nothing else. Not one word! It makes me panicky."

"Not panicky, surely!"

He kissed her. "Oh, no, don't worry. I merely talk. I can say anything to you, can't I? After I've talked to you, I feel easier."

"Don't be heavyhearted." Elizabeth stroked his hair.

"It's not so bad as all that." He laughed.

"Many envy you."

"Do you really think so?" He sounded doubtful. "Many–maybe. But many more are saving themselves for later."

"Can it be–?" she broke off.

"Naturally!" he cried, not without a trace of anger in his voice. "All the younger officers, all the younger diplomats, the ministers are split into two factions. The ones want to achieve whatever they can now, the others wait for tomorrow or the day after."

"They will have a long wait," Elizabeth replied, but her tone lacked conviction.

"A long wait?" repeated Neustift. "Who knows? Who can pretend to know in advance? Seventy-seven . . . an old age. You can't deny that."

"Wilhelm I lived more than ninety years," she rejoined. "And Friedrich II ruled but three months." She breathed deeply. "Franz Ferdinand . . . I can't tell you why, but I cannot, I simply cannot picture him as Emperor."

"Oh," Neustift snapped his fingers, "it's easy enough to explain that feeling. We were born, went to school, grew up, married, had children. . . . And during all that Franz Joseph was Emperor. For us there just is no other. His face, his figure, his manner . . . they call it knightly. Wrong! Imperial, it is, imperial! Majesty . . . you yourself spoke of it a moment ago. He is in our brain, in our blood, in our soul!" The major smiled. "Just like our military horses, we all carry his name indelibly stamped on us. No wonder, then, we have no room to picture another as Emperor."

"Habit." Elizabeth stared down at the ground. "Habit. Perhaps something more. Perhaps we are the last who . . ."

"What do you mean?" Neustift checked her. "After us there will be others. And others will be sitting on the throne."

"Of course," she agreed. "But I mean, perhaps we are the last who shall have such a deep-rooted conception ... something so personal . . . such a personification of an Emperor. Franz Joseph was eighteen when ..." She hesitated. "And Franz Ferdinand is already past fifty."

Neustift rubbed his chin. "If he should get the scepter today, tomorrow . . . that might happen any time and he is eating his heart out for it ... then—then everything is over for me."

"For you?" She was astonished. "Why for you?"

"Franz Joseph's adjutant," he said briefly. "What could I expect? In the face of the hatred the Archduke feels for everybody—he calls us all Franz Joseph's creatures. I am one of them."

"Are you ambitious?" Elizabeth asked lightheartedly.

He did not jest. "Right now I am. I should like to become a general. A long way from major. A very long way." He sighed. "Oh, if only a war came."

Elizabeth half shrieked: "War!"

"Have no fear," he reassured her. "As long as Franz Joseph is alive there won't be any war. He is too old."

She laughed, at ease again. "And he has never been lucky with his wars."

When Neustift returned from the State dinner a few hours later, he was in ebullient spirits.

"I've met another majesty," he recounted. "Quite a different type, but undeniably a real majesty. The King of England!" He waxed enthusiastic. "At first we secretly laughed at him and made fun of him. He looks almost like a Jew. Especially in the uniform of our Hussars. And with his fat paunch. But then, Elizabeth . . . he has about him something of a great merchant prince, just a trace. Very much of the great cavalier, too. And he is an epicurean, a man full of the joy of life. But beneath his light manner there is an earnestness that lends to everything he says and does a beautiful dark background. He isn't easily described. And clever! He has a biting, sparkling wit. And tact. And sensitiveness, too."

"You make me curious," Elizabeth murmured. "Your admiration seems . . ."

"I admit I am enthusiastic. Maybe because I, like the others, underrated him at first. Honestly, he is above and beyond the virtues I've just described."

His wife interrupted him with faint irony. "That shows you have a keen insight into human nature, my dear, finding all these virtues in so short a time."

"Child," he retorted, "a monarch who is the guest of another monarch hasn't very much privacy. A naked man is well-dressed by comparison. His intentions are palpable, or else you notice right away that he is trying to hide them. Since a king can freely dictate his behavior, his character can readily be sized up by what he does and says. His mold involuntarily fits his nature, and betrays his qualities. If, however, he is an actor and selects his own part, then the style in which he plays it is the *carte d'identité*."

"You have developed remarkably, darling, in the short time you have been adjutant," Elizabeth interposed.

"Think so?" Neustift grinned. "Maybe. This perpetual

vigilance sharpens the instincts, the inner eye. But we are not talking about me. I tell you, it is a joy to know such a man as Edward VII is on the throne. All his virtues, his practicality, his gallantry, good cheer and cleverness, all that is overshadowed by a noblesse, a loftiness, an unapproachable something that impels veneration. Yet he is gracious; you feel he is remote and still somehow you feel intimate with him. You should see how he treats his people. So simply and naturally.... And if you stand opposite him, you are spellbound ... but in a pleasant way, without being embarrassed. Elizabeth, I don't have to tell you I love our Emperor; nor do I take the liberty of making comparisons. But Edward is a modern king, as kingly as can be, a true modern majesty, and in that sense perhaps the only one alive!"

The next forenoon King Edward appeared in the Court Box at the Spanish Riding School. He sat between Franz Joseph and the Heir Apparent, both of whom wore the uniforms of Austrian generals. Edward came in civilian clothes and wore his simplicity as nobly as his elegance. Now, in the twilight of his life, with his white head and his high slim figure, Franz Joseph looked as impressive as ever. Against that, King Edward's comfortably filled figure, his clear, intelligent, aristocratic face and his dark beard intershot with white made a striking contrast. But the impression the two monarchs made was equally compelling. Franz Joseph's manner, for all his freedom and his personal grace, seemed constrained by a conscious sense of supremacy, possibly accentuated by his upbringing in Hapsburg-Spanish etiquette. Edward, on the other hand, was completely relaxed, carefree even, *sans gêne;* he ventured far along the paths of normal human conduct and in spite of that lost none of his high-born attributes.

In their company Franz Ferdinand was eclipsed. His broad fleshy figure betrayed the strength of an ox, but lacked grace and nobility. His countenance— low forehead, short bristly hair, thick, dark brown mustache like a sergeant's—lacked all trace of spirit and of breeding; a face that revealed only brutal energy and unbending will. So plainly were those traits written over his features that they practically obliterated all marks of higher gifts. Only the waxen complexion and the hard unyielding glance of the night-dark eyes bespoke a powerful personality. In the Court Box, in such close proximity to these two rulers, he was obviously the least mighty, and yet the only ominous one; his mere presence radiated foreboding and dread.

The assemblages had risen at the entrance of the two monarchs. As they were welcomed by the Heir Apparent, the orchestra hidden behind the escutcheon played *God Save the King.*

For a moment before he sat down Edward was absorbed in the sight of this vast hall.

"Superb," he remarked to the Emperor, "these dimensions, these simple and yet gorgeous adornments. Really superb!"

Franz Joseph smiled.

"Fischer von Erlach, isn't it?" Edward queried. His host nodded.

"I already know the Riding School," Edward said to the Heir Apparent.

Franz Ferdinand was surprised. "Really? When has your Majesty been here?"

Edward smiled. "While waiting." He leaned toward the Archduke and whispered: "As you know, I was Prince of Wales for a long time. A very long time. Console yourself, my dear friend."

Franz Ferdinand assented throatily. "Yes, your Majesty, everything has its end. You've only to live long enough."

Trumpets. The horses appeared, the horsemen offered the time-honored greeting, and the play began.

The English King was in nowise *blasé* and did not spare his hands.

"This is magnificent!" he cried. "This is marvelous!"

At Florian's entry Edward was all expectation. "A superb animal. An extraordinary creature. What effortless, thorough mastery!" He didn't sit still for a moment. "What a graceful *courbette*! Charming! This stallion is not merely a beauty, he is a genius!"

Franz Joseph leaned over. "He is the one I wanted to show you."

"Oh, I am tremendously grateful."

Since Edward had spoken to him, Franz Ferdinand was quite buoyant. "Majesty, you are too kind," he belittled. "You can see as much in any of the better circuses." He wanted everyone to know how little he cared about owning Florian.

The Emperor ignored the remark, but Edward protested with surprise: "My dear Franz, there you are mistaken. In a circus! There is nothing in the entire world to compare with your Spanish Riding School. Nothing!" And as Florian was about to make his adieus, Edward applauded violently.

Ennsbauer and Florian retired amid thunderous handclapping.

Franz Joseph had seen through his nephew's utterance. Sour grapes. Unruffled, he casually said to his guest: "Two hundred years of breeding and training."

"Yes," Edward enthused. "Otherwise such a thing could not be achieved."

Franz Ferdinand laughed, his good humor expanding. The future was his. It lay just ahead, directly before

his eyes; just like this arena. As wide, as empty, as ready
for action, this future of his. And like the multitude
in balcony and gallery, humanity waited impatiently
in fear and in hope upon the deeds he would do—he,
Emperor Franz II of Austria! He laughed.

"Someday, your Majesty, all this waste must go. . . ."

"That would be wrong," Edward protested heatedly.
"You would destroy something unique."

With three fingers of his right hand Franz Joseph
carefully brushed his mustache, controlling his distem-
per. "Nobody can destroy this," he said softly but suc-
cinctly. "No successor of mine will be so blasphemous
and stupid."

In consternation Edward stared at Franz Ferdinand
who winked.

Florian just then was led in again on the long loose
rein by Ennsbauer. The shimmering white horse wore
practically no trappings. The side-pieces on his head,
more massive-looking than before, and the purple rein
like a bloody stripe along his snowy back; that was all.
At first Florian was shown between the pillars, doing

the Spanish stride on the spot. Then he pranced and glided in all his paces through the arena, even lifting into the *levade*–a heroic moment.

Edward used the very word–heroic. His whole being shook with admiration.

"Don't you find," he asked the Emperor, "that this affects you erotically and heroically at the same time?"

"I admit the heroic," was the smiling answer.

"No," pursued the King, "this naked horse . . . trembling with power and passion and restraint . . . and the man beside it–that's like a man with his beloved. . . ." He applauded heartily.

Franz Ferdinand breathed heavily. The words of the King had stirred memories of a vanished past. Enchanted anew, he watched Florian. But he could not bring himself to applaud the horse and rider.

Chapter Twenty

A WRITTEN ORDER HAD ARRIVED from the equerry, whereupon Ennsbauer mustered the horses.

"He, of course," he decided, stopping in front of Florian, "is the outstanding one. In fact he would be best alone."

Wary and full of fears ever since the affair with the Archduke, Anton listened. What was in store for Florian?

"He has been working here for three years now,"

Ennsbauer spoke while he stroked Florian's forehead, "which isn't very much, really. But with him it is equal to five years of ordinary work. His time has come."

Anton was terrified.

But when he learned that Florian was to return to Lipizza to be mated, to have offspring, he breathed easily. Intoxicating joy swept through him when Ennsbauer answered his timid question bruskly. "Of course, you ass, you'll have to go along. You and this beast of a dog. You three are inseparable."

During the days leading up to the time of departure, Anton showered Florian and Bosco with tender discourses.

Everything had awakened in Anton. The four years they had spent together at the place of Florian's birth, childhood and youth, the carefree existence, the wide meadows, the invigorating, salt-laden air that wafted over from the sea. . . . In his dull brain these memories began to seethe. To return there was a homecoming. It was even a triumph, for Florian returned crowned with laurels. Anton's early dreams had all come true.

For hours he held Florian's head in his arms, his mouth pressed to Florian's twitching ears, and whispered: "Lipizza! Do you remember? Lipizza! A baby you were! A lovely, helpless little fellow! Do you remember? You were hardly born when the national anthem was played! Do you remember? And today Emperors and Kings know you. Now we are going back to Lipizza. Lipizza, dear Florian! Do you understand? Lipizza!"

Patiently Florian listened to the tender words, moved his delicate ears, while his eyes shone opalescent in the semi-obscurity of the stable. Anton would have sworn an oath that Florian knew the meaning of every word, and that Bosco did also.

He lifted Bosco, pressed him to his breast and whispered to him: "We're going to Lipizza, Bosco. In Lipizza we shall be together again. Isn't that nice? You will recognize the meadows and the trees and everything . . . you will be happy, won't you? Won't you, Bosco, my little one?"

Bosco wagged so vigorously during this speech that his tail beat sharply against Anton's hip. He stretched and turned his tapering head, and washed Anton's smooth face with his tongue. Then he yawned, bashful with enthusiasm, and comprehending the question by its melody, he launched into a long drawn out yowling that sounded both mournful and gay.

On the meadows of Lipizza Florian at first stood stunned. Years had passed and he had known nothing, had seen nothing, except the short distance over the cobbled ground from the stable to the Riding School; had never breathed any air other than that in the old courtyard where during the summer months he had been exercised, mornings. Now he stood upon a meadow, breathed the sea breeze, the perfume of the trees, the tang of the limited freedom which is yet untrammeled— for the truly wild, untrammeled freedom his forebears had lost and forgotten in unthinkably far-off ages. A long line of ancestors had helped Florian to conquer his most fundamental instincts, through the alchemy of breeding reshaping them into instincts of service and subservience to man's will. In his soul, though, the bond with Nature had never weakened. Restored to the open he became fiery; the shock of renewal sharpened his temperament; his blood flowed more freely as the intoxicating freshness about him stimulated his senses. Although his aroused and growing exhilaration was hampered by his Hapsburg-Spanish education, the control was superficial; just as, for example, Franz Joseph's merriment was held in bounds by Hapsburg-Spanish decorum. In this sense Florian could be accepted as a sort of Hapsburg prince.

Bosco, the fox terrier, romped about him as of yore whenever he galloped across the grounds. Without reins, without fetters, bare and free, he could ride the wind! Soon Bosco began to pant, his tongue hung far out of his mouth and swung with the racing tempo of his pulse like a galvanized leaf. In Vienna Bosco had grown deplorably fat. He had had no opportunity to run as a fox terrier must to retain his shape. He had usually lounged around, loafed, stretched on the strong-smelling but agreeably warm straw. He had not been allowed in the Riding School. To run along the street or saunter about like a vagrant had ceased to be attractive after he was once almost run over in the vaulted passageway; and he had retained a deathly fear of the terrible Viennese streetcars which, in his estimation, made much too much noise anyway. Anton had never gone walking and for this reason never taken Bosco out or given him a chance to live rationally. Thus Bosco had become the Imperial Stable fox terrier, grown fat as an old lackey and known no other terrain than the old gray Court and the stable. There he had chased after his own scent, learned to distinguish the smells of medicines and liquors which were stored in the magazine for the adjacent Court Apothecary. That boring him soon enough, he had come to use the courtyard only for the essential things.

Now Bosco stripped off his enforced laziness in a trice. The wide meadows, the free roaming horses, Florian who acted increasingly impetuous, Bosco's own resurgent memories demanding reacquaintance with earthy things soon whipped him into shape again. The more fat he sweated away, the slenderer he appeared, the more wind and verve he regained.

Florian's meeting with Nausicaa, the companion of his youth, the elemental force with which his love broke forth, was as grandiose as a thunderstorm, as unsuppressible as a broad high, consuming flame; it was a mighty spectacle of Nature. Florian was hardly to be recognized. His whole body trembled, his veins swelled and traced bluish serpents along his white skin. Foam fell from his lips, his nostrils distended, his eyes became bloodshot and blazed with a wild luster. He snorted incessantly, bucked, and pawed the sod with his hooves so that great clods of earth and bunches of grass flew. His neighing sounded like metallic thunder and rang over Lipizza so imperiously that all the horses stopped in their tracks. The stallions and the mares listened to this masterful, seeking voice and were thrown into a turmoil of lust and impotent jealousy.

Florian was the supreme lord of Lipizza. He was obediently unfaithful and tyranically insatiable. Not Nausicaa, any longer, nor any other one possessed his love. He bestowed it upon any and all whom they brought to him. He enjoyed the female as such, the other sex as the other sex. And he reveled in his own malehood, squandered the vast stored-up force of his loins and did not grow tired of it. Afterward he would go rushing in his gliding gallop across the green carpet of the grass, challenging Bosco to race.

He teased Anton as he had never done before, came obediently at his call or when Bosco fetched him, suddenly to jump sidewise like a foal and pound off again, raising clouds of dust under his feet. Or he went sneaking up behind his friend, shoved him unexpectedly, then stood there innocently, almost laughing at Anton's surprise, and would circle him in a mad gallop. Sometimes he threw himself to the turf, started rolling around, and struggled with his four legs lifted to the sky, enjoying it most when Bosco imitated him like mad or barked in rage at this "Land of Cockaigne" existence.

Time passed. Florian had to return to Vienna. But this time it was different from his first arrival at the Spanish Riding School.

Anton accustomed himself readily to the routine of the service. He was a man. He knew the purpose and goal of vacation, the purpose and goal of the resumption of work.

Bosco soon rehabilitated himself in the narrowed sphere of activity. He was a dog and therefore ever ready to endure all the adored master of his fate inflicted or bestowed.

Only Florian, now grown mature, prouder, healthier, more eager for physical activity than ever, felt uncomfortable. He was as docile as ever, and as ever he obeyed the inner submission to the rider on his back; but it had ceased to be a labor of love. Of course, he could not clearly comprehend the state he was in. But his sojourn in the open, the joy of freedom under the heavenly tent, were unforgotten. That was now in his blood and fiber. He hated dozing in the stable. He hated seeing nothing but the arena. Hated having always to run in the oblong square, never getting any farther than from the stable into the dark narrow corridors of the Riding School, and from there across the yard, under the archway, back to the stable. . . .

Florian became morose.

After a few unsuccessful attempts, Ennsbauer advised the equerry: "Florian is done."

Count Bertingen wanted details. How? Why? Sick? Completely finished? Only with the High School? How did he know?

"One just knows," Ennsbauer said. "He used to be different. He guessed, knew everything instinctively. Now he hesitates. All of a sudden he's lost his uncanny instinct. He refuses to respond. I've got to help him as much as I do a beginner. He doesn't enjoy his work anymore. Nor do I enjoy riding him."

"Since when?"

"Well—since he returned from Lipizza."

"Give him time," Count Bertingen suggested. "Maybe he needs rest."

The riding master frowned darkly. "I know the usual rest periods. I gave Florian a longer one, even though he doesn't need it. He needs a different mode of life."

"Well, then . . . to the carriage. Send him over to the Imperial Stables," Bertingen decided.

Ennsbauer nodded.

Count Bertingen's face showed a trace of a smile. "Then we are both right. First you. Now I. After all, he has accomplished enough here, this Florian. Now he shall pull his Majesty's carriage."

When the equerry had left, Ennsbauer stepped into the front yard of the Riding School and looked around to make sure he was alone. In a gust of rage he broke his crop in two. Bent and tore the leather-covered bamboo so that splinters and tatters hung down from it. "God damn it!" he muttered between his teeth.

Gabriele Menzinger found him in miserable humor.

"What's the matter with you?" she asked him lovingly.

Acidly he barked at her: "Stupid question! I haven't got Florian anymore."

She was helpless and could only sigh: "Dead? The poor thing."

He mimicked her: "The poor thing.... Dead.... You are a silly goose, my dear. I haven't got him any longer. Does that mean he's got to be dead?"

Gabriele laughed. "Well, if he is alive, then it isn't so terrible."

Ennsbauer's rage increased. "Not so terrible! You talk as you are . . . utterly stupid."

"Don't be so uncouth," she said sharply. "I am not your stableboy."

"My very lowest stableboy," he shouted, "the stupidest, would understand what it means for a horse like Florian to become a—a cab horse! An ordinary common, cab horse!" He took a deep breath. "If you had a partner, with whom you've shared triumph after triumph, and he joined another theater or left Vienna, you would feel like the devil, too."

"I? I?" Gabriele Menzinger shook with laughter. "Beside myself? Why would I be? You are precious! My partners don't mean a thing to me. Nothing! If my partner shared my success I couldn't endure it. I'd be glad to get rid of him."

"Then I don't know." Ennsbauer growled. "Is it just you who is a louse, or are all actors vermin?"

They were both in the stable now.

"You don't see," Gabriele said softly. "We come from different worlds."

"This much I see," he grated: "you *are* a louse!"

She looked around. "Where is Florian? Let's visit him, shall we?"

She said that very quietly.

"Leave Florian alone!"

He grabbed her all of a sudden, pressed her to the wall. His hot face close to hers, he panted: "I want you."

And she, with an enigmatic smile: "Why not?"

His grip on her tightened. "Now? Right away?"

She lifted her face so that her breath warmed his cheek. "Yes. The carriage is waiting."

"Let's go."

He fairly dragged her.

Chapter Twenty-One

TWO DAYS AFTER FLORIAN WAS LED to the Imperial Stables.

Ennsbauer was not even there. The leave-taking occurred without much ado. From the Mews came a stableboy. Anton fastened a blanket over Florian, called Bosco, and they were on their way.

The years had flown. . . .

Anton passed them just as Florian did. Not so dully as the other stablemen imagined, for his days were full. He had enough in Florian and Bosco. His simple nature did not require more. While the weeks slipped into months, the months into years, without his noticing, he had never a desire for anything beyond the stable, beyond Florian.

An unheard-of event happened, this early morning, as Anton led Florian across the outer square of the Palace for the first time. The inner court, with its towering statue of Emperor Franz, he had penetrated a few times in the past, and had casually peered through the three open low arches into the distance. He had never had the impulse to explore. To the contrary, a timid feeling that it wasn't befitting a mere stableman to be so venturesome had always held him back.

Now he was profoundly moved by the vast space. Broad grass plots spread before him. Rows of trees crossed and intersected. Mighty cupolas, turrets and roofs glistened from afar. The wide street that lead straight toward the arches enclosing the court was flanked by two monuments of bronze horsemen about to gallop on their bronze horses right down into the street. Alluringly scented lilac bushes blossomed about the statues and lent them a paradisiacal note.

Overcome by this sight, Anton decided to address the stableboy who had come for Florian. "You . . . what is your name?"

"Wenzel," the boy replied. "Wenzel Kralick is my name. And yours?"

Anton gave his name, pointed to the monument at the left and inquired who that was.

In his Czech accent Wenzel gave the desired information. "That's Prince Eugen."

Anton recollected. "I see . . . *Prinz Eugenius, der edle Ritter.*" He thought of the age-old soldier's song. Nor did he know much more about the conqueror of the Turks.

He pointed to the other monument. "And this one?"

Wenzel hiked his shoulders. His erudition was no more profound than Anton's. "Don't know. I think his name is Karl. He was prince, too, or something."

They reached the Ringstrasse. Anton stopped uncertainly and Wenzel instructed him: "Straight out."

With Florian they crossed the street making toward the park, in the center of which, between the two museum palaces, Maria Theresia gazed down from her throne.

Anton tugged at his new comrade's sleeve. "And she . . . ?"

"Say, you never been here?" Wenzel asked, astonished.

"Never," Anton confirmed vehemently, as though to protest his innocence of a crime.

"Well, then"—Wenzel, more astonished than before, now felt very superior—"so that you know . . . Empress she is, name Maria Theresia."

"Oh," Anton muttered reverently, "I've heard of her all right."

Of Maria Theresia, too, he knew only the shining glory of her name. In silence he trudged through the gardens, observed with disapproval how Bosco dared to scamper around. Anton could not suppress a twinge of embarrassment at having to walk here. He felt like a vagabond who accidentally finds himself in a royal palace. With abashed eyes he looked around, gaining only blurred impressions of what he saw. The idea of asking Wenzel what purpose the two colossal palaces really served, he quickly gave up. He considered Florian the only one worthy of walking here, and felt half excused by reason of Florian's presence. For Bosco's impudence he had no excuse whatsoever.

Having traversed the Lastenstrasse and reached the Imperial Stables, Anton sighed and breathed more freely again. An incredible fairyland presented itself to him, a place of fabulous sumptuousness and awe-inspiring grandeur; yet Anton knew at once that he belonged to this world and that he would readily feel at home.

Hundreds of horses stood here in endless rows of magnificent stalls. Lipizzans whom Anton greeted like friends, Irish palfreys, Kladrubers, Arabs, hunters, Hungarian, English and Russian carriage horses. Roan, fallow, mottled, jet black. Heavy and light horses. Ponies with tousled manes. High-limbed brown mules, white and pearl-gray asses carrying the dark cross on their backs. What was the Spanish stable with its thirty Lipizzan stallions against this multitude?

"Forty little saints!" The devout oath escaped Anton, who was in seventh heaven and forgot all about the noble art of the stallions.

Bosco simply arrogated to himself a place beside

Florian. They tried to chase him, but he didn't bother to move. Tired after the long walk, he sank into the straw at Florian's feet. There he remained. He did not know that Anton had somewhat helplessly explained the friendship between horse and dog, nor that Florian's fame was great enough to make everyone respect his love for the terrier. He was with Florian and stayed with Florian.

The equerry arrived just as Florian was being harnessed.

The other horse, also a Lipizzan, was called Capitano and was three years older. He sniffed curiously at Florian's face and showed him sympathy, which Florian accepted in all friendliness. Now the two, Capitano and Florian, stood side by side at the shaft of the carriage and nodded solemnly with their heads; with all the beautiful reticence of their temperament they pawed the ground and waited for the signal to go.

The equerry gave the order to fasten the ropes. Anton worked on Florian and Wenzel on Capitano; they were speedily done. The reins were adjusted and the loose loop was placed on the dashboard pole.

Count Bertingen waited until the horses had completely calmed down and stood at rest, head by head, back by back, croup by croup. Then he compared their points with great care.

"They match," he decided, "just as I thought. They will make an excellent team. Exactly the same height and length. Capitano's gray croup and cannons don't matter."

Then it happened that the usually mute Anton exclaimed, inanely proud: "Yes, there has never been a horse like Florian."

Under the astonished expression on Count Bertingen's face he turned scarlet and laughed in doltish embarrassment.

The old official who had supervised the matching up of the team whispered to Bertingen: "Excuse it, your Excellency; the lad is good and not at all impudent. He simply loves Florian so much...."

"Why, Councilor," Bertingen smiled, "he wasn't impudent . . . just anxious . . . and I rather like that." Louder, he said: "Now it's just a question of how Florian behaves." With these words he climbed aboard the chaise, took hold of the reins and said while unscrewing the brakes: "We'll see whether he understands at once, or whether we'll have to work with him."

Bosco began to bark and sprang to Florian's nose. Anton wanted to catch him but Bertingen waved him back: "Leave the dog be." He clucked with his tongue and the two horses pulled.

Florian had poised his ears backward to catch every sign of the driver. He held the bit between his teeth, and trotted as smoothly as Capitano. In his way of lifting his feet and setting them down one close to the other, he gave evidence of his training in the cadenced gait of the Spanish School.

The equerry drove around and around through the spacious yards. Florian could scarcely feel the whip on his back, on his flanks. He who had mastered every pace in the Spanish Riding School did not dread the whip; to him it was a subtle sign language in which the driver spoke his wishes.

Florian and Capitano exchanged quick glances. The

latter's eye held an appreciative light: "I like you. Bravo. You know your business."

And Florian's good humor grew. He liked trotting gaily beside a comrade, competing in pace and posture. It was fun. And how pleasant out here in the open, bathing in ever-changing sunlight and shadow. You breathed easier. You felt the earth under your hooves more intimately than in the Riding School.

Bosco soon had enough and ran toward the group among whom Anton waited. There he lay on his forepaws and let his tongue loll.

At a smart clip the equerry drove up. A tiny movement of his wrist and the two horses stood riveted to the ground, snorting loudly, their heads nodding and foam flying. Not another step did they take. Quiveringly self-controlled, they knew they had to stand, stand like iron.

Fastening the reins, to the step and tightening the brakes, the equerry waited another moment and jumped down. He walked forward to Florian, patted his neck, and gave him full praise. "It really went well.

Like an experienced carriage horse. Soft-mouthed. Very attentive and very willing."

Councilor Stepanek stroked Capitano. "But this one, your Excellency, does help him a bit."

"Certainly. And yet—I didn't notice any particular sign of help. . . . It's a rare accomplishment." Bertingen looked around. "Is Gruber here?"

"At your service, your Excellency!" spoke up a well-built man who looked elegant even in his drab-colored every-day livery.

Konrad Gruber was Franz Joseph's personal coachman. For more than a quarter of a century he had sat on the driver's seat when the Emperor rode in the carriage. Twenty-three years before Konrad Gruber had happened to be driving the Emperor all alone in a closed carriage. No *chasseur*, no adjutant . . . alone . . . somewhere. . . . And in a deserted, unguarded street a man had run toward the carriage, his hand raised threateningly. It could not be ascertained whether he brandished a pistol or a bomb. A stroke from Gruber's whip had lashed across the man's eyes and blinded him. A second stroke had driven the horses off at a mad pace. Nobody ever knew of this incident. Only Franz Joseph, Gruber and the secret police who saw to it that the man disappeared forever. A few months later Konrad Gruber had been awarded the golden cross of merit by the Emperor himself, over the heads of all the Court officials. He was in the Emperor's grace, unshakable in his position, had seen his second first chamberlain and third equerry, no one of whom dared oppose him. Konrad Gruber knew his power and its limitations. He was shrewd, tight-lipped and unaggressive. When it came to the State coach and the horses for Franz Joseph, however, he brooked no interference. That was his own personal jurisdiction, and there he exercised absolute authority, without changing his mien or saying an extra word. Equerries and other excellencies, counts and princes might come and go as often as God wished—that disrupted nothing in the vast, complex, well-organized Court life and did not affect the well-being and the security of the Emperor. Only the two firm steely hands and the watchful eyes of the State coachman could not be replaced. Konrad Gruber felt superior to all courtiers.

"Well, my dear Gruber," Count Bertingen suggested, "you try the new pair."

Across Gruber's lantern-jawed face, because of its fine modeling and intelligent expression looking more like a prelate's than a coachman's, flitted a covert smile.

"At your service," he murmured in a low tone.

Slowly he approached the two horses, examined their harness, took them by their heads and peered gravely into their eyes; just as if he were alone with them. He looked imposing as he stroked Florian over forehead and nose. He was a big man, had stemmed his tendency toward fatness by exercise and massaging. Ever since he had first driven his Emperor's carriage he had abstained from alcohol, and had remained unmarried in order to devote all of himself, with all the fanaticism of his nature, to the Imperial service. He did love good food, and plenty of it. He made gourmandizing the only pastime of his solitude; for he even spurned the friendship of men.

Despite his size he swung lightly onto the driver's seat. In the same motion he grabbed the reins and whip, released the brake and drove off at a brisk pace. So sudden had been the start that the horses had bent their hindlegs slightly and heaved upward in front—a gesture at once wild and solemn.

Florian ran fluidly.

Konrad Gruber diminished and then accelerated the pace. Florian didn't dream of galloping. In one of the smaller courts a sheet of white paper lay on the ground. Gruber had prearranged that. In the sunlight it lay there and fairly shrieked, fairly exploded with a cruel glare. As Gruber drove toward it, a breath of wind stirred it. It moved like a living thing. Florian snorted with fright, reared and wanted to run away but could only shove sidewise, held by Gruber's iron wrists.

A lash of the whip stung his neck and back. Sharp, like a cutting knife, it burned like hellfire.

It was the first punishment he had ever known in his life. His stunned surprise banished his fright about the paper. The searing, maddening pain concentrated all his nerves on his neck and back.

Gruber guided the carriage in a sharp circle, and

drove toward the sheet of paper once more. Just as he hadn't given Florian time to rear and plunge, so now he did not give the mincing animal the slightest chance to revolt against the whiplash.

The whip tickled Florian's thigh. He understood instantly; now he knew the power of that whip, and, encouraged by Capitano, he fell into a quick trot. Without a hint of hesitation he made for the fluttering sheet of paper. He snorted briefly only as the driver egged him on. That was all.

Gruber would have liked to say "bravo" or "good horse" or something like that. Instead he compressed his lips so that his mouth formed a narrow line in his smooth copper-hued face. He drove into the other large court, gave the horses their heads, made them describe a turnabout, and came back to the small court. Two sheets of paper were lying there dancing in the soft breeze. The horses neared them. Florian knew what threatened him if he should try again to avoid the white terror. His quick perceptions told him that he had far less to fear from the two white dancing sheets than the man he served. He controlled himself, and only let out one irrepressible snort. In an unbroken trot he reached the sheets and thundered on, trampling them under.

Three and four times the animals circled the court-yard and came at the white rustling sheets of paper. Capitano remained unruffled; he seemed to notice nothing. Florian kept nodding his head, moving his ears, rolling his eyes; but he kept step. With a turn of his head Capitano tried to quiet his companion. There was no second streak of whip-fire, no danger underfoot. Florian grasped the truth and finally passed over the white terror as calmly as Capitano.

Satisfied, Gruber drove toward the stable, hopped off the board and ordered: "Unhitch."

"Well?" Count Bertingen asked, seeing the coach-man was loath to say anything. "What do you think?"

Gruber replied: "They'll do, your Excellency." Then he saluted, doffing his top hat with an air, and disap-peared.

The equerry went over to Florian. "Wringing wet," he remarked.

Anton had noticed the welt running from Florian's neck along his back. Horror-stricken, he looked at the count. Bertingen turned silently away.

But Anton soon had cause to think better of Konrad Gruber.

Whenever the Emperor returned from Schönbrunn to the Imperial Palace, or if they telephoned to the Mews to say he remained at Schönbrunn and would not need a carriage, then Herr Konrad Gruber would order Florian and Capitano harnessed to a phaeton. And he would drive out through the city or along the Ringstrasse into the Prater, down the main driveway, around the Lusthaus, and back again.

Anton was outfitted in simple drab livery, given a top hat with a gold border and a gold cockade, and permitted to come along. In this garb he thought he looked as grand as any prince.

Gruber began to like the quiet unobtrusive lad. Reticent himself, he esteemed Anton's silence. Himself fanatically loyal to the service, he appreciated the ardent self-effacement with which Anton worked. Konrad

Gruber loved horses, and horses only, and therefore he was touched by Anton's love for Florian. Gruber knew men thoroughly, particularly the stable personnel, and was held in fear by all. Only Anton never showed any fear. He had no equal for diligence, obedience, trustworthiness and unselfishness. Gruber held these qualities in the highest regard. He also fathomed Anton's simplicity. And when, to top everything, it was established that Anton was a Styrian—a countryman of his— then Gruber gave him his complete trust. Anton never heard a kind word out of Gruber, so he did not suspect how close he was to this important man; nor did he sit in judgment on the man inasmuch as he always accepted everything, good or bad, stoically and without any meditation.

Every time Florian and Capitano drove off, and Anton in the phaeton shooed him back, Bosco fell into a state of melancholy. As often as Anton got into his livery and donned the top hat, Bosco's desperation mounted. For he knew he would suffer hours of dreary loneliness. So whenever preparations began he sat in front of the stable door and whimpered softly until his two friends disappeared.

One day Gruber pointed his whip at Bosco and said: "Take the dog along."

Completely baffled, Anton hesitated and then lifted the still more baffled Bosco into the carriage. The terrier uttered one brief yelp, then scrambled up on the small seat in the back where he squatted contentedly and watched out of his intelligent eyes, now Florian, and again the passing stream of carriages and pedestrians in the streets. From that time on he went along regularly.

That day Anton began to admire and love the forbidding, mighty Konrad Gruber from the bottom of his devout heart. He never had the courage to address him, though. And when he crouched, much lower down, next him on the dickey, he would actually have considered it impertinent to speak one word to Gruber.

Gruber drove the two beautiful horses through the clamor and chaos of the city as carefully and skilfully as if evading deathly perils. Florian and Capitano were responsive instruments in his hands, obeyed his slightest wish so quickly and so reliably that it became one of Anton's greatest joys to watch them.

Sometimes Gruber drove the carriage by the Maria Theresia monument directly toward the Imperial Palace. Then again he passed the Parliament, the municipal building and along the Schottenring. Anton observed these monumental edifices without the slightest conception of their purpose. On the Parliament he liked the horsemen and the quadrigas which seemed to drive straight into heaven from the gables. The winged horses of the Opera ridden by harp-playing figures struck him as comical. He smiled wryly every time he passed them. He did not know that this building housed the Opera, any more than he could have said what an opera was. When they took the route across the city in a straight line from the Kaertnerstrasse toward the quay, Anton gazed with pious wonder up at the church on the Stephansplatz, at the tower wrought out of earthly heaviness into delicate grace, rising to the clouds. He needed no one to name this church and this tower. They spoke their own impressive language and Anton knew at first sight: St. Stephan's.

He noticed that the policemen, and even the Palace
gendarmes in their proud uniforms and their helmets
crested by black horsehair plumes, knew and saluted the
state coachman. Gruber acknowledged these greetings
either by a slight nod or by lowering his whip. Anton
liked the orderliness of this procedure. It deepened that
comforting feeling of security. He also noticed how the
policemen at the street crossings attempted to clear the
way for Gruber's phaeton. The rhythmical, undiminished
clip at which the horses crossed intersections he esteemed
and appreciated for what it actually was: special privilege.

Anton's particular pleasure was when they passed
the railroad crossing behind the Praterstern and the
wide, straight, main thoroughfare lay before them . . .
the green shadowy crowns of the old chestnut trees, the
smooth, gray, endless ribbon of the street. Here Gruber
held the carriage to the middle of the road and dictated a mad pace to the horses. No longer were their
steps short and minced. The thin legs were thrust far
forward and ate up the ground in big chunks. Florian
and Capitano tore along, clearly enjoying their speed.

The fastest fiacre, the fleetest Hungarian *Jucker,* the best Russian team were all left behind. That was Gruber's purpose; that was Florian's and Capitano's passion. They never failed. And Anton rejoiced.

When the horses were granted a respite, to walk around the Lusthaus on their homeward way, the two Lipizzans danced as nimbly as if they had just quitted their stable.

Bosco, however, suffered slight attacks of vertigo due to the swift pace, and now recuperated by yawning continually.

There was one exciting moment. In the narrow Rotenturmstrasse an automobile coughed, snorted and wheezed toward them. Gruber heard it from afar and took the horses in hand. It was just as well that he did. For, as the automobile approached and sounded its claxon, Capitano lost his head. He rose on his hindlegs, like the horses of Prince Eugen's monument, and would have plunged into the first show-window had not Gruber expertly shortened the reins and checked him with his iron grip. Capitano made a second attempt to rise, and failing again, surged forward and tried to run away. That, too, failed.

In the meantime the clattering automobile passed, leaving only a smelly cloud of smoke in its wake.

Had Capitano in his momentary lack of composure been the stronger, the shaft would have rammed the back of a hack and perhaps injured its passengers. Luckily Florian had remained calm, and had become still calmer when Capitano made his second break, attempting to compel his mate back into the obedient trot. That had made matters much easier for Gruber.

Once more Gruber's mouth formed the thin horizontal line in his bronzed face. He lowered his forehead as if to ram something, but he did not raise the whip; he had no intention of punishing Capitano. He registered satisfaction over the fact that Florian had not forgotten the paper lesson and was apparently resolved not to be terrified by anything, or, what amounted to the same thing, to let any terror get the better of him. A single stroke of the whip had done this to a blooded animal unaccustomed to punishment!

Capitano went unrebuked. Automobiles were something of a novelty, were fearsome and unpleasantly noisy. Capitano had been maddened by the shrieking and groaning monster rather than terrified by it. On this score Gruber heartily agreed with him. He refused to beat a Lipizzan because of one of those infernal machines. Nevertheless, Capitano had to get rid of his nervousness in the proximity of these running teakettles. So the next time they went out they encountered one automobile after the other; Gruber had seen to that. And Capitano soon got over his revulsion.

The equerry showed up, once, as the phaeton stood ready.

"I want to see personally whether we are prepared."

Anton was shunted to the rear of the carriage. Doubtfully he took his place. He didn't dare take Bosco along, even though the little dog already wagged longingly around the wheels. Gruber, however, to whom the difference between himself and this Count Bertingen wasn't so great, plucked the little dog from the ground the instant before the equerry had sent the horses off, and handed him up to Anton.

They went along the Ringstrasse into the Prater. This time there was no thrilling race down the main thoroughfare, although Florian and Capitano made a mild attempt to fall into the stimulating tempo.

On their return Bertingen, as he climbed down, gave the dog a marked look, and a none too friendly one to Anton. But he withheld any comment. To Gruber, who stood waiting, he said: "Well, my dear Gruber, I think we are ready."

"Tomorrow these two will serve his Majesty," Gruber replied, as if he had long ago made up his mind to that.

Afterward he asked Anton very casually: "How does his Excellency drive?"

Anton shrugged his shoulders. "The horses do everything by themselves."

Gruber chose not to show his pleasure.

Chapter Twenty-Two

EARLY NEXT MORNING THE OPEN landau with the gilded spokes stopped at the inner staircase at Schönbrunn. Capitano and Florian drew it. Gruber, in a dun-colored coat, each tip of his bicorne over an ear, held the reins.

The horses' pawing echoed down from the vault. Their ears moved convulsively, they were waiting impatiently for the signal that would set them going.

Franz Joseph, accompanied by his chief adjutant and his *chasseur*, appeared. He was ill-humored and did not glance at the new pair. The adjutant wore a long face. He saw nothing at all. As soon as his Emperor sat in the carriage, the morose-looking *chasseur* climbed to the driver's box, and the horses trotted quickly through the corridor and turned a sharp corner to the courtyard.

As soon as their nodding heads came into view, a sentry shouted: *"Gewehr heraus!"* three times, for the Emperor was entitled to a triple salute. Three times the shout rose like the crack of a whip, dissolving in echoes through the wide square. The last one had hardly died away when the command rang out and the drums beat the general march. The two officers saluted, their sabers flashing three times in the sun; and the front-line soldiers slid their hands down behind their gun belts in presenting arms. The flag dipped. It was a military ceremony, solemn and impressive.

Once again Konrad Gruber compressed his lips, his mouth a thin line. He knew exactly what to do, not under orders but by his own tact. The carriage rolled slowly along the middle of the courtyard toward the wide-open gate.

At the sound of the drums Florian executed his

Spanish stride, moved his ears in expectation of music, and rocked his beautifully molded white body from his hocks, taking tiny steps. Capitano tried to imitate him. Their necks bowed low one moment and proudly aloft the next, the two horses turned the departure from Schönbrunn into a triumphant spectacle. In passing, Franz Joseph ran his eyes over the company of soldiers and leaned back against the cushions as the carriage reached the street outside.

Konrad Gruber knew what he wanted to do.

The Emperor had not noticed Florian, nor seen Capitano. Gruber was hurt and resolved to compel the Emperor's attention. Gradually he raised the pace, did it so smoothly that his passengers did not notice. Obliquely cleaving the Volksgarten, and open only to the Emperor, was a paved short-cut from the street. Konrad Gruber covered it faster than he had ever done with other horses. Upon reaching the Rudolfsheimer Hauptstrasse which led to the Mariahilferstrasse, the horses began to race. They tore along with the gliding smoothness of birds in flight.

The Emperor could not help noticing this extreme

pace. He noticed it by the way men tearing off their hats to the royal coach, or just standing agape, disappeared like leaves blown away by a storm. Franz Joseph smiled. He could not adapt himself to the new motorcars, but he loved sweeping along like this straight through the ranks of human beings to whom he was close and yet beyond reach, who longed to see him and who saw but his passing silhouette.

He was silent. His face grew milder and finally turned gay.

The Gürtel was passed in no time, in no time Mariahilferstrasse had been reached. The Emperor bowed from the carriage. Would the little girl again be there? Yes, there she stood at the streetcar stop, waiting for her tram. And for the Emperor. A ten-year-old schoolgirl. Slim and of aristocratic bearing. Fresh and pretty. With clever gentle eyes. Each time she made a curtsy and laughed. And the Emperor each time smiled back at her. He could not say what it was, but somehow this child reminded him of his wife, of Elizabeth as a young girl; and that moved him.

"Have Gruber stop," he said this time.

The general-adjutant called to the *chasseur* who whispered in Gruber's ear. The horses slowed down and came to a halt, standing like posts rammed into the earth. There had been scarcely any jolt.

Upon the Emperor's gesture the little girl approached, without shyness, quite naturally, like one accustomed to daily association with the Emperor. Her simplicity held no artifice. It was dictated by childish trust.

The adjutant had opened the collapsible step. Unhesitatingly the girl climbed into the carriage and sat down opposite the Emperor.

"Proceed."

The horses flew over the pavement on invisible wings.

"What's your name?"

"Gretl Saxl."

She answered firmly and blushed deeply to the heart-shaped line of her black hair at the forehead. Her chest heaved and her heart palpitated, but her young mouth and her clear eyes laughed.

Franz Joseph laughed, too. "Gretl Saxl . . . what a merry name."

"Oh, yes," she said without removing her eyes from him. And all the while an inner voice, which she alone could hear, kept on telling her: "The Emperor! The Emperor! The Emperor!" She found it difficult to keep down her elation.

"You are going to school?"

"Yes."

"Where is your school?"

"In the Fourth District." She gave the address.

Franz Joseph lifted his hand, the adjutant transmitted the information to the *chasseur*. Gruber did not stir when he heard these instructions, didn't even indulge in a smile, but merely pressed his chin back against his chest. He had ousted the Emperor's ill humor; in that he had succeeded.

"Do you like to study?"

The girl grew serious. "Not always," she confessed.

When Franz Joseph laughed at this, she, too, tried to smile. But by now she was highly self-conscious.

"What lessons do you like best?"

She had an answer ready: "Biblical history and German."

"That's nice. Biblical history. Beautiful. You are a good girl?"

The child shook her head and kept silent.

The old man was astonished: "No?"

His gaze fixed her eyes. Again she blushed. Slowly the blood crept into her cheeks, up to her forehead; an open, and at the same time, bashful confession. Reluctantly she said: "Not always."

"But," replied the Emperor, "children ought to be always good."

Her eyes contradicted him. "Oh, that's entirely too difficult," she said impetuously.

It was the Emperor's turn to smile again. "Difficult? Why so?" He was altogether too remote from childhood; he not only pictured childhood as a fairyland, but all human beings as "good." Only "good" people existed for this unworldly old prince. Those few that were disturbing, were dangerous and had to be done away with. To be good, was his people's duty. . . . So he imagined. There had been sporadic occurrences before which even he had had to bow, without comprehending them or being in accord with them. Parliaments and national demands and political upheavals and majority struggles and such things, which he called rubbish. In his opinion they prevented peaceful rule just as dust or rubbish clogged and hindered the operation of a machine. It was entirely a question of being "good"; that was self-evident and accepted. Difficult? Why so?

Eye to eye, the little girl insisted: "One can't always be good."

He was amused by this schoolchild. "Why, Gretl Saxl, if you promise me that you will always be good . . . me, you understand? . . . then it will be possible, won't it?"

"Maybe. . . ." Her answer contained doubt.

Their eyes, the shining light blue eyes of the Emperor and the dark ones of the child, smiled into each other. "So, promise me."

She couldn't resist the kindly old man. "Yes, I promise, I'll always be good. But . . ." Now came the loophole. "But I don't know whether I can keep my promise."

"Why, Gretl!"

She heard him, heard his implied accusation. . . . "It

is impossible to be always good," she complained, and retreated into the desperate question: "Are grown-up people always good?"

The mild glance that met her consoled her. What did this child know about this old man who was so lonely, so naïve despite a vast fund of experience with human sins, frailties, vices? "Listen, my child, you have promised me that you will always be good. You won't forget your good intention, will you?"

"Oh, never.... Never!" she stammered. "I will always think of it ... and always try."

"Well, then, everything is all right."

"Thank God." Straight from her pure heart came the words.

She remembered, just as the horses stopped, that one said "your Majesty," to the Emperor. Yet by the dictum of some strange inhibition it seemed wrong to her and she didn't dare to. And so, suddenly timid, she murmured: *"Küss' die Hand...."*

Gretl Saxl skipped from the Emperor's landau. She turned quickly to curtsy, to wave her hand; but her eyes met nothing else than the fluttering white plume on the *chasseur's* hat and the glittering sheen of the gilded spokes.

Leaning far back, Franz Joseph sat in silent meditation beside his adjutant. He did not regret the whim that had swept into the little girl's life an ineradicable mark of the Imperial presence, a memento of his grace. On the contrary, his whole being was suffused by a warmth bordering on gratitude; he would have been conscious of this, had he thought about it even for a moment. He had been refreshed by the free and artless manner of the child. He would doubtless have found it unbearable to have everybody approach him thus, meet his eyes so imperturbably, so disarmingly. As a rare occurrence, however, as a brief and exceptional incident, this child had been diverting and stimulating.

Franz Joseph's now excellent humor infected the adjutant, the *chasseur* and Konrad Gruber. Even the horses shared the good humor. Florian and Capitano sped over the Ringstrasse. When they turned in at the outer gate of the Palace and were hailed by the guard and the drum corps, they lessened their pace, and pranced through the green vastness of the Heldenplatz. People came rushing from the side streets, waving their hands and hats as they stood bareheaded at the curbing. Under the middle arch of the old castle went the white team and on to the Franzensplatz, the wide, gala inner court-yard. Once again the greeting of the Guard rang out amid the beating of drums, gleaming sabers deflected the sunlight and lowered banners rustled silkily.

Describing a semi-eight around the statue of Franz I the team drew to a halt in the vestibule of the Prime Minister's wing, stamping and foaming. The Emperor descended and studied the horses.

"That's Florian," he said. And Florian affirmed that with a few elated nods.

"At your service, your Majesty," Gruber acknowl-edged.

The Emperor laughed. "He answered before you, Gruber. And who is the other one? ... Oh, yes, Capitano. I know. They run like the devil, these two. We'll keep them, won't we, Gruber?"

Again: "At your service, your Majesty."

Franz Joseph stepped back the better to observe Florian. "He is really faultless. He was the best one in the Riding School. The very best. Triumphs like Caruso's. And one fine day he lost interest. Temperamental, like all great artists. Well, Gruber, we two gain by it."

"At your service, your Majesty." Gruber hardly ever said anything else to his master. Let Franz Joseph chide or jest—that was his right. The coachman never over-stepped his bounds. And he remained in the Emperor's grace.

In the vestibule at the foot of the staircase the adju-tant stood at attention. The *chasseur,* hat in hand, waited by the carriage. Konrad Gruber did not have to doff his hat. He sat on the driver's box, held the reins and watched the horses, relieved of any formality which might upset the performance of his duty.

"Very good, Gruber." Franz Joseph smiled up to him. "I was very pleased with the way we drove today. Wait in the stable and give the two a chance to rest."

"At your service, your Majesty."

Gruber had known, untold, the order of the day. The fact that the Emperor expressed it in person only indicated his particular pleasure.

Very slowly he drove back to the stables.

Chapter Twenty-Three

TO ANTON THE COLORFUL LIFE OF the Mews was a pleasant diversion. He was ever absorbing new experiences with never-failing eagerness. Nothing could perturb him. Whatever concerned horses was related to him; but these stables he believed capable of any miracle. At no time curious, he kept to himself and devoted himself exclusively to Florian, or else played with Bosco or groomed other horses entrusted to him, this latter competently but without any special enthusiasm. Florian . . . everything centered in Florian. Anton passed the numerous stablemen politely. He had no friends. He sought no friendship. Of the many coachmen he greeted when the occasion arose, only one really existed for him—Konrad Gruber. And this one didn't ever think of showing Anton the horses, the mules or the asses, the gala carriages, the historical old carosses. Nor did it ever occur to Anton to look around for himself or to get someone to show him around. Consequently it took him a long time to realize what was accomplished here.

There were carriages for the Emperor's retinue and for the Court supernumeraries. Coupés, open four-seaters, huge, wide-bellied calashes to fetch the choirboys on Sundays from the Piariste Monastery to High Mass in the Palace Chapel (Anton, incidentally, never saw the boys clad in their decorative uniforms, *epée* at side, stepping into the carriages as large as children's nurseries), commissary carriages with very high driver's seats and nothing but a wooden platform behind them; and smaller, somewhat similar vehicles which were drawn by the brown mules (these *mulis* wore outlandish harness, red-tasseled red nets over their ears and necks, and on their narrow collars tiny silver bells; to Anton they looked, thus caparisoned, ready for a costume ball).

Anton's interest was really captured by Gruber's attempts to arrange for teams of six or eight horses. Invariably the State coachman placed Florian and Capitano at the head of the team. If six horses were to pull the carriage, Gruber rode astride Florian; if eight, he directed them from the dickey. The Lipizzan stallions used for this purpose—Gruber matched them up expertly—were all good friends. To be grouped together before a coach became a gala occasion for them. They displayed their noblest motions. They were happy to do joint service, regardless of the object; to be together was enough for them.

It made Florian extremely mettlesome to drive through the vast stable buildings with Capitano at the head of such a group. He was first. He had the absolute conviction of belonging in front. For this reason he was sweet-tempered, friendly to his companions, and contented with his lot.

The same ambition rages feverishly in man and beast. With one difference. Subterfuge, intrigue, falsehood remain alien to the beast. How frequently a man who really belongs in the ruck wriggles on to the forefront by chicanery, bending or breaking justice, forging ahead by sheer nerve and lack of scruple, or by ignoble commercial enterprise. That man knows what he has done, and in his heart cannot suppress the accusing knowledge of his own trifling value. It thus becomes impossible for him to enjoy, or rise to, or be content with, his rank. He always feels insecure, and tries to hide this feeling from himself and from the world, to stifle it under meretricious gaiety, under false highflown talk, under challenging conceit. Always and in all circumstances is conceit stupid and the sign of lack of talent. Intelligent and gifted people are strangers to it. Animals, as distinguished from men, know but one way of achieving front rank—by open competition. The capercaillie, the stag maintains its premier place by right of greatest ability, and steps down if one comes who is abler. Animals are simple; and they know of no falsification or trickery. They obey the superior without reserve.

Florian was first. By tacit competition in the service of the master this fact had evolved. The master did by deliberate arrangement what he could not help doing. Florian had been first at the Spanish Riding School; and he remained first before the coach. The other horses were measured and valued by him. They themselves, purely by intuition, ranked themselves behind him, cheerfully recognized his supremacy, showed him devotion and received in return every sign of a hearty and reliable friendship.

Anton could not contain his joy when Florian led a team of six. Gruber sat in his saddle and led them briskly through the yards. Bosco ran ahead. On such occasions he never barked. He had a deferential respect for these three pairs of white horses thundering behind him, and for Gruber who was a rider then and not a driver. The terrier did not leap up to Florian's nose but silently extended himself to keep a few paces ahead of his friend. However, when the carriage rumbled back to the stable, and the harness had been taken off and Florian had followed Anton into his stall, then Bosco could restrain himself no longer and broke into loud rejoicing. The three were united; just Florian, Anton and Bosco, as they had been together for years. No others. Anton and Florian silent, Bosco full of talk, full of fun.

A team of eight always went slowly. Gruber drove with special care. He watched every movement of the thirty-two legs, the eight necks and heads, the eight tails so much like standards. Bosco paced ahead as if being led on a leash.

Little Bosco knew far more about the stables than Anton did. When Florian and Capitano were hitched to the carriage with the golden spokes, and Gruber appeared wearing the gold-braided bicorne, then Bosco squatted near by, watched the preparations with ears upright, and did not run along when the carriage rolled off.

Through interminable hours Bosco wouldn't budge

from Anton's side. By and by he became more careless, though, strolled into every nook and corner of the
Mews, peregrinated through the yards. Anything that
had four legs Bosco soon knew far better than Anton
ever could. He knew, in the stable housing the black
horses, a reddish brown bulldog whose fierce expression
belied his extreme friendliness. Bosco had a sharp tussle
with him when they first met. He displayed such reckless courage that the bulldog promptly sued for peace
and their future relations were most cordial. With the
mules lived a few *pintschers:* iron-gray fellows with long
matted hair and pointed, solemn faces that gave them
a marked resemblance to petty officials. Bosco knew
nothing of clerks and the like, but he quickly perceived
that these relatives of his had little esprit, no inclination
to play and no sense of humor to speak of. He therefore limited himself to a cool exchange of the ameni-
ties. There was a chipper Spitz who pleased him more
and who in turn took a great liking to him. Fox terriers, his nearest kin, betrayed the usual attitude among
close relatives: blood enmity, cousinly envy, and a subtle

understanding which compensated for many things.

During the years at Lipizza and at the Spanish Riding School, Bosco had given no thought to his own kind. After the cramped stable and the small court behind the vaulted thoroughfare, he now found himself surrounded by the Mews with their roomy yards, their high and massive buildings and living quarters, their multitude of horses, dogs, carriages and human beings. His horizon had widened. His attachment to Florian and Anton remained as intrinsic and intimate as ever. From these two creatures he was inseparable. And yet, although nobody troubled about him or thought to interfere with his fate, changes came: crises of the most fundamental nature which no one, outside of Florian perhaps, knew about. Anton noticed a little something. But it was left to Bosco to battle through his own emotional conflicts unaided.

Blame Pretty for that—for all his happiness, for all his pain and sorrow.

She was a slender, delicate thing belonging to a family of smooth-haired terriers. On her white skin she had yellowish brown spots bordered by black, and similar spots above her leaflike ears dividing the top of her head, so that a fine white stripe ran down to her white, black-bordered snout and shiny black nose. Her dark eyes were full of roguishness.

A ravishing beauty, she had all the wiles and was well versed in the art of love. These dangerous attributes she hid under a guise of complete innocence, thus instinctively following the trait of every true woman to become the more alluring. Her temperament was stormy; she could be crazily playful, although the erotic element stirred at the bottom of her very nature; she could be tenderly endearing and coldly repelling in two moments—just as her moods dictated. She changed from minute to minute; none of her suitors ever really knew what mood she was in.

With Florian away for hours at a time, and Anton taken up with work, Bosco sallied forth on expeditions through the stables, making and renewing all sorts of acquaintances with dogs, horses and men; and in this fashion he met Pretty. He succumbed to her charms in one fell swoop. He was enmeshed in that all-consuming passion that befalls the mature man who has till then despised and scorned everything female. He was thrown into a state of erotic obsession.

Together with him Pretty would chase through the stables and across the immense yard, tumbling about in coquettish playfulness. She lay on her back and let him sniff her all over, laughing at him and with her tiny red tongue kissing his eyes, his lips and his forehead. Once, however, Bosco caught her playing the same game with Tobby, the black and white terrier. She appeared so innocent and guileless, it was hard to suspect her of any deliberate infidelity. Yet Bosco was hurled into an abyss of unspeakable sorrow. The ravings of jealousy seethed within him. He lunged madly at Tobby, sank his teeth into the surprised and cowering creature's neck and gave no quarter. The blood that spouted from Tobby's wound tasted warm in his mouth, somehow aggravating his rage, robbing him of the last shred of decorum.

Pretty had made off. Things having become serious, she took the discreet and cautious course; retired, lay down coyly on her pillow and gave every overt sign of being a good little dog.

His wound had scattered all of Tobby's good sense along with his courage. He knew no better than to yowl in pain, alarming the vicinity.

The two dogs were doused in a pailful of cold water, a tidal wave that knocked the breath out of them and, for a few moments at least, the fear of drowning into them. Tobby fled. Just as Bosco was about to laugh at his comically retreating rival, he received a kick that actually lifted him into the air. On bent legs, his belly close to the ground, he limped into Florian's empty stall. Soaking wet. In pain. Miserable. Never before had he been mistreated by man. Now he had lived through the tragedy of disappointed first love, had fought his first real battle, had been drenched to the bone and driven out. And he was all alone.

He felt ashamed as never before in his life.

Anton discovered him trembling in the straw, lifted him, wrapped him in a towel and rubbed him dry. Rolled in a warm blanket he laid him outside in the sun. Throughout this entire procedure Anton asked over and over: "What have you been up to? What happened to you?"

Bosco stuck his intelligent face out from under the enveloping woolly mountain, and would have liked to tell what evil things had befallen him, but could only whimper. Anton stroked his forehead and murmured: "There, little one, be quiet. It'll pass all right. Good Bosco. Nice Bosco."

That soothed the disturbed soul. It almost consoled him. Almost. For there was the inexorable boundary-line between man and animal, that impassable barrier in the face of the closest intimacy. Anton had no inkling of what had inwardly shaken Bosco. He left the dog, went back to his work, and considered the trivial incident closed.

But it wasn't closed; Bosco was still madly in love. And jealousy ate at his heart. True, he had emerged victorious from the combat with his rival. That was proved by the way Tobby and all the other terriers evaded him, retreated whenever he came seeking Pretty.

Pretty lavished great tenderness on him, and inexhaustibly, in hoyden, coquettish play, now showered him with love and again repelled him with hateful disapproval, but invariably was glad of his presence. He was completely under her spell. His jealous tantrums grew milder, and disappeared. He ceased to have any reason for them. Yet he had no peace. His existence swung like a pendulum between bliss and despair. On top of that, he had pangs of conscience before Florian. After each happy or unhappy tryst with his beloved when he returned to Florian he squirmed and writhed before his great friend, whipped the straw with his tail and begged forgiveness. Of his adventure, of his passion he told nothing. He simply begged forgiveness.

Florian lowered his beautiful head, on these occasions, and sniffed at him kindly and knowingly, scented Pretty's perfume and guessed Bosco's fate. It befell every creature.... Of course he forgave him, even tried by a teasing snort to assert that such matters did not require forgiveness but understanding.

Chapter Twenty-Four

CAME A DAY OF UPSETS, OF QUARRELS, of excitement in the Mews.

Emperor Franz Joseph was sick at Schönbrunn. He had contracted a cold. The news sounded serious, thanks to certain Court factions who set exaggerated rumors going. The faction surrounding the Heir Apparent became mysteriously active. People who hoped for Franz Ferdinand's accession carried their heads higher, their necks stiffer. They gave orders where hitherto they had learned the habit of silence; they domineered where heretofore they had hemmed and hawed. Their actions implied that the succession to the throne had as good as taken place. The faithful servants of the old Emperor suffered all these things browbeaten and resigned.

On the morning of this day Anton rushed into Konrad Gruber's room. Gruber had just shaved and eyed the intruder questioningly.

"Florian is gone ... and Capitano, too!" Anton stammered.

Gruber's mien asked him to tell more.

"I put them in harness—" Anton explained. And still getting no response he added in his own behalf: "Orders from the councilor. . . ."

Silence.

Now Anton spoke haltingly: "For—the Archdukes—Franz Ferdinand. . . ."

A wave of a hand and he bolted from the room.

Gruber grabbed the telephone and called Schönbrunn. . . . No, the colonel of the House Ministry would not do. He wanted to talk to the chief adjutant.

At once! . . . When he heard that official's voice, he reported what had happened, quietly and clearly. But his voice quivered with wrath.

The adjutant chuckled. "Not really! . . . Such impatience. . . . And, praise God, much too soon."

Emboldened by anxiety, Gruber asked: "Is he better?" his voice unsteady.

"His Majesty is out of bed. But don't tell anybody."

That was that.

Konrad Gruber had to sit down. His knees trembled. He mopped his forehead, breathed deeply, and then started to pray, silently. His head lay on his devoutly folded hands. Only his lips moved.

Later, just as he finished dressing, the telephone rang. An order from Schönbrunn, in the name of the Emperor: "Demand the immediate return of Florian and Capitano. These horses, and all the private horses of his Majesty, must be used only for his Majesty's purposes."

The colonel of the House Ministry repeated: "And *only* for his Majesty's purposes."

Fully dressed, Gruber left his room and walked over

to the main building to call on the councilor. On the way he observed that a few coachmen, stablemen and lower officials greeted him less respectfully than usual; some of them ignored him. He made a mental note of each one. He compressed his lips so that his mouth formed a cruel gash.

The councilor kept him waiting purposely. Gruber knew the man wanted him to feel "through." When finally he stood in front of the desk, the councilor toyed for a long time with his papers before he asked disinterestedly: "What do you want?"

Without mincing words, Gruber said: "Have his Majesty's horses been ordered to Castle Belvedere?"

The councilor somewhat amusedly looked out of the window: "I am not accountable to you."

"Wrong!" Gruber was slow and precise of speech. "If you have taken the liberty—"

"How dare you!" the councilor shouted. "Who are you? An ordinary coachman! You don't seem to know that your glory is at an end? And you are impudent? Get out!"

Konrad Gruber held his ground; an immovable boulder the councilor could not dislodge by shouting. After a short pause he said with the same equanimity: "*Your* glory is at an end—if you have sent the Emperor's favorite horses to Belvedere."

Pale as a corpse the councilor listened. If Gruber spoke so definitely and unflinchingly he must know more than the others around the stables. The miracle might have happened. The eighty-year-old Emperor might have arisen from his sick-bed a healthy man.

"I am transmitting his Majesty's orders," Gruber continued icily. "The team is to be brought back at once, and like all the other personal horses of his Majesty must not be used for any other purpose whatsoever."

Without another word he walked out.

The secretary had heard the councilor shouting and had put his ear to the keyhole, overhearing Gruber's words. As Gruber passed through the anteroom the man bowed deferentially.

Full of desperate zeal the councilor telephoned Belvedere, telephoned wherever Franz Ferdinand might be. In a panic of haste he gave orders to send the regular carriage of the Archduke, as quickly as possible, to Breitensee. The Imperial equipage he had already ordered home from there.

As gun-cotton lights the hundred candles of a candelabra—in one puff—word of these occurrences made the round of the Mews. Just what happened at Schönbrunn, nobody knew. But everyone knew that Franz Joseph had given an order. That was enough.

Gruber stationed himself at the entrance of the stables to await the return of his horses.

Anton sat on his small portable bench in front of the door, Bosco at his feet.

Gradually a group of people came from the stables, from the carriage sheds, from the offices, and gathered around Gruber. When it was apparent that he would not engage in talk but wanted to be alone, they kept their distance.

The Imperial carriage arrived. At a comfortable trot Florian and Capitano swept up. They caused the same sort of sensation as on a first appearance.

While Anton unharnessed the horses, Gruber took a good look at the driver, Pawlitschek, who usually drove the Heir Apparent. Gruber did not say one word, but he silently vowed that Franz Ferdinand would have to get used to another driver; hereafter Pawlitschek would ride on servant and kitchen carts.

The voice of the councilor intruded upon his thoughts. "Well, there they are again, the favorite horses of his Majesty. Now everything is in order, isn't it?"

Gruber did not hear him, refused to hear him.

The councilor gulped, stepped directly up to Gruber, and said in his most unctuous tone: "It was a mistake, nothing but a mistake. Things like that can happen, after all. I beg of you, don't cause me any trouble. We always got along so well together...."

Tight-mouthed, Gruber turned his back on the man, followed Anton into the stable, and shut the door behind him—something that wasn't done at this time of the year.

A week later the councilor was pensioned—without the customary service medal, with every indication of being in the equerry's bad grace. As for the coachman Pawlitschek, he drove heavy freight.

From the Belvedere, however, emanated a story its hearers accepted partly with gloating and partly with sympathy. Franz Ferdinand, it ran, had by no means been thrown into a tantrum by the incident. Quietly, deeply moved, he had thrust his hands toward the skies. The incident with the horses was immaterial to him; but the unexpected and complete recuperation of Franz Joseph had shaken his soul. "Never! It is not my destiny. He lives! He lives eternally! He will outlive me!"

Deaf to all consolation, he kept repeating: "He will live so long that it will be too late. So long that the realm will be irrevocably lost."

Chapter Twenty-Five

FLORIAN, CAPITANO AND A HOST OF other horses—brown Kladrubers, Hungarian Juckers, ponies and Haflingers which served for mountain climbing—were unloaded early one morning at the station of Ischl.

There wasn't much time for loafing. Anton could just get a glimpse of the verdant landscape. Florian and Capitano had to be fed, watered, and after a lukewarm bath groomed with brush and currycomb.

The intimidated Bosco sat near Florian in a corner of

the new stable. Gruber had instructed Anton not to allow the dog to roam at large in the park, for the children and grandchildren of the Emperor had dogs of their own; and it was better to be careful. Anton had then taken Bosco aside and for the first time catechized him sternly. Bosco didn't understand a word, but Anton's earnestness and unusually long speech had a shattering effect upon him. He was all broken up.

Court gendarmes with their horsehair-plumed helmets had taken up their positions in the park and at the doors of the Imperial villa. The House Ministry, the adjutants were installed; postal, telephone and telegraph clerks were carefully instructed; as a matter of fact most of the functionaries knew the routine from years of practice. The private detectives of the Secret Police sauntered around the grounds of the villa, along the streets and on the esplanade of Ischl. They prided themselves on their impenetrable disguises. In truth, the most rustic villager spotted them at a distance of fifty paces.

In the afternoon the Emperor arrived. On the station

platform the stadholder, the district commander and the burgomaster stood in readiness. Just outside the station a large gathering waited; natives and summer guests.

In the midst of the hubbub the Imperial coach, driven by Gruber and drawn by Florian and Capitano, kept driving round and round on the roomy square in front of the station. The people cheerfully drew back on every side. Such fiery steeds couldn't and shouldn't stand still. They realized that. Florian's and Capitano's heads, the curve of their proud necks, the gold-braided bicorne Gruber wore, the empty seat for the *chasseur* beside him—made a picture of joyous expectancy.

When the train chugged into the station, Konrad Gruber held the carriage at the exit. The horses heard the shrill hiss, the powerful hoarse breathing of the engine, and swung their beautiful heads higher, making the metal of their traces jangle melodiously. The cries of acclaim that burst forth did not fluster them. Gruber had them firmly in hand; they stood like statues as Franz Joseph came through the exit. He took his place in the carriage. The general adjutant sat at his left. The agile *chasseur* climbed to the driver's box.

They set off at a pace appropriate to the occasion. In concert, their leg action reminiscent of the Spanish stride, the two white horses took the chalk-white ground under them. The vociferations of the throng, the waving of hats and kerchiefs bothered them not at all. Their measured gait, the gleaming, gold-spangled white of their bodies, the liveried coachman on his perch, the flowing white plume of the *chasseur's* hat, the close phalanxes accompanying the carriage and partly hiding it from the public's gaze, lent a very distinct, a very Austrian, a musical impression which, completely summed up, spelled Franz Joseph.

The mountain air of Ischl refreshed Florian. Like a man who has been drinking champagne and by it been lifted into an ever airier frame of mind, so were Florian's flagging spirits revivified by the odor of pine, of resinous damp wood, of lush earth, mixed with the snowy breath from the mountains. He had never run through woods, never trotted along the bank of a trout stream.

Now there were excursions along the smooth road to Ebensee, with the River Traun murmuring just below. There were drives through the leafy Weissenbacher forest whenever Franz Joseph went hunting.

To Florian it was of course immaterial that at such times the Emperor wore a short Styrian coat and Styrian hat, that Konrad Gruber was less pretentiously garbed than usual, and that the *chasseur* and the gun-loader wore the simple green hunter's costume. But that the carriage he and Capitano drew was lighter, that he could feel. Also that the man who sat in the carriage, this man who meant so little to Florian, was alone most of the time.

Florian drank deeply of the scented air of the Weissenbacher forest. The grassy clearing before the hunting lodge enchanted him. He had never seen such a meadow . . . encircled by towering old firs, and overgrown with sweet grass and strong-smelling herbs. The many mixed scents stimulated him pleasantly and made him curious. He did not know that the forest abounded in stags, hinds, foxes, hares, martens, fitchets and weasels. Wild animals were as alien to his ken as true freedom. And so, coming across their spoors for the first time, he was not able to explain them.

As his soul interpreted and loved music—instinctively—in much the same fashion, only by no means as definitely, did he sense the benign and happy abandon that pervaded the forest. Rushing with Capitano along the Ebensee road, and turning left in Mitter-Weissenbach to climb the steep curves of the path always meant the meadow before the hunting lodge, and Florian always felt sure this had been arranged for his special benefit. He took the sharp incline, took the long steep climb to the Kapellenberg, with incomparable vim, carrying Capitano along at the spirited pace as if they had been on an even grade all the way.

Once when they trotted back to Ischl from an evening's hunt they came, in the deep dusk of the forest, directly upon a stag. The light from the carriage lanterns flickered over his ruddy skin and crown of antlers. Then he bounded into the thicket and disappeared.

With a quickened play of their ears and surprised

eyes the two horses had spied the shadowy figure. Florian wanted to ask Capitano: "Do you know who that is?" But Capitano asked the very question first. Before they could puzzle out an answer the whole intermezzo was over.

Whether they drove to the Hotel Elisabeth, over to the villa of the Emperor's daughter, Gisela, or elsewhere, Florian enjoyed this furlough from the strained going between high stone walls on paved streets. He enjoyed the quaint abiding charm of this village set like a jewel in the midst of forests and mountains. His enjoyment, of course, was not the product of his brain; he simply showed his gratitude for the freer form of existence in the more intense exhilaration of his being.

It was in front of the Weissenbach hunting lodge that Franz Joseph, as he climbed from the carriage, commended Gruber: "The horses are better than ever."

"At your service, your Majesty."

"I think Florian particularly is in excellent shape. Don't you think so?"

"At your service, your Majesty."

The Emperor smiled. He approached Florian and stroked his neck. Florian bent his head and sniffed at the old man's pockets.

"What do you want of me? Sugar? Do you have any sugar, Gruber?"

"At your service, your Majesty."

They were by themselves. The Emperor, Gruber and the horses. Far to one side, a councilor, the game warden and the hunting retinue were waiting.

Gruber gave his master a few lumps of sugar.

"The other one is splendid, too," said the Emperor, "but this Florian is simply marvelous. Absolutely marvelous!"

Konrad Gruber remained silent; after all, he hadn't been asked.

In the stable Florian invariably looked for Bosco. He and the dog had agreed that this stable was the best and the most comfortable they knew.

Anton was a happy man. He found himself in a landscape that reminded him of his Styrian home. High wooded mountains, topped by stately crags at which the snow still licked with its white tongue. In the distance the glacier of the Dachstein was visible. If Anton wandered along the Salzburg road he saw farmhouses in the deep broad valleys. It was years since he had seen a farmhouse. At the suggestion of a few colleagues and under Gruber's brief order he had fared forth on his first walk; it was climaxed by his coming across a peasant's abode. After that he frequently took the road toward Pfandl, went even beyond it when the Emperor was hunting. He made sure always to ask Gruber's permission beforehand, and he always took Bosco along. The dog enjoyed the long uninterrupted walks, the explorations he could make, the many amusing and critical adventures that befell him.

The two companions did not bother about each other on these walks. Each was certain of the other; they were linked together even when one disappeared for a short while.

Bosco experienced all kinds of gallant episodes.

And for Anton suddenly there was Kati.

Her name was Kati Pinchelberger and she was the

daughter of a small farmer; almost thirty and a widow; a big-boned, full-bosomed woman with broad hips, thin hair and freckles all over her coarse healthy face.

Anton spoke to her of his homeplace.

Why hadn't he stayed at home on the farm? she wanted to know.

So he told her about his military service, about Lipizza, about Siebele, about Florian and about the Emperor's stables.

"Well, then you have a good job," Kati stated prosaically.

He had never questioned the security of his position, never troubled his head about that. He talked and talked about Florian, and since he now had found the chance to pour out his heart and Kati listened to him, he liked her.

He had never had the desire to talk or to open his heart to any human being. Now, though, he felt that it did him good. Once he summoned up all his courage and asked Kati to come to the stable to see Florian.

She replied matter-of-factly that she could do so

only on a Sunday. And so she came next Sunday after mass. Anton was overcome at sight of Kati in the festive raiment of the Ischl peasants. In his estimation she looked ravishing. They sat together in the stable and looked at Florian.

"A horse like that," Kati opined, "is no good for work in the fields."

"Florian isn't made for that," Anton replied. "But he is beautiful, Florian is."

Kati couldn't deny that. "Yes, he is," she said.

"And so good," Anton appended.

In that, too, Kati agreed with him. "Sure. Sure." But she argued: "Why shouldn't he be good when he is treated so well?" And after a longish pause, she decided: "Only the Emperor can have a horse like that." She changed the subject. "Does the Emperor talk to you much?"

Anton was shocked and informed her that the Emperor had never talked to him.

Sitting next to Kati in this fashion it occurred to him that it might be rather pleasant to have her for a wife. He mulled this over for a long time without being able to express it. In the end Kati came to his assistance and said without beating about the bush:

"Two people like us would make a nice pair, wouldn't we?"

"Maybe," he murmured, and grew pale.

"Then I'll stay with you to-night," she informed him.

And he answered timidly: "As you please."

Next morning, after Kati had gone home, Anton fell to thinking. His habit of being with Florian, of caring for nothing else in the world except Florian and Bosco—no—that habit he couldn't give up. Would a wife stand for that? Would Kati who was so blunt and so definite let him remain with Florian? He did not know the answer. He couldn't see his way clear. He was afraid. He would have liked Gruber's opinion. He regarded Gruber as the pinnacle of wisdom, the well of all experience. But he did not dare address him or seek his advice. Anton considered his own affairs and his own person not worthy of mention.

He met Kati again, twice, without touching on

marriage. He felt easier both times when the meetings passed off so smoothly. Finally he had to quit Ischl and didn't even have the chance to say good-bye.

Franz Joseph journeyed to the Imperial maneuvers in Moravia. Florian and Capitano were dispatched there a few days ahead. The Imperial headquarters were in a medieval castle that looked romantically like a robber baron's roost. Everything there was weirdly beautiful. The deep moat encircling the castle, the thick walls, the portcullis, the century-old ivy which clothed the facade in a tenuous green garb, the inner court-yards, the stables that looked like deep caves and yet contained red marble mangers. These stables smelled of rats and mice, which threw Bosco into a state of feverish anticipation.

Of the maneuvers Anton had as much idea as any common soldier has; that is, none at all. But he recognized the different regiments from the patch of color on the soldiers' collars. And it was jolly to witness the military scene, which did not concern him, while he sat in front of the stable door in the courtyard.

On the other side of the fosse Franz Joseph's host, the manorial lord, had erected a long low wooden shed for the guardsmen who came the morning of the Emperor's arrival. Gruber went to fetch his master from the distant station. An hour later the automobile of the Heir Apparent rolled into the courtyard.

At length the Emperor arrived. The Guard presented arms.

Thereafter there was little for Florian and Capitano to do. The reason was that the new Chief of Staff, Conrad von Hötzendorff, a favorite of Franz Ferdinand, no longer made the maneuvers a mere spectacle for the monarch. Fierce and warlike, with surprises that came hourly, the operations of the troops stretched over a vast terrain. And the Emperor, if he wished to see something, if he wanted to be present at decisive moments, must needs use the hated automobile.

A magnificent motorcar waited for Franz Joseph in the castle. He owned it but had never made use of it. Two chauffeurs went with it. Konrad Gruber shunned any contact with them. Here conceit met conceit. Here the stubbornness of yesterday was pitted against the superciliousness of a new epoch. Gruber despised the machine drivers who in turn looked down at a mere coachman.

For three days Franz Joseph sat in the automobile. But when Franz Ferdinand proposed that he return to Vienna by car, he didn't deign to answer, merely shrugged his shoulders. To his adjutant he said: "The ideas this Franz has ... incredible!"

The Heir Apparent laughed. "Emperor Ferdinand refused to travel by rail and the present Emperor can't get accustomed to automobiles. Well, when I am emperor everybody will use cars—or fly!"

Chapter Twenty-Six

I N THE FALL FLORIAN MADE HIS FIRST public appearance with Capitano at the head of a team of six.

Czar Nicholas II of Russia came for a visit. He threatened to cancel everything if he were not driven in a closed automobile from the station to Schönbrunn. Under no circumstances would he risk an exposed ride through the streets to the Imperial Palace. Schönbrunn was immediately made ready for the Russian "Little Father" who lived in constant fear of assassination. As for the closed automobile, that Franz Joseph adamantly refused. He held absolutely to the tradition of transporting visiting sovereigns through the capital by carriage *à la Doumont*. He had neither cause nor intention to show his people distrust; and the closed automobile would assuredly be so construed. Neither Franz Joseph nor the Czar of all the Russians had any ground for disquietude; Nicholas need fear nothing in an open carriage.

Nicholas conceded this point only after the ambassador earnestly made clear to him that Franz Joseph shared the same danger, if any, as he, and was in this fashion giving guarantees at the risk of his own person. But he made further difficulties by demanding a double *spalier*: artillery, in the first row, the horses and men facing the sidewalks; then infantry, their guns primed and ready for action and pointed at the houses and the people along the way. There should be little room for the populace to move about. Furthermore, plainclothes policemen were to be distributed among the spectators.

Franz Joseph did not approve of such Russian measures, but ultimately he agreed, only remarking casually that he did not put much weight on the strict execution of his orders.

It was late September. When a chestnut dropped into the Emperor's carriage, he laughingly ordered that all the ripe fruit be shaken off the trees standing in double rows in front of Schönbrunn lest a chestnut fall into the carriage and hit the Czar. God forbid! Nicholas might swoon on the spot, or have an epileptic fit.

The Czar came. The poor state of his nerves was apparent from the outset. The train rolled into the station with all its windows heavily curtained. Nothing stirred while the military band played the Russian national hymn. Franz Joseph waited on the long narrow runner stretching to the door from which the guest was supposed to emerge. But there was no door there; only the side of a car.

The archdukes waited, lined up in a row. The members of the Russian Embassy waited. The ministers and other dignitaries waited. A select Court gathering waited. The drums and trumpets reechoed from the glass dome overhead. The band continued to play the Russian hymn.

Waiting.

Franz Joseph looked helplessly around.

After a while, at the far end of the train, the Czar's bodyguard climbed down, a Tartar giant in a scarlet kaftan, his cartridge belts across his chest, the high gray astrachan cap on his head. Unhurriedly he walked along the row of cars and passed Franz Joseph whom he pushed aside with a sweep of his arm. Taken aback by this unparalleled audacity, the Emperor hopped a step backward.

And still the Russian hymn blared forth and mingled with the echoes falling in fragments from the high glass roof; an exciting cacophony.

At an even pace the Tartar walked to the very front, to the first carriage, the windows of which had been rendered opaque with white paint. He opened the door.

Behind it stood Nicholas in the uniform of an Austrian Dragoon. Slim, pale, timid, he stood there, not stirring, until Franz Joseph rushed up. Then he stepped down quickly and gave the Emperor a hasty embrace, clutched him by the arm and dragged him along. He did not bother about the Company of Honor, about the gentlemen from the Embassy, the archduke, the officials and the courtiers. Almost at a run he left the platform, forcing Franz Joseph along at half a run. In the general consternation, which was accompanied almost sarcastically by the thunder of the Russian hymn, a general finally succeeded in silencing the band. The solemn Imperial reception had been turned into a farce of fear and stupidity; it dissolved in disorder.

By that time the carriage bearing the two rulers started toward Schönbrunn—a magnificent carriage *à la Doumont;* the floor rose in an elegant curlicue toward the driver's box. Franz Joseph and Nicholas sat in it as in a saucer. Just behind them fluttered the white plumes of the two *chasseurs.*

Konrad Gruber relished the grandeur of the *à la Doumont* team. He knew this to be a vestige of feudal times when the high nobility used to drive daily in such manner. He knew also that where four horses were ordinarily used, six were the prerogative of a monarch. Everything connected with driving that accentuated regal prerogative, he held inviolate. He had a reverence for the noble scale of the carriage and for the team he guided. The perfect union of sublimity and discretion, the greatest magnificence and the utmost simplicity, could not but impress. Of that he was convinced.

He rode Florian, rode him for the first time on a public occasion. He resented the artillery display. Like Franz Joseph, he was displeased by the well-nigh complete absence of the public; he badly missed their amazement, admiration and *vivas*. He was angered, even as Franz Joseph, by the way the few spectators present were squeezed close to the walls of the houses. Knowing the slow pace Franz Joseph desired on such occasions, he kept it even slower than usual. He did not need to fear Imperial displeasure on that score, of that, too, he was convinced. Let this rabbit of a Nicholas tremble with impatience. Konrad Gruber was glad of it.

Florian carried his rider as if he were a feather. Devoid of any conception of human things, Florian had no idea who sat in the carriage. He had the same joyous feeling he would have had at a festival arranged for him. He was the first in the triple row of six horses. Ahead of him the street was clear. No carriage, no pedestrian, nothing. The street seemed to wait for him.

To the right and left he could descry the heads of the horses in front of their cannon. Brown Wallachian mares. Not a single stallion. There they stood to admire him!

He almost walked. He mustn't run, he didn't want to run. To trot was always sport, yes; to pass other horses running along the same street, and leave them, behind, was something he could not do with five others. He and Capitano, yes, had shared that thrill together often enough. Unhampered speed, an unhampered flow of power and health—they had tasted it in the streets of Vienna and in the woods near Ischl. Now it was entirely different. And since free rein didn't belong here, he didn't miss it.

Florian knew the signs, knew every bit of help he received from Gruber. By his willingness he had regained the beautifully unique harmony with his rider that he had known in the days when he used to dance under Ennsbauer at the Spanish Riding School. Moreover, he had kept all the force of his disciplined existence, the leadership over the five other horses. His inherited intelligence told him that being in the company of his five cousins was participating in a ceremonial procession; that therefore the subduing of his fire; the subjugation of his temperament was his task. This knowledge, coming from subconscious organs of intelligence, was itself not conscious; nor in the terms of any language. His musical sensitiveness effortlessly and unthinkingly achieved in him an attunement to the demands of this hour; expressed itself in the rhythm of the short cadenced steps and filled him with the sensuous pleasure of self-obliteration in a melody.

When Florian reached the wide-open gate of Schönbrunn and was gently guided across the white yard to the inner staircase, every joint and sinew of his tapering legs and shoulders was a spring. His torso rocked his rider like a lulling cradle. His head was raised high, his eyes shone, his small ears fluttered. All of Florian had become one paean of joy. The cries of the guard, the rumble of the drums were a demonstration in his praise, a hail to his success.

Chapter Twenty-Seven

COUNT BERTINGEN WAS NO LON-
ger equerry. He had resigned on account
of fatigue and ill health. He wanted to
end his last years in peaceful repose at his
castle in the Croatian oak forest. After little more than
a year and a half he flickered out like a burned-down
candle. Thus did Franz Joseph's servitors, exhausted and
done in, step back one by one into obscurity; burned-
down candles.

Franz Ferdinand figured out who of all the generals,

ministers and courtiers of the Emperor lingered on. Only a very few, to be counted on the fingers of one hand. And they were all younger than Franz Joseph. Some of them had not yet been born when he ascended the throne; they had made their whole careers under his rule, become old men. He alone, Franz Joseph I, the Emperor, lived on, indefatigable, erect, fresh, brimming with the unbroken will of the suzerain.

Franz Ferdinand admired him even while he hated him. What a blessed life! At eighteen he had become Emperor. When other youths still sat on their school benches, Franz Joseph already had a boundless wealth of power in his boyish hands. As a boy he had made mistakes. That was only natural. Making mistakes as a young man of thirty, after twelve years of rule, he had given conclusive proof (Franz Ferdinand consoled himself) of his lack of greatness. He had had bad luck on the battlefields, in politics, with his family. He simply had lacked the irresistible personality to shunt bad luck aside. He had lacked the gift of turning difficulties into advantages. Had lacked vision, perspective. He was a simple honest man. (Franz Ferdinand had no use for simplicity and held simple honesty in very low esteem.)

For more than six decades, already, had this magnificent Imperial existence of Franz Joseph endured. The end, near as it ought to be according to human reckoning, never seemed to come any nearer, like a mirage.

Franz Ferdinand had passed the fifty mark. He was in a state of desuetude. He had been Heir Apparent for more than two decades. Not an easy situation. Rather tragic. It was torture, tantalizing torture, to witness the decay of the realm, to have the plans and the methods for succoring the realm and preserving the dynasty— and to be shackled.

He wished nobody's death. His piety forbade that. But his impatience, his gnawing, searing impatience was understandable. He wanted to drive Franz Joseph into abdication; but Franz Joseph was tough and had no idea of retiring. God in heaven! Franz Joseph stood in the lingering shadows of a blessed life. He stood alone. He had burgeoned into majesty from his earliest youth. He was now the personification of majesty, the quintessence of

majesty. For decades he had lived in a cold lofty solitude, alone, wrapped in his majesty; not a happy man,
obviously not, but a monarch who faced his immense
fate with a clear conscience.

Franz Ferdinand often consoled himself by vowing
that the crowns he would inherit would give him, too,
diligence, toughness and long life. He told himself this,
time and again, and liked to hear his wife say it, his
father confessor, and all his sycophants and supporters.
Despite this forebodings ate at his heart and would not
be stilled for long.

The new equerry began his incumbency. Prince
Buchowsky was a youngish man, slightly over forty,
and extremely handsome. His ivory-tinted face was
adorned with a thick black mustache. Soft black eyes
looked out from under long lashes. He was considered
the most brilliant rider in the Army. He understood
horses as well as the shrewdest horse trader. He had a
lively gay temperament and great initiative.

However, everything remained as it had been,
because everything had to be as it had been.

Konrad Gruber had known the prince for years and treated him with measured respect but not with servility. The prince handled Gruber jocularly.

"Well, my dear Gruber," he said in the beginning, "I think we two will get along together."

Gruber kept silent as usual.

"Don't be afraid," the prince pursued, and smiled so that his perfect white teeth shone under his black mustache, "I won't interfere with you. You've been turning your hurdy-gurdy for quite a long time and to the satisfaction of his Majesty."

About Gruber's lips played a furtive smile.

"But," the prince concluded very seriously, "I'll stand for nothing from you, either."

Gruber stood motionless. His cheeks paled under the weatherbeaten patina of his face.

"And now show me the horses which are entrusted to your care," the prince ordered.

"In the stable . . . or—?" Gruber murmured.

"Out here, of course. One after the other. Florian first."

Gruber disappeared. Immediately thereafter Bosco bolted from the stable door and casually sprung up at the prince who acknowledged this effusion with a loud halloa.

Then Florian came out. He was all alone, without a guide and stark nude. At Gruber's orders Anton had taken everything off the horse. Snowy white, he stepped out into the sunlight.

"Florian," Buchowsky called. "Florian. I am very pleased to make your acquaintance. Come here to me. Come."

Florian thrust his head aloft, snorted gaily and stared at the prince with obvious curiosity. The nobleman stood five or six paces away, the gold braid glistening on his uniform. He wore the light coat of the Arcieres Body-Guard, which only few wore.

"Come on," Buchowsky coaxed. "This time without sugar. Just for politeness' sake."

Florian approached and touched the prince's breast softly with his mouth.

"That's right," the equerry laughed. "We're all good

friends. I am delighted. I feel quite honored. Of course, I've known you for a long time. Just as one knows a famous stage star. Nice of you to be so condescending."

Anton grinned. Gruber's mien remained inscrutable.

The prince stroked Florian on nose and forehead, along the back, across his croup. He walked around him, patted his firm limbs, tickled his loins to send a trembling over the light skin, slapped his chest and finally took his head in his hands.

A small cabriolet driven by Elizabeth entered the yard. Next her sat Neustift, and perched between them the little boy, Leopold, now in the uniform of the Theresianum.

Buchowsky faced them. "My first visit!" he declared.

"Our last," Elizabeth replied.

They climbed down. Anton rushed over to assist them.

"Yes, please hold Caesar," Neustift said to him. "And how are things with you?"

"Thank you very much, Captain," Anton answered, and hastily corrected himself: "Beg pardon, Major!"

Elizabeth joined the prince. "We want to pay a fare-well visit to Florian. Yes, to Florian. An old sweet memory ties us to him."

"And I have just introduced myself to him," the prince informed her jokingly. "A matter of duty."

"Of course you know," Neustift said, "that my time as adjutant is over."

"I know," said the prince without releasing Florian. "My time begins. That's how it is. One goes. Another comes."

"We are lucky," Elizabeth said, "to find both you and Florian."

"Yes . . . it's all a matter of luck," the prince replied, playfully serious. "Are you staying in Vienna?"

"I told you we came to say good-bye," Elizabeth explained. "My husband has four weeks' leave of absence. We are to spend it at home in the country."

"But before then"—Neustift drew little Leopold in front of the prince—"we've got to install this young man at the Theresianum."

Leopold saluted.

The prince held out his hand. "Will you be a good boy at the Theresianum?"

"Very good!" Leopold assured him in earnest.

"Too bad," the prince looked down disapprovingly. "To be good is bad. Very, very bad."

Fixing the astonished boyish face, the young eyes, with a somber stare, he continued with feigned gravity: "Take my advice, my boy, be as bad as you can, don't stand for anything. Fight with your comrades, throw the silly books in the fire. That's the surest way of getting somewhere."

"Fine advice that is," Neustift said, displeased, while he diverted his son's attention to Florian. "Grand advice! I thank you very much for it."

"Why," Buchowsky protested, "everybody gives a child so much good advice that he's bound to get sick and tired of it."

"And so you want to give bad advice?"

"My dear friend, I'll tell you something. Advice like mine impresses a youngster, but he never takes it seriously."

"Let's hope not," Neustift punctuated.

"Let me finish," the other begged him politely. "You preach all the virtues to a boy like that, and he'll become a rotter. Tell him to be a rotter, and he will automatically be good. Besides that, everybody becomes what he is by nature and by what his surroundings make him."

Neustift could not help remarking: "Our youngsters are entirely too well off. Unfortunately, one might say."

"Quite right," Buchowsky agreed. "But you might as well leave the 'unfortunately' out. Who knows how long it will last?"

Prodded by curiosity, Neustift inquired: "Do you mean you actually know something definite? Is there to be a war? Is there any chance? Wouldn't that be great!"

"That would be great," the prince said mockingly. "War—great! That's too much for me. No, my friend, as long as the old man is alive we'll have peace."

"Unfortunately," Neustift sighed.

"You and your everlasting unfortunately!" The prince turned to Elizabeth who stood beside Florian. "Now then," he said, "we shall combine hello and adieu."

Elizabeth surveyed the prince, enterprising and proud. "I wonder how you're going to do that."

"Gruber!" Buchowsky ordered. "The saddle."

"Forgiveness, your highness," Gruber demurred. "His Majesty has given orders. . . ."

"You shut your mouth!" the prince interrupted calmly. "You talk when I ask you. In five minutes you will have Florian on the track." To Neustift he said as if nothing had happened: "We'll wait for Florian inside."

They crossed the yard and entered the covered riding track which was part of the stables.

Konrad Gruber stood stock-still in surprise.

The new equerry had barked at him as though he were the lowest stableboy, and had disposed of Florian in a momentary whim. That was insufferable. He caught the helpless, undecided look on Anton's face and regained a hold on himself: "The saddle," he ordered.

Gruber had come to the conclusion that he must make no protest. The battle was much too one-sided. He was the weaker, in spite of everything, and would obey.

Led by Gruber, Florian appeared on the track.

Buchowsky examined the harness, stirrups and reins. Then he swung with easy grace on Florian's back.

Horse and rider began to go through the paces of the High School. Florian felt the master and vibrated with readiness. His memory—the memory of his muscles—had retained each step and movement. To be allowed once again to perform those paces was pure joy. As in the past, he set one foot carefully before the other, swayed and swung gracefully from his joints. As in the past, his hind feet during the circular turn remained veritably nailed to the spot. With pure joy he rose high up, forelegs bent.

Elizabeth and Neustift gasped in admiration. Little Leopold said, enraptured: "Ah!"

And when Florian, during the change of figures, during the intervals of rest the prince gave him, insisted upon maintaining his Spanish stride as of yore, Buchowsky laughed to his friends as he passed them, and cried: "Fantastic! Upon my soul!"

It was indeed farewell. It was the last time that Florian rode the *Hohe Schule*.

Chapter Twenty-Eight

ONCE MORE THE SPRING SUN began to pour down its warmth after the long winter. Blue skies smiled upon Vienna, the tips of the church steeples gleamed and the cupolas shone. In the outer court of the Imperial Palace lilac bushes bloomed again, snuggling against the statues.

Florian was in rare form. Gruber treated him with tender consideration; Franz Joseph, who never had his horses wait when the weather was humid, did likewise;

and Anton's customary care had a great deal to do with it.

Bosco once again belonged among the contented. The years had taken but little toll of his lively temperament. His gallantry, however, was practically stilled. His love for Pretty sank into the limbo of forgotten things. What did she mean to him now? Hardly a memory. After her last litter of puppies she had grown fat and lazy and old, seeming to realize that she lacked her onetime attractiveness. Bosco clung to his friend, Florian, and to his adored master. He led a blissful, satisfied existence.

Anton fared similarly. He had long since ceased to think about the strong and willing Kati. She had given him brief happiness and for a while filled him with oppressive anguish. That was a thing of the past.

A letter came from home. His stepmother wrote that his father was old and ailing. Anton should return home, he was needed for the work. He read the letter three times, read it slowly and as laboredly as it was written. Then he laid it away in an old soiled envelope

among other documents he never looked at. He wrote
no reply. What for? His father's wife was a stranger to
him, and his father as forgotten as if he had long since
died. Go home? Leave Florian? That was not worth
thinking about.

During the first few days after the receipt of the
letter; when its import dawned upon him at recurrent
moments, he went to Florian, put his low forehead against
the white neck, buried his simple face in the white mane,
and whispered: "No, no, no ... I am not going away from
you! Certainly not! We'll stay together ... that's all."

At such moments Florian turned his head to him
and drank in his friend's image, the while Anton
stroked the warm, velvety nostrils and assured him:
"You don't need to be afraid. I couldn't leave you." And
Bosco braced himself with his forepaws against Anton's
shins and emitted a plaintive yip.

They were agreed. To stay together was best.

One day Anton was summoned to the livery room
by Gruber. Whenever he received an order outside his
regular routine, he was startled; and as always when

startled he buried his feelings deeper than usual in stupefaction and disinterest. Only his eyes blinked.

It was nothing bad.

He had to try on a white flax peruke from which two horizontal curls drooped at the temples and which ended in a short queue tied by a black silk riband. Then he had to get into the ornate Hapsburg livery. The peruke on his square peasant's head gave him an extremely comical cut, while he stood there in his shirt. After that came patent-leather pumps, very light pumps called *escarpines;* and he was shown how to buckle the short black silk pants around the knees after pulling up the white stockings. He also was shown how to fasten the white jabot-ruffles around his neck. Their light, curly, half-starched cascades rippled down his chest. At last he arrived at the crowning glory, a thing that made his eyes wide with admiration: a long frocked coat of vertical black and gold braid. The cloth of precious brocade was as dark as a summer night, and was richly embroidered in gold with the Double Eagle which kept reappearing and glistened like the sun. From his left shoulder hung a yellow band heavily interwoven with gold.

The tailor busied himself with Anton, selected the fitting pieces, helped correct slight faults with needle and thread, and finally poured a bagful of white cotton gloves on the table so that Anton could choose a pair that would fit.

When they were ready Anton was completely changed. Now, oddly enough, he would have looked foolish without the peruke! As it was, he was the picture of ceremonious dignity.

During the proceedings his astonishment had frittered away as no danger seemed to threaten, although he still wracked his brain over the why and wherefore of all this.

Konrad Gruber sat near by, observing everything intently. He went over the black-and-gold clad Anton searchingly and finished with a terse: "All right."

Anton watched him rise and leave. He did not dare to ask a question. Nor did he take the liberty of seeking enlightenment from the tailor or his assistant. He did not speak. He was never talkative and always felt most collected when not expecting a word from anyone. In silence he shuffled back to the stable. There he asked the tormenting question of Florian: "What do they want to do with me? Do you know?"

Florian threw him a soulful glance that sent a deep peace into Anton's breast.

That afternoon the equerry came.

From one of the unused corridors a large carriage was rolled out and given a long, careful going over. Anton from afar only half surmised that the monstrous thing on the high wheels was something akin to a carriage. However, when six white horses were picked out and two more added, he concluded that it was indeed a carriage.

Anton was not one to associate ideas, was unable even to guess the simplest relations. He knew what actually was, what visibly existed and what he could touch with his hands. Constantly in the company of Florian and Bosco, reticent, and in spite of his kindness thoroughly unsocial, he never more than half heard, often heard not at all, things that were being said around him. He might long have known that another Feast of Corpus Christi was approaching, and that it was to be celebrated with unusual pomp. During the winter the stablemen had often talked of it, but Anton paid scant attention and had forgotten.

Corpus Christi dawned.

At six in the morning Anton along with seven others, coachmen and stablemen, stood ready in his impressive black-and-yellow livery, his white peruke on his head, his rough hands encased in white gloves. The seven others smoked cigarettes which they hastily stamped out at Gruber's approach.

He inspected them all and said to Anton: "You'll lead Florian."

Anton did not fathom that it was an extraordinary distinction to be permitted to lead one of the carriage horses, particularly one of the front pair. He remained silent and let Gruber pass. To him it was only natural that none but himself should lead Florian. In a long column they marched to the Imperial Palace.

It was a dreamlike sunny June morning. Not a single cloud ruffled the azure sky. Refreshed by the dew, the young foliage of the trees and the bushes rustled, the flowers and the grass around the monument of Maria Theresia swayed. The roofs and the towers of the capital lay ahead of them as they crossed the Ringstrasse, and the heart of Vienna seemed to smile at them expectantly.

The outer court of the Palace stretched in empty immensity before them. From the Volksgarten came the scent of flowers. In the inner court, around the statue of Emperor Franz, a multicolored group of horsemen were assembled. Many of them had dismounted and stood chatting. When at exactly seven o'clock the bells in all the churches began to chime, the riders swung into their saddles.

The Emperor, followed by the archdukes, and preceded by the Court dignitaries, came out and stepped into the carriage.

Under triple command, the Guard presented arms, the drums beat, and at the very head of the procession two heralds on horseback blew the general march. They held aloft their long silver trumpets from which hung the black and yellow embroidered pennons of the House of Hapsburg, and the high silvery tones reechoed from the cupolas of the Michael's portal.

A squadron of the Arcieres Body-Guard rode behind the heralds. They were followed by the Trabant Foot Guard in scarlet coats, their halberds under their arms. In an old-fashioned calash drawn by four brown horses sat the first chamberlain, alone.

Finally came the carriage of the Emperor. From this point back an ambulant *spalier* of Court gendarmes, carrying guns, flanked the procession.

The Emperor, with the Heir Apparent at his left, sat in the stately carosse which Karl VI had built. The resplendent body of the coach hung on immense, wide belts, shaking lightly on the springs. The wood of the carriage doors, which had been painted by masters of the Baroque, reached only as far as the white damask of the seats. Large crystal panes sparkled on both sides, and their frames bore the top. Thus the Emperor and his heir sat in a moving show-window. Lips sealed, they sat side by side. They had nothing to say to each other. Both might have been thinking of the faraway time when Franz Joseph had driven to St. Stephan's in this very carriage accompanied by the Crown Prince. To both of them it must have appeared as God's will that Rudolf slept for over twenty years at the Capuchines.

But each of them interpreted God's will differently.

That was the high wall that separated them as they sat so close together, driving through the stationary rows of troops, amidst the city's multitudes kept in order by the soldiery.

Shouts and *vivas* arose, a cloud of sound which rolled along the way of the Emperor.

On the frame of the carosse, between the gilded wooden springs, on a board inside the high lacquered wheels, stood three lackeys clad in gala livery, wearing tricornes on their white perukes. They held fast to the wide fringed belts which were there for that purpose. The richly draped driver's box, in front, was occupied by Konrad Gruber, who also wore the gala livery, the tricorne and the peruke. His coppery face was horizontally cleaved by tightly closed lips; his eyes, contracted into narrow slits, were all attention and care. In his hands he held the reins of the eight stallions. These eight Lipizzans were richly caparisoned in gold and purple, and carried bouquets of waving white ostrich plumes between their ears. Each was led by a stable-man holding onto a wide gold ribbon.

Anton held the ribbon in the ordained manner. One hand high up near the bridle, the other hand letting the dangling ribbon play freely enough to preserve its decorative line. He was ever on the alert, for Florian kept raising and lowering his beautiful head in a proud gesture that made the crest of ostrich plumes nod impressively.

The horses walked slowly in measured strides. For Florian this was still another festal pageant, the most gorgeous and the most solemn he had yet lived through. The silvery fanfares of the heralds, at the van and rear of the procession, alternately blowing the general march, sounded like tones turned into sunbeams. The pealing of the church bells sent a solemn clangor rushing high through the air. The *vivas* burst forth wherever Florian appeared and enveloped him in warm invisible waves.

Florian gazed everywhere, enchanted. His shimmering, dark eyes took on an expression of complete rapture, as he walked on, the Kohlmarkt, the Graben, the Stephansplatz floating together into an indistinct picture of unearthly splendor.

He gave himself up altogether to the triumph he took to be his own and Capitano's. He walked with chained fire, with spirits difficult to quell; walked in the cadenced gait of the Spanish School. He would have loved to rise on his hindlegs, to show what magnificent feats he could do; would have loved to prance and share his happiness, his joy of living, with the onlookers. But there was the rein to which he had to submerge his sparkling mood. Thus did his blood respond.

And there was Anton, who was fired by the joy flaming in each movement of Florian's muscles and rippling along the ribbon halter, and who held Florian back from his passionate impulses with a tender loving hand.

Anton couldn't see much. Only the petals strewn along the route of march, only Florian's neck and restless head. Before his eyes, too, swam blurred and indistinct the rows of soldiers, the packed humanity. The pageantry and tumult stunned him.

Behind the State carosse rode the equerry and Franz Joseph's adjutants. In other carriages, drawn by teams of six horses, came the archdukes. And back of them a swarm of pages in light costumes; noble youths, gay, carefree and proud; boys who were aware that someday they would rule the realm as their fathers and forefathers had ruled it once. They were followed by the Hungarian Guard on horseback, their unsheathed curved sabers in their hands, garbed in gold-embroidered coats, skin-tight breeches, saffian boots and gem-encrusted bandoliers, and wearing panther-skins across one shoulder, fastened on their breasts with jeweled buckles. On their heads they had brown bearskin caps crested by white aigrettes.

Bringing up the rear came a squadron of Dragoons in their high-slung parade helmets.

Before St. Stephan's came a long halt. Meanwhile,

the procession, which had a long way to go and many altar stations to pass, finished its circuit. The State carosse stopped at the side of the church. Gruber remained motionless seated throughout.

Anton passed the hours in soft talk to Florian, in quieting him.

The way back was, for Florian, a hotly desired repetition of this colorful parade.

Afterward, leaving the Imperial Palace and returning by way of the Maria Theresia monument to the stables, gay military music sounded behind them, accentuated by the tireless beat of the big drum. The metallic broad *tzing* of the cymbals ripped through the rousing strains of the Radetzky march. These were the troops that had stood in double rows along the route of the procession and had paraded by Franz Joseph in the inner court.

Florian began to dance.

Chapter Twenty-Nine

THE YEAR CIRCLED. IT STOLE ALONG on the chill dark of the winter, donned the vernal garb of a fairy spring like a young girl preparing for her first ball . . . and then the summer came and brought the burning sun, the glowing sky; summer early ripe and voluptuous. All the world indulged in the reckless sensation of being alive. Only few sensed, and fewer foresaw, the impending disaster.

It was a fateful summer.

Bosco did not live to see it. That may mean nothing

in the world of men, in the world of more or less important events. Nothing whatever. A dog. Small, white, with black spots on his head and back. A terrier—there are more than enough of them—belonging to the son of a peasant who had become a stableman. That this little dog was clever, staunch of faith, pure of soul, that within his breast could be found no trace of suspicion, of egotism, of falsehood, that he was finer and more companionable than many a man, could mean nothing to anyone.

Only Florian, the Lipizzan stallion, answered Bosco's abiding love with love. Only Anton, his savior, was attached to this dog.

It was when Bosco, at the beginning of the winter, bumped into the wall a few times and missed the stable door, that Anton noticed he had lost his sight. He had grown old, this once lively Bosco. Old and lame. He jumped and ran no longer in his impetuous way. On stiff legs he crept along slowly and timidly, ventured only a few steps into the yard and then returned to the stable and Florian. No gay antics did he perform for the benefit of his great white friend. Instead he stood quietly at his hooves, sniffed his legs and whispered soundlessly up at him. Florian bent his head far down to his little comrade, blew his warm breath over the spotted head and evidenced his distress over the little one's pains and aches.

When the terrier occasionally raised his voice it sounded hoarse and had no jubilant ring in it. Sometimes he cried quietly. He sighed when he lay down, sighed when he curled up to sleep. The sole expression of his love, of his willingness, of his enthusiasm was his silent laughter: his wagging. That alone he preserved. He wagged spiritedly when Anton discovered that he was blind, lifted him in comforting arms and set him down by his plate. He wagged while he ate. He wagged when Anton pressed him to his breast as he had done in the dim days of Lipizza.

Again and again Anton murmured: "Don't mind it, Bosco, don't mind it."

Once in the course of the winter Anton gathered up the courage to show Bosco to the veterinary on the latter's regular round of the stables. The veterinary gave the dog one glance and said briefly: "What do you want with the cur? Have him killed. It's time."

He did not see how Anton writhed under these words, under this disdainful death sentence. When the veterinary had gone, Anton carried Bosco to Florian, stood next his white friend with his blind dog in his coiled arm and said softly: "What do you know ... what do you know!"

He let Bosco wash his face with his tongue, and Florian's, too.

When the spring sun laughed across the world and grew steadily warmer, Anton led the dog carefully into the open, as carefully as one teaches a child to walk; there he prepared a cushioned bed for him, and laid the feeble little terrier down to let the sun warm his tired body. Bosco sighed deeply or whimpered to himself. He heard everything, he smelled everything. When Anton approached to see to him, Bosco wagged his tail at the first sound of his steps, and beat the cushion with his tail as cheerfully as he could.

As often as Anton carried the dog outside, Florian followed them to the end of the stall and peered after them with grateful eyes. When they returned he received them effusively and bent down to Bosco as if to ask: "Was it nice? And how do you feel?"

Sometimes, although more rarely than of old—for Franz Joseph drove but seldom—it happened that Florian and Capitano left in the morning and stayed away until late in the forenoon. When they returned and were unhitched, Capitano walked right into the stable, but Florian stood for quite a while at Bosco's couch. There, with wagging tail and solicitous snorts, they held a brief, friendly conversation.

Well into May, one night, Florian awoke, disquieted, got up, and after sniffing Bosco all over began to snort loudly. Anton was on stable watch. Hearing Florian, he left his cot and came running.

Bosco lay on his side near his accustomed place; he seemed quite flat, almost flush with the ground; his head was buried in the straw and a cramp convulsed his limbs intermittently.

As far as space permitted, Florian stood aside, pressed against the wall. His large eyes were full of fear, his mien ghastly, his bearing showing every trace of horror.

Bosco tried to groan but emitted only half-strangled sounds. So he wagged his tail feebly. It was like an apology and a farewell.

Man thinks animals know nothing about death and dying. And sometimes this appears to be true. But it probably only looks that way and is one of the errors resulting from man's overbearing attitude. Because man does not understand their language, he thinks animals cannot talk. Because man does not understand the behavior of dumb creatures and does not admit gifts of the spirit and of the soul in them, he explains all things by the one word, "instinct," a word that has become well-nigh meaningless and is basically arid of meaning. Man discerns only the very last desperate awe in expiring animals, if he does that. And thus he is convinced that the beast knows nothing about annihilation and has no knowledge of death.

Yet Florian knew well that death was at work close by him. The quiet battle, in which Bosco was to be the loser, had roused him from his sleep, while Anton has had to be awakened by his snorts.

Bosco wagged weakly. The cramps ceased. A trembling shot through his frame. Then he grew taut. With a clumsy motion Anton, kneeling down, eased Bosco's head and looked into his vacant eyes.

"Over," he whispered. "Over."

Florian, who never shied, seemed about to lose control of his nerves. With minced and hesitating steps he neared his dead friend, bowed his head, inhaled and reared back sharply. Anton could not calm him; the horse pressed out of the stall, looked around with wild eyes, rose on his hindlegs, threatened to jump over Anton. Anton had to give in. He had to lead Florian to the other end of the stable and open an unused stall.

Morning dawned.

Anton carried poor Bosco outside. For the last time he held the cold, white little bundle in his arms. Not a word passed his lips, his face showed nothing. His sorrow lay deep in his breast, tore at him like a flame; it could not find expression, it sought no outward expression.

Florian did not lie down again. His nervousness did not abate as the dawn grew into the new day. Hour followed hour. When the sun shone full through the window, Anton, who stood leaning against the horse's neck, told him slowly:

"Now we two are alone."

Chapter Thirty

THEY WERE SOON AT ISCHL.

In Vienna Florian had not ceased to look for Bosco. Or else he kept his eyes on the corner where Bosco used to sleep and indicated thus that he mourned his dead comrade.

Drearily Anton passed his days. He missed the fox terrier, missed the ministrations he had given the poor sick, blind dog. Whenever he saw Florian in that corner of the box, he would put his hand on his croup, hoping thereby to console himself and Florian. Or he would simply stand with arms hanging. But most of the time he would hurry away lest he meet the questioning dark eyes.

Anton hoped that he would forget his grief during the sojourn at Ischl. It was not to be. Even in the railroad car Florian began to think again of the dead companion of his youth.

In Ischl, Anton did not resume his walks. He found no joy in wandering through the landscape without Bosco.

The stay at Ischl was abruptly curtailed.

Franz Ferdinand and his wife, the Duchess of Hohenberg, had been murdered.

Anton hardly remembered the Heir Apparent and had no idea what great hopes were thus blasted. On Corpus Christi Day, Franz Ferdinand had ridden in the State carosse next the Emperor. That was all Anton knew.

Murdered.

During the ensuing days the ghastly event, the double murder, was excitedly discussed in the stables and in the living quarters; the murders of King Humbert of Italy and of King Alexander and Queen Draga of Serbia were cited as examples. And Anton mused: to be murdered—that is the fate of kings and princes. Why? He didn't break his head over this riddle. He accepted the state of things. Anything that did not concern Florian did not concern him either.

Orders to return to Vienna failed to upset his stolid self. Well and good—Vienna.

And in Vienna he groomed Florian as lovingly as ever.

Uneventful days came for Florian. Only rarely did they telephone from Schönbrunn for the carriage. Franz Joseph hardly ever drove out now.

The new Heir Apparent came with Prince Buchowsky.

Archduke Karl Franz Joseph was a young man, simple, kind and unobtrusive. In him was no trace of the universal fame of his father, Otto, of his overweening hunger for life and his senseless frivolity. He had the simple bourgeois make-up of the Saxon-Wettins and looked like his uncle, King Freidrich August.

Having become Heir Apparent, he had the right to

a carriage, a team and a saddle horse from the Imperial Stables.

"I probably won't need a carriage," he told the prince. "My wife and I use an automobile."

"I know that," Buchowsky replied, "but your Imperial Highness is aware of his Majesty's aversion to automobiles. . . ."

"Yes," the Archduke smiled, "for official functions, then . . . send me the same carriage, and the same—" His youthful face fell dark, adopting suddenly a funereal look. Then, animated anew, as if pushing his dreary thoughts aside: "My riding horse must naturally be lighter than . . . than . . ." Again he didn't finish the sentence. He had meant to say: than the dead Franz Ferdinand's.

They entered the Riding School and the equerry gave orders that the horses be introduced.

The new Heir Apparent felt neither the active nor the passive resistance his slain predecessor had contended with his whole life long.

A few days later a storm of excitement swept over

Vienna, over the entire realm. It blew from the Russian border to the Lake of Constance, from Tetschen, the northern rim of Bohemia, to the Bocche di Cattaro on the Adriatic.

In the stables everybody was gripped by terrific nervousness which spread like a contagious disease. The men were driven to useless, yet feverish tasks, although nobody, from the prince to lowest stableboy, could have said what purpose this activity served.

Anton alone remained quiet and stolid as always. He did his duty. He couldn't do other than his duty. The memory of Bosco wrenched his soul and he looked for consolation to Florian. Otherwise he sat in a semi-stupor on the little bench before the stable door. And there, more than elsewhere, he was tormented, recollecting Bosco's bed in the sun. Otherwise he thought about nothing.

Unintentionally he overheard a conversation between the prince and the Neustifts.

Elizabeth and her husband had visited the prince here. They came up to the spot where Anton sat and he jumped up, stood at attention, and tried to greet

Neustift and Elizabeth with the old smile; but the faint smile he might have forced was forgotten. Their serious countenances prevented it.

"Sit down, Anton," Neustift ordered. Obediently Anton sat down again and pressed his shoulders against the wall.

"No," Neustift spoke excitedly, "whether you grieve for Franz Ferdinand or are glad he is dead—I know there are such people."

The prince interrupted him: "His huntsmen, if you please—it's not a question of the higher-ups, the lower-downs, of political adversaries—his own huntsmen danced when the news arrived from Sarajevo."

"How horrible!" Elizabeth cried out. "Just as in *Wilhelm Tell* . . ."

"What do you mean?" the prince asked, and Elizabeth recited, "'Has madness seized these people, that they would make music to celebrate murder?'"

"Right you are!" Neustift broke out. "Horrible! He was a stern master, this Franz Ferdinand. For his underlings, perhaps too stern. To servants, a master who insists upon his due may very easily appear a tyrant. But since Franz Ferdinand's death the huntsmen are not the only ones who have gone mad. No, and it's not just his official staff. Nor just the people. It seems that all of Europe has plunged into insanity!"

"Where will it all end?" Elizabeth sighed.

The prince was about to reply when Neustift said rapidly: "Who can say? I want to explain to Buchowsky what I have said from the first. I am deeply moved by this murder! And it must move every decent human being, whether he was for or against Franz Ferdinand. A man of force, of energy, of far-reaching plans for the future, of impatient desire for his work. . . . A rare man, and—say what you may—an extraordinary and important man. . . ."

"You are all enthusiasm," Buchowsky said with cool sarcasm.

"I am shaken!" Neustift cried. "I had nothing to hope for from Franz Ferdinand. On the contrary! But that a man like him, just before he has the chance to say his first word, should be silenced for all eternity—that overwhelms me!"

Elizabeth said, looking at the ground, "I have never been able to picture him as Emperor." Very softly, she repeated: "Never."

In a matter-of-fact tone the prince recited the facts: "Two pistol shots—two bulls'-eyes! History has seen nothing like it!" He shrugged his shoulders. "Fate!"

With mounting passion Neustift again flung his words at the prince:

"And how they buried him! Is that fate, too? The Heir Apparent of a great empire! The victim of inexcusable neglect . . ."

"Whom are you accusing?" The prince's tone became caustic.

"I accuse no single person," Neustift defended himself. "I establish what has happened. Franz Ferdinand knew how badly guarded he was. He sensed what would happen to him. Before his departure he received the Last Sacrament at his own castle."

"What does that prove?" Buchowsky challenged. "Emperor Ferdinand was forced by Metternich at the beginning of the Revolution of '48 to drive through the streets of Vienna. Ferdinand received the Last Sacrament, too, at that time . . . and nothing happened to him."

"Oh, my dear friend," Elizabeth said, "eighteen-forty-eight is not nineteen-fourteen. And Vienna, even a rebellious Vienna, is not Sarajevo. . . ."

The prince bowed. "I happen to know that. The two pistol-shots Princip fired are a signal. The beginning of a new epoch."

"But why," Neustift could not resist asking, "why has the old epoch been buried so shamefully?"

Buchowsky rejoined: "The old epoch, my friend, is still sitting on the throne. If you mean Franz Ferdinand—that was a future gone, a dawn without sunrise."

"Did one have to do away with it so—so disgrace-fully?" Neustift asked loudly.

"Artstetten," the prince answered soothingly. "His last wish. A grave in Artstetten instead of the Capuchines. That had to be respected."

"Respected!" Neustift echoed curtly. "The two cof-fins lying around in the small station at Pöchlarn, surrounded by the volunteer fire-guard, veterans with their steins and their sausages! Respected! Then the crossing to the other side of the Danube. The *cortège* on a float in the midst of lightning and thunder. The horses plunging and trying to jump into the water...."

"Who can help that?" The theme became distasteful to the prince. "The hand of fate."

"Madness from beginning to end," Neustift insisted. "The whole world has gone mad."

"If only," said Elizabeth hesitatingly, "if only this cup will pass from us."

"War?" Neustift stiffened.

"Quite possibly," Buchowsky replied uneasily.

"War!" Neustift almost sang. "That would be a way out. That would be a salvation!"

Elizabeth faced the prince. "My husband and I understand each other very well. Really. In everything. Only in this we shall never agree."

"Why, my dear," Neustift retorted, "you must understand! I am a soldier. What am I good for? If we have a war I shall become a general. And then ... and then ..."

"And then?" Elizabeth took up in profound sorrow. "Who knows what then? Who? But that there will be hordes of widows and orphans and cripples . . . that we know beforehand. It is the only thing we know for sure."

"Think," her husband argued, "think! Our boy is still little. Someday the war will have to come. Better now than when he is old enough. . . ."

"A strange point of view," mused the prince.

"Only an appeal to a mother," Neustift shot back. "Only to make her accept the idea of war."

"Never!" Elizabeth shook her head. "I'll never accept the idea of war!"

Anton had heard everything and understood nothing. For him this was an alien language.

As they left, Neustift clapped Anton on the shoulder: "Anton, get your military papers in order. It might become necessary."

Anton stood at attention, having understood hot a single word, and stammered:

"At your service, *Herr Oberstleutnant!*"

Chapter Thirty-One

THE INNER COURT OF THE IMPERIAL Palace was thronged with people.

When the guard was changed and the colors handed over, the military band played a few bars of the national anthem. This was the formality. In the middle of the anthem the band always broke off. Today, as usual.

But today the people sang on. Alone at first. Then the band joined in. Stanza after stanza they sang, jubilantly and sorrowfully, and when they came to the passage: *"Lasst uns seiner Väter Krone schirmen wider jeden Feind,"* the Palace walls shook with *vivas* and *hochs*. And at the end: *"Österreich wird ewig stehn,"* a storm of enthusiasm broke loose.

All eyes were fixed on the Emperor's windows. Everybody hoped to see the familiar, beloved old face that was dearer to them at this moment than ever before.

But Franz Joseph was not at the Imperial Palace. Henceforth he remained invisible to his subjects.

During the early afternoon hours a rumor passed electrically through the streets: Peace!

Toward nightfall came the spectral truth: War!

Once more the streets seethed. Groups of men roamed them, singing, shouting, befogged by patriotic intoxication.

In a few days came the manifesto: *"An meine Völker."*

The conflagration burst out in sky-high flames.

General mobilization was decreed. Thousands upon thousands had to leave wives, children, parents.

Anton, too, had to say farewell.

The call to the colors hit him like a bolt from the blue. He had given all this no thought because he was not accustomed to thinking. He had not imagined that he, like all the others, was a pawn in a vast chess game. He had taken heart in the conviction that no power on earth could separate him from Florian.

Konrad Gruber tried to reassure the dumfounded man.

"Doesn't mean a thing," he said. "Just a short maneuver."

"But," Anton stammered, "but . . ."

"Don't worry," Gruber said, "in two or three months you'll be home again."

"Two, three months," Anton groaned. "That's so long, so terribly long. And . . . and . . ."

"Don't worry! We'll take care of everything here." And when he saw that Anton's face became a mask of anguish, he added: "What's the difference? It's only a matter of a few weeks. That's all. The war can't last long."

He offered his hand, for the first time. Anton clasped

only the finger-tips with his work-gnarled hand, and was deeply moved. He did not dare utter another word.

"Come back hale and hearty!" Konrad Gruber said. It sounded like an order. Anton silently vowed to obey this order, too.

He went into the stable once more. Holding Florian's muzzle in his cupped hands he stared long and silently into the great, dark, shining eyes before turning away.

That was his farewell.

Amid the tumult of troops waiting to be entrained he remained alone. Around him hundreds of women and girls, swarms of children. Everyone embracing, kissing, weeping and shouting. No woman, no girl, no child bothered about Anton. No tear was shed at his departure for the battlefield and no kiss lingered on his mouth or cheek.

A drunken soldier fell on his neck and held fast to him. Anton was startled but didn't move; he held up the fellow who babbled incoherent words into his face: "Brother, we'll show 'em. We'll swallow 'em like sandwiches, the dirty dogs. . . ."

The band played one march after the other, obviously to drown out the loud sobbing and wailing of the women and children. The spirits of the soldiers surrounded by their kith and kin had to be kept up, too.

The drunkard let go of Anton. "You're dumb." He cursed and fell on somebody else's neck.

Anton stood there all alone and listened to the martial airs, lively, stormy, courageous rhythms, ricocheted around by the big bass drum, and bathed in a shower of musical sparks from the crashing cymbals. The horns lilted the military strains in high long breaths. The bombardon carried them on its broad bass back. And the wood-winds adorned each march with tonal arabesques, threw octave-high somersaults, nestled close to the tune or fluttered above it. Without intermission one march followed another. *Under the Double Eagle, Prinz Eugen, O du mein Österreich.* They enforced good humor, they whipped up the spirit, they caused a concordant tumult. It was a gallant, high-hearted occasion.

Anton listened attentively.

Of festival he could see nothing. Upsurging youth-

ful force sounded here and there; yes. An occasional
sanguinary cry to battle was accompanied by shouts
induced by alcoholic temerity, by mob courage, by
deliberate self-intoxication. Shrieking, men fell into the
song, men desirous of making their leavetaking from
mothers and wives easier. They acted reckless and gay
and unafraid. The military music helped them. Anton
did not notice anything of that. The marches knocked
at his ear-drums but gained no admittance to his heart.
He was obsessed neither by courage nor by fear. The
happenings around him meant little to him. He was not
bound to all this. His simple soul did not seek to grasp
the situation. It so happened that he had put on the uniform. It so happened that he was assigned to the infantry. It so happened that he was about to start on a train
journey with many other soldiers—bound somewhere. It
had to happen so. A colossal, undeniable "had to."

Anton was a nonentity, a stableboy whom the mad
torrent rushing through the world carried away from
his homeland into the unknown distance. This nonentity, called Anton Pointner, which despite its obscurity

had known a limited happiness of its own, a human destiny, didn't dare entertain the idea of protest. Anton abandoned himself without resistance, without a trace of resistance.

While the train rolled through the night, while comrades around him chattered, laughed, sang and dropped off to sleep one after the other, he sat in a tomb of silence and stared at nothing.

Florian . . . Konrad Gruber . . . the beautiful, peaceful existence . . . the wide yards of the stable. Anton drove these images from his mind, forbade himself to remember.

A young man in the midst of the sprawling soldiers suddenly launched into the national anthem. His fresh tenor voice sang the hymn as bravely as children sing patriotic hymns in school. He sang in the darkness of the car to reassure himself, to give himself courage.

Anton recalled that distant dawn at Lipizza. Florian, new-born, lay in the straw unable yet to rise. Captain von Neustift came to the stable just as the national anthem sounded.

"Siebele . . ." Anton murmured. "Siebele . . ."

The words the young man was just singing penetrated to his consciousness: *"Gut und Blut für unsern Kaiser, Gut und Blut für's Vaterland."*

That was it! Now he knew. It was the most natural, the most obvious thing. It was this "had to." Having nothing else to give to the Emperor, he gave his blood. His blood?

Who would want Anton's blood?

Who could want to shed his blood?

What would result, what would be gained, what would be saved after his blood had been spilled?

Anton's head was awhirl and hung heavily against his chest. He fell into the depths of dreamless slumber.

Chapter Thirty-Two

FLORIAN RARELY QUITTED THE STABLE.
Now and then the Emperor drove out; from
Schönbrunn to the Imperial Palace; then
to several hospitals to visit the wounded. It
affected him. And he was old. The war dragged on. The
end was not in sight. So he kept to Schönbrunn.

Once Wilhelm II visited him. Franz Joseph sent
a representative to the station at Penzing to receive
and escort the German Kaiser. There was no Guard
of Honor, no team of six *à la Doumont*. Kaiser Wilhelm

arrived in Schönbrunn by motorcar. The soldiers had more serious duties than to form guards of honor.

The horses were no longer used. It was deemed unwise to show these luxurious creatures to the populace. Now that nobody saw Franz Joseph anymore, rumors and jokes about him ran from mouth to mouth. They said that Franz Joseph had died, only he was not aware of it because no one had the heart to tell him. And such like nonsense.

But Franz Joseph lived on, in clear sight of his fate. Among the warring Central Powers he was one of the very few whose eye peered unflinchingly into the future. For the first time during his long reign he read the future clearly. In his old age he had become far-sighted.

At Gorlice the army broke through the Russian horde and recaptured Galicia for Austria, in fact penetrated far into enemy territory. In commemoration of this victory a woman friend of the Emperor gave him a statue of Nike.

When she visited him later, Franz Joseph greeted her with upraised arms. "For God's sake, *gnädige Frau*, I beg of you, take back your gift. You mean well, I know that, and I thank you from the bottom of my heart. But please take it back."

"Oh, your Majesty," the lady stammered in consternation, "such an important victory . . . one's simply got to be happy."

"What does it mean?" Franz Joseph cried. "What do you call a victory? To be glad? Really happy? *Gnädige Frau*, there is no cause for that at all. We are going to perish. I am not a pessimist, certainly not! But I know what is and what is going to be."

"Your Majesty," the lady broke out in confusion.

With profound sorrow, with all the exalted majesty that was his, he said: "We are standing at the abyss. Only one thing is left: to perish honorably."

He knew the demoralizing effects of the hunger blockade, knew the people's diminishing powers of resistance, the inner corrosion going on relentlessly. The longer men were in the trenches, the longer they were kept there, the more terribly Death reaped harvest among them.

Franz Joseph looked the Medusa-face of the future

straight in the eye, saw the onrushing disaster, the fall of his dynasty. And he was silent.

Beyond that he worked, he did his duty.

The stables waited. One year, a second year. In vain. None but old men busied themselves there now. The younger ones were all at the front. Among the younger were fifty-year-old men. The horses, however, were ignorant of the war; they had been untouched by the famine so far.

Konrad Gruber drove Florian and Capitano around in the yards, and exercised also the other personal horses of the Emperor. He rarely spoke a word. He forced himself to be hopeful, to think of pleasant things. But his heart was heavy, although he wouldn't admit that even to himself.

The entire Imperial Court, the stables included, was like the face of a stopped clock, without movement. Everything had become aimless, meaningless.

Chapter Thirty-Three

AUTUMN NIGHT FELL, OUT THERE on the Polish plain where the trenches of the Austrians and the Russians faced each other. Dark starless night. But no peace. The torturing thunder of drum-fire had broken out to cover the attack. A hell of bayonet, hand-to-hand fighting.

Tumult. Groans. Wild outcries. Pistol-shots.

Finally a tramping, a clattering, and murmurs lost in the distance.

And at the very end, silence and darkness.

Here and there a groan, a sigh, a death rattle.

Anton lay on his back and did not move. He breathed painfully and could not stop it when his breath turned into throaty rasps. His whole life long he had been a quiet man, never noisy, and he remained to the end of his existence quiet, unobtrusive, alone and in the dark.

His body had been torn apart by shrapnel. When shrapnel knocked him down he had hardly felt any pain. Only surprise. He was surprised to find himself too weak to rise. Patiently he suffered. Waited. The stretcher-bearers would come and fetch him.

He felt his body and his limbs. Wet. . . . Then he gave it up, for even groping with his hands proved terribly difficult.

And his blood flowed. . . .

During his lifetime he had appreciated but little the glory of the realm, of the earth, of the landscape. Now Vienna, St. Stephan's, loomed up before him. The square, that wide square before the Palace laughing in the sun. Over there Maria Theresia sat on her throne. That was all. For those symbols he gave his blood. He hadn't shed his blood voluntarily. It was that overwhelming, that devastating "had to."

Anton was not thinking of that. Nor of his ebbing life. Only the marvelously beautiful pictures he had carried in his soul awoke and passed in review before his mind's eye now that he was so wide awake.

And he thought of Florian. Of the strong, gentle, intelligent Florian whom he loved and who loved him. Here, right in front of him they were, Florian's great limpid eyes, shining with affection. Anton felt the velvety lips, the rose-tinted, fine, quivering nostrils. His fingers played in the dank ground as they would have over Florian's muzzle.

When morning came Anton lay quiet, his eyes wide open. But he saw the rising sun no more.

November came sluggishly. One afternoon—it was already dusk—all the church-bells in Vienna, all the church-bells in the wide-flung empire began to toll. Franz Joseph had lain down to his eternal slumber.

At his ascension to the throne, sixty-eight years before, the lands under the Hapsburg crown had writhed in blood and fire. He sank into his grave while, more fiercely than then, blood and flame seethed around him.

He sat at his desk, at Schönbrunn, and signed papers when the black wings of death fluttered hoveringly over him.

"I am tired," he said. They were his last words.

He had never before admitted to fatigue. Untiringly he had stood staunch and refused to admit defeat, be the blow never so crushing. This time he really was deathly tired, and as soon as they had brought him to bed he closed his eyes. As a man of duty, which he always was, he postponed the end long enough to receive the Holy Sacrament. Then he fell asleep.

So used up was his eighty-six-year-old body that his cheek crumbled and remained in the hands of the men who took his death mask.

Franz Joseph had to be borne to the Chapel of the Imperial Palace. Konrad Gruber drove the eight massive blacks which drew the heavy carved hearse. For thirty years he had driven the Emperor. That function he now performed for the last time.

Prince Buchowsky, till now the equerry, retired into private life; whether voluntarily or by order of Emperor Karl, nobody knew. Enough—the prince was on hand no longer. His successor had not yet put in an appearance at the stables. The ceremonial of an Imperial funeral was traditional, however. The councilors knew what to do. Gruber was the novice in this case.

They handled Gruber with silk gloves. The councilors and the stable personnel had worked in conjunction with him for many years, had shown him esteem; and now they adhered to their attitude. No longer was the situation as in time of peace, when Franz Ferdinand still lived and it was expected that the sick Franz Joseph at Schönbrunn would not rise again. Then Konrad Gruber had undergone all the humiliations of a fallen star, only to triumph a few days later over the envious and the hostile. He girded himself for similar barbs, only sharper, cruder than then. He alone in these stables would grieve for Franz Joseph, he thought.

But no, all were intimidated and humbled by the prolonged war; they could no more be sure of their future than Gruber could; they themselves felt like fallen stars. Konrad Gruber noticed their depressed spirits, their commiseration, their tact. It did him good to be spared pointed remarks and malevolent digs. He maintained silence, and in his hopelessness welcomed the forbidding harmony of universal hopelessness.

As the eight heavy, ebon horses were made ready, he stood by, his weather-bronzed face as pale as it could ever be. He wore the black livery of mourning, the black coat with the enormous black fur collar, wore the white allonge-peruke and the black-bordered tricorne. Not a word did he speak. He climbed up on the coachman's seat and took up the multiple reins.

He thought: "This is my last ride." All the while the carriage rolled along through the dreary evening toward Schönbrunn leading the train of old-fashioned, cumbersome calashes, he thought only this: "My last ride."

In the meantime a small gathering had formed in the courtyard, nobles, diplomats, functionaries of Franz Joseph. A feeling of fidelity, an obligation of reverence, and an inner recognition of their also being *passé* compelled them to do honor to the dead Emperor on his last ride to the Chapel.

Prince Buchowsky strolled with Elizabeth around the statue of Emperor Franz. "Your husband has been appointed a general," he said. "Congratulations."

Elizabeth, whose face was hidden by a veil, answered bitterly: "A fit occasion to be congratulated."

"Oh, that." The prince seemed slightly taken aback. "Excuse me. . . . You are right. But it was your husband's highest wish. And I . . . I just heard of it. . . ."

Elizabeth did not reply.

After a short while she whispered half-hysterically: "Oh, I wish I were dead!"

The prince took her arm. "Good God, what is it?"

She straightened up. "Nothing. Nothing at all. Only, I have had enough. More than enough."

"Don't you want to tell me," he urged her.

She shook her head.

"Has anything serious happened?"

"Oh, nothing at all," she replied. "Hardly worth mentioning. We have been at war for more than two years now."

"Elizabeth!" he exclaimed.

But she went on as if she hadn't heard. "We shall have war for God knows how long."

Buchowsky was upset. "I don't understand, Elizabeth. . . . I don't understand."

"Quite so," she laughed tragically. "Nobody understands anyone else. That's just it. That's what causes this awful misery."

He stopped walking. "What's the matter with you? Speak, I implore you. . . ."

She kept on walking, so he had to follow. "Speak? I am speaking all the time. I am speaking because my heart is bursting. I speak—and know all the while that it is useless. You don't understand. Nobody understands. And I . . . don't understand, either."

The prince countered.

"These are accusations—" He checked himself.

Her agitation grew. "If it were possible to accuse anybody, oh, then it would be easy. I'd feel much easier then. It is pleasant to make accusations, to make solemn, fiery, challenging accusations. You see yourself as just, you take yourself to be good and the others for sinners."

"Well?" Buchowsky demanded. "What am I supposed to answer?"

She protested. "Nothing! Nothing! Does anybody in this world, in this bleeding, mutilated world, know an answer? They are all good, decent people—my husband, too. He is a general—and therefore at his goal."

"Present—arms—"

From the outer gate the order drifted across, melancholy, funereal. Three times it was repeated in the semi-darkness of the wide square. Muffled drums followed.

"He is coming," the prince said, his voice choked.

Hastily the two walked over toward the gate, took up their position close to the first arch, and gazed toward the Schweizerhof. Few people were there. They greeted each other mutely.

Behind them the sentry called out three times: "Present arms!"

The drum, covered with black cloth, sounded harsh and bony.

The *clop-clop* of the horses' hooves, slow, rhythmical, echoed in the darkness, a darkness made the more ghastly by the fitful gleam of the lanterns. Two lamp-carriers on black horses emerged through the middle arch and turned right toward the Schweizerhof.

Now the eight black horses, at the head of the solemn *cortège,* appeared, moving slowly over the ground. The loud rumble of the heavy, richly carved wooden hearse sounded like a series of groans, sobs and unearthly wails—not to be stilled, without end.

His hands motionless in his lap, Konrad Gruber guided the eight blacks as carefully, as intently, as if this Franz Joseph who lay stretched out behind him in his coffin were still alive, still a monarch, able and ready to praise his efficient servant. Masterfully Gruber executed the sharp turn of the eight horses, from gate to gate, from the inner court to the Schweizerhof.

Reddened by the cold, his face bore the same self-contained expression as usual, with the lips pressed into a thin gash. But two liquid lines glistened downward from his eyes to the corners of his mouth. Incessantly, tears purled down his cheeks. Konrad Gruber could not dry them.

"Now," Elizabeth said, "a new epoch begins."

"I liked the old one better," Prince Buchowsky answered. He donned his top-hat again.

Chapter Thirty-Four

TWO MORE YEARS.

Not: two short years. Nobody would have the courage to describe them as short. Just the opposite; they were two interminable, torturous, chaotic years, strewn with hate and misery, with blood and destruction. And then, in one convulsion, everything broke down. The realm. The throne. The war.

Florian learned to know the hateful drudgery of existence. During these two years it was quiet and bare in the stables. The supply of oats diminished, and at last there was none left. The high-born horses began to show their undernourishment.

But among the people the hunger was far worse. Children died of exhaustion although they were fundamentally healthy, were able and destined by God to bloom and to grow. Therefore, there was scant pity left for beasts. Hearing of lions, of panthers, of elephants, of giraffes that died in the drawn-out agony of starvation in their cages in the zoological gardens, people shrugged their shoulders. How many human beings lay in their beds in the throes of death, and dragged on, emaciated, wracked by suffering, to the bitter end?

That was but part of the cruel conduct of war: the blockade of all the wells of life; an empty trough while the wide world without had an overabundance of food and wealth.

Horrible tragedies took place quietly, unnoticed, like ordinary events. Terror became the content of every-day existence. Men gave way to a stupefaction of horror, despair and deprivation. Yet at the root of their torpor lay pitilessness. Few there were who felt pity for the animals, for the innocence of the dumb suffering creatures.

"They don't need horses anymore," Konrad Gruber told himself as he wandered aimlessly through the Mews.

He stopped to see Florian and touched his protruding ribs.

"My dear Florian," he whispered, "they don't need me anymore either."

Gruber had become talkative, but he talked only to himself and to the favorite horses of the late Emperor.

Florian turned his drooping head. Gruber held him by the forehead, by the locks of hair hanging down between his ears. To the questioning dark eyes which stirred him to the depths, he said: "No, no. Waiting is of no avail. He'll never come back. He is better off than you and I. It's all over for him."

He meant Anton.

Florian pushed his nose against the man's breast, softly, intimately, in a show of friendship. Only there was in this gesture no longer any playfulness and mirth, but a fervent plea for help.

Gruber stared into Florian's grief-stricken eyes, breathed hard, and whispered: "Yes, yes, we're through, you and I. Quite through."

The new Emperor used an automobile and special trains wherever he went. No horses for him. He lived at Laxenburg, and in a simple house at Baden. He shunned the Imperial Palace, and the Viennese saw him but rarely.

When the catastrophe came he retired, with his wife and children, to the hunting castle, Eckartsau. Thence the Imperial family went abroad under the protection of foreign officials who had but yesterday been foemen.

The horses in the Mews were sold at auction, all of them. There was no Emperor anymore. No Court. No Imperial Stables.

So!

From his tiny room far out in the suburbs, where he now lived, Konrad Gruber came to attend the auction. He had grown old, had lost his erect bearing; a used-up, broken man who would not admit he was used-up and broken.

The dealers and cabmen who had collected showed him deference and esteem. For more than thirty years the personal coachman of the Emperor Franz Joseph! They still revered the memory of the old Emperor, even if they did not say so aloud.

Gruber joined the cabman, Lorenz Schleinzer, pointed at Florian and whispered: "Take my advice and buy that white horse. There is no better."

Schleinzer listened to the description Gruber gave him of Florian: Favorite horse of Franz Joseph whose carriage he had always drawn; incomparable trotter; soft of mouth; followed the slightest command.

Later, as Lorenz Schleinzer was leading Florian away, Gruber cautioned him: "One thing I must tell you. . . . No whip. Florian does not need it. He isn't used to it and won't stand for it."

Schleinzer protested, as if this were an accusation: "Why, Herr von Gruber! What do you think of me? I ain't beating my horses, never!"

Gruber nodded, pulled his hat far down over his forehead, pursed his lips, and went.

Lorenz Schleinzer was a kind-hearted man of fifty, a man who bore good-will toward his fellow men and also toward his horses, who loved well being and for whom well being meant an occasional bottle of wine. Whenever he was on the border-line between sobriety and inebriacy, and had to hide his condition from his fare by all kinds of ruses, he invariably fell into a wild senseless rage. And at such times he turned into an insensate tormentor of his horses.

At first everything went well enough with Florian. The new milieu was somewhat distasteful, of course. The narrow, dingy, fetid stable, where the dank stagnant air made breathing difficult, was by no means a pleasant change from the magnificent stable he was accustomed to. There was too little straw to soften the cold hard flags under him when he lay down to rest. He sorely missed the marble trough always full of fresh water. He had to wait until the stableman, a grouchy old boozer smelling of liquor, brought him a pail of water. Often he did not quench his thirst because the man simply pulled the pail away whenever he thought Florian had had enough.

Two other horses occupied the stable which could hold five; a jaded iron-gray, purblind and stupid, who forever dozed and took no interest in his companions; and a foxy mare, a mischievous, sickly creature, obviously a spinster.

When Florian greeted the iron-gray, he didn't get an answer. That was Hansl's way. The mare, who bore the ill-fitting name of Lovely, snapped at him in salutation.

The work Florian had to do was extremely arduous. In harness for hours at a stretch, with the bit between his teeth, he stood at the hack stands. Hour after hour. In rain, in cold, in the scorching sun. His thin blanket offered scanty protection against inclement weather. When rain or snow fell heavily, his head and neck became wringing wet. His legs grew painfully stiff. It was especially bad when Schleinzer tore the covers off and Florian's naked body, suddenly exposed, began to shiver. Florian would warm up while running. But when he had to stop, abruptly, with panting sides and steaming back, he began to freeze, and kept on shivering even after the blanket again covered his wet back.

Worse troubles arose when he was hitched up with the iron-gray; for Hansl loved to amble, or, at most, weakly simulated a half-trot. The whip, cracking about Hansl's ears, occasionally nicked Florian also.

But matters became really critical when he was in the company of Lovely. She behaved as if it were impossible to keep step with him. She was forever changing the pace. She plunged and tugged and at length fell into an execrable gallop. Schleinzer then proceeded to whack her, which caused her to snap at Florian. Often, while standing absolutely still, she broke out as if intent upon running away. But she never succeeded in carrying Florian along. On these occasions, too, she had to be subdued by Schleinzer—sometimes with words, often with a heavy beating.

One day when it had rained and Lovely wanted once more to indulge in one of her peccadillos, she lost her footing on the smooth asphalt and fell. She lay on her side, back down, and began to thrash around like mad. Florian pressed to one side to evade her flying hooves. She did not try to find her footing, or consider for a moment rising; she just stupidly struck out with her legs and actually landed on her white partner. At this moment Schleinzer, who had jumped down from his seat, undid the harness and rescued Florian, otherwise Lovely would certainly have crippled him.

This time Lorenz Schleinzer did not need liquor to stimulate his rage. The mare's behavior was enough. He pulled madly at the reins, once Lovely had regained her feet, and favored her with hissing smacks. She became at once ruly and obedient.

Several strokes fell on the innocent Florian's shoulders and croup. Such pain as he had never known tore into him; and this, together with the feeling of humiliation and injustice, caused him to stamp his hooves in despair and refuse to go on.

Just in time Schleinzer recollected Gruber's counsel. He climbed down hastily and started to stroke Florian's long forehead and nostrils. But Florian reared his head high in the air, stared terrifiedly into the distance, and had to be forced down by his reins.

"There, there," Schleinzer murmured soothingly, "it wasn't as bad as all that. A miscarriage of justice, let's say. It's nothing at all, at all."

Mollified, Florian snorted aloud. Nevertheless it happened again, shortly thereafter. Schleinzer was drunk. In causeless wrath he kept on beating the horses, cursing the while with all the vituperative violence only a bad-humored Viennese cabman can muster.

The iron-gray who accompanied Florian this time did his best to satisfy his master. But Florian simply stood immovable. Stroke upon stroke rained down on his back, on his flanks, on his ears. Every inch of his body smarted like a raw wound. His whole body, emaciated by malnutrition, burned with terrible pain. And his soul writhed in humiliation. He did not take a single step forward. He would rather have died than submit to this miserable treatment.

The waiting customers voiced their impatience. Schleinzer was half insane. He beat still harder.

Suddenly Florian rose, stood almost perpendicular for an instant, fell down on his forefeet, took the bit between his teeth, and began to buck. His hooves drummed against the carriage, against the driver's board.

"What kind of a stubborn beast is this?" was asked from inside the carriage. "He ought to be at the knacker's."

Schleinzer had to give in. Florian pulled once more. But he would never again be reconciled.

Florian was not so young as he had once been. He was close to twenty now—not so old for a stallion of his race, since Lipizzans attain forty and even forty-five. But misery finished him much sooner. He experienced the lot of many, many a man, who after a well-guarded, comfortable existence, is unexpectedly confronted by poverty and despair on the threshold of old age. Accustomed to do his full share of work, if given the proper rest and recreation, life's descent, instead of sparing him, bequeathed him only sorrow, mortification, friendlessness and maltreatment. No moment of rest was his toward the end.

Chapter Thirty-Five

"THEY'VE GOT TO GIVE US BACK OUR estates! God damn them," Neustift fumed, "they're our property. Our inherited property!"

"Not so loud about property," Elizabeth admonished him. "These days it isn't any too safe to shout about one's property."

They were walking along the Herrengasse in the direction of the Michaclerplatz.

"And even if we get our estates back immediately,"

she argued, "what are we going to do with them? They are overburdened with debts, they produce nothing. Where shall we get the money to make them productive?"

"Just the same," Neustift growled, "they are our property. Ours by right!"

Elizabeth laughed. "No. The right belongs to the victor. You were an enemy general." And as an afterthought: "And anyway—right? Who gives us the right, these days?"

He shook his head gloomily. "Elizabeth, we can't discuss things calmly with each other any longer. Whether you want to or not—opposition makes for opposition."

"I hope not." She smiled. "We are bound by so many unforgettable memories. Nothing would be more terrible for me than to find us becoming really opponents. But I am telling you one thing, and I shan't recede one step from that: I will never allow you to implant your attitude in our son. Never. Not another word. Never!"

"And why not?" he demanded. "I want the boy to know loyalty! Loyalty to his origin, to everything that has been. Loyalty!"

Quietly, full of determination, Elizabeth answered: "You are mistaken, my dear. And no mistake is as devastating as a mistake with one's own child."

"Leopold is no longer a child," he corrected.

"Adolescent, for all I care." Her words tumbled out. "Youth, if you want to call it that. So much the worse. So much the more dangerous. You will remain loyal. As it seems, you have to remain loyal, even though it would not be a breach of loyalty to submit before elemental catastrophes. . . . Well, never mind that. Now we are not discussing you. You're suffering enough for your loyalty as it is."

"I suffer," he complained, "hellish torment."

"And that hellish torment you would hand down to your son?" Her voice betrayed nervous excitement. "With the boy it isn't a question of loyalty or disloyalty. He must be spared any conflict with this day. Another, a different world is being born. We don't know it, we don't even guess what's coming. You and I—we submit, or we protest futilely. That's our affair. But my son is young. He can and he must grow into this new world

without prejudice, without taking sides. Sides! An inex-
perienced, unripe youngster. What knowledge, what
rectitude, what superiority it takes to judge in such vital
things, to side, to find clarity in this chaos!"

"Today," he retorted, "every schoolboy has his political convictions."

"Really?" She took that up. "Really? Suddenly you
point out today's attitude—which you condemn! Well,
I don't condemn it at all, today's attitude. I understand
it. I even feel admiration for today. And as a mother I
love youth. I want to give it all the freedom possible,
every right, every demand which it has by nature. But is
this thoroughly political-minded youth responsible for
itself? Right? Is it possible that these schoolboys, these
twenty-year-old boys, if you will, who know nothing
of life, who know nothing of the interrelations, of the
development, of the fate of humanity, who have experienced nothing, who have suffered nothing—is it possible that these children represent a firmly grounded
conviction? We have watched the bloom and the decay
of an empire. We have gone through the débâcle and

stand practically helpless in the face of it. And suddenly youth is supposed to know everything better and is supposed to arrive at its own decisions! Instinct? There is no instinct for things of that sort. Not in such a general way. It's the sickness of today and the temptation of those who are easily led into temptation. I do not want my son to grow sick, I do not want him to be led into temptation."

Neustift changed the subject. "Do you know where I could find Buchowsky?"

"At the Spanish Riding School. There everything is as it was before." Elizabeth smiled.

"Yes," he declared, "I heard about that. Lipizza is lost. But they have saved a number of horses, and in Piver, which I believe is somewhere near Graz, they have started a new stud-farm. I wonder whether it will last."

"Certainly it will," Elizabeth said confidently. "The Riding School was always crowded. And the Lipizzan stallions were adored!"

"Thank God for that!" Neustift sighed devoutly. "Even if we have gone to the dogs, I am glad something is left of the old magnificence, that something of the old splendor shines in this darkness. They will carry on their beauty, the brave Lipizzans; carry on the fine art of riding, the secrets of pure breeding. There is something good in that. Something good for a time which will never be able to produce anything as perfect."

Chapter Thirty-Six

LORENZ SCHLEINZER HAD LEARNED to drive an automobile and passed the test. Horse teams had become so scarce that people on the street stopped in their tracks and stared at them. Schleinzer drove his car through the streets and was satisfied. Now he was able to take people places faster than ever before. Just step on the gas, and the car flew!

"This is better business," he observed to himself when hardly a half hour passed before he had another fare.

Florian stood alone in the stable and starved.

The flayer had called for the iron-gray, and Lovely had gone to the butcher.

But Florian somehow still looked impressive and Schleinzer felt an irresistible reluctance to send the Imperial animal to such a horrible end.

"By thunder!" he complained as often as he filled Florian's manger with food. "What the devil am I going to do with this damned nag? Couldn't even get any- thing for him these days. Not a stinking copper."

A timely coincidence brought about a solution, brought salvation for Florian.

Schleinzer drove a pair of lovers into the Wienerwald. They didn't want to drive too far out, merely wanted to walk by themselves a bit among the trees, and later to eat together at the Kobenzl. At Sievering Schleinzer passed the last inn, and continued up toward the Hermannskogel. Where the street to Weidling branched off, he took the direction toward Scheinblingstein. He drove and drove.

The pair in the taxi could not make love while rid- ing. The man was a shrewd grafter who had got rich during the inflation. He owned his own car but decided not to use it today, lest his chauffeur talk of this excursion to the servant girl or his valet, and in that fashion relay it to his wife. The girl was a young, rather pretty dancer in a cabaret. She wasn't as yet in the habit of giving herself for money; a meretricious comedy of affection had to be played first.

By the fence of a farmhouse they stopped.

"Wait here," the gentleman ordered, and helped the girl to alight. "We'll take a little walk and will be back soon."

Left alone, Schleinzer proceeded to grow bored. He climbed out of the car, stepped across to the gate in the fence, and shouted: "Hallo!" He had to repeat that a few times before a man appeared and asked him what the matter was.

"Can I get something to drink?" Schleinzer asked.

The man replied that he had no license; a glass of milk which he offered was rejected with shudders. The man laughed good-naturedly and invited Schleinzer to come in; he would be glad to give him a glass of schnapps.

They sat together in front of the wide, comfortably squatting farmhouse, and the man, who apparently liked having company, waxed eloquent.

He had been in the war. From the first to the last day. And nothing had happened to him. No wounds. No gas. No sickness. The four years' struggle had had a happy ending for him. For on his return home he had told the woman who lived here about the death of her husband, and had stayed on ever after. First he had helped with the work, and after a few months he had married the widow. He, a poor stableman. He, Karl Wessely, with no hope of being taken back into the Imperial service, since there was no Emperor any longer. What luck.

Now this beautiful farm here belonged to him, Karl Wessely. At least it was as good as his. For, damnation, he was master in the house!

He pointed all around.

Encircling the house was a meadow. Then came a narrow strip of wood, and a second meadow, which sank and rose again like a green wave. From here, the top of the mountain, one had a wonderful view. Far down, swimming in a blue haze, lay the city of Vienna. But Wessely didn't speak of that. And Schleinzer paid no attention to it.

Six cows stood in the barn. Many chickens ran around. Geese were on their way to a narrow rivulet that ran through the fields.

Wessely delivered milk to the city; butter, eggs, and now and then fowl.

Shrewdly Schleinzer asked how these deliveries were made.

Well, by God, Wessely confessed, before the war there had been a horse on the place. They still had the cart. But now the innkeeper next door undertook to deliver to market. Not regularly, though.

Schleinzer began: "I've got a horse I can't use no more. A hell of a fine horse. A Lipizzan. Cheap, I'll tell you, a real bargain."

Wessely looked baffled. "A Lipizzan?"

"And a genuine one, too," Schleinzer emphasized. "A stallion. You know, it once pulled the carriage of Emperor Franz Joseph!"

Wessely sprang to his feet and shouted into the house: "Mali! Mali! Come quick!"

A thin wizened woman, prematurely old, appeared and stared suspiciously at Schleinzer. When she had heard the offer she insisted on seeing the horse first.

Wessely described the Lipizzans, told many tales, pointed out the advantages that would accrue from driving daily down to the market in Vienna.

Frau Mali admitted that a horse was desirable. "But it's got to be healthy."

"The horse is all right," Schleinzer said dryly.

"Well, then," said Mali, who seemed to be in love with her husband and doted on him, "all right. You know something about horses, go and look the beast over."

Thus Florian became the property of the couple, Karl and Amalia Wessely.

When Wessely brought him home he knew, of course, that it was Florian, the admired, the renowned Florian, once the pride of the Spanish Riding School. Wessely exhibited Florian to his wife as one does an impoverished prince or a genius gone to the dogs—a prince, even though impoverished; and, though gone to the dogs, a genius.

Florian stood on the grass and inhaled the smell of the verdure, the scent of the wood. Again he was offered kind words, was gently stroked again . . . after a long, long time.

A feeling of happiness stirred timidly in his heart. His head rose, his beautiful neck regained a bit, a wee bit, of the proud stiff curve of yore. The bottomless pools of his eyes, which had been full of despair and fear, once more shone with a joyous light.

Gratefully he accepted the large chunks of bread which Frau Mali gave him, kissed each piece daintily out of her calloused hand. He was hungry. He didn't think of sugar. It was so long since anyone had given him sugar. And Frau Mali didn't even think of offering him sugar.

Karl Wessely couldn't say enough in Florian's praise.

"Mali," he cried, time and again, "that's Florian! And he belongs to us now. You don't know what that means. . . . Florian! Understand? Florian!"

But then he put Florian in the cowshed. He didn't have any other place for him.

Now Florian trotted down to the city every morning. Not into the elegant sections, nor through the magnificent streets he knew; he reached only their periphery. To Ottakring or Hernals. There the milk, the butter and the eggs found their purchasers. Florian pulled the cart on which the tin cans clanked. The high, stout, iron-rimmed wheels rattled deafeningly on the cobblestones. Harnessed to a shaft meant for two horses, the harness itself shabby, Florian and the cart made an incongruous sight.

Nor did Florian have the noble bearing of long ago, when Ennsbauer had ridden him or Konrad Gruber driven him. The privations of the war years, of the years following the war, the heavy work and the evil treatment he had endured at the brutal hands of the cabman Schleinzer, had slackened his resilient nature, had blunted his sensitive instincts.

Wessely was nevertheless inordinately proud to have a horse of Florian's rank. He would never have dared to dream of possessing such aristocratic property, he who belonged to those people favored by the upheaval. But in spite of his satisfaction and in spite of his innate respect for Florian, he beat the noble animal now and then, without rhyme or reason, simply because he held a whip in his hand. That Florian had to live in the cow-shed was not Wessely's fault; he had no better quarters to offer him.

Florian accepted everything, even the whippings. As first he protested, meekly, without tantrums. But even this he gave up. He trotted to the market-place and patiently stood around in the midst of many other carts and horses for hours. The company was really what tormented him most. They were more unpleasant to him than the cows. The cows remained strangers, and in their doltish fashion were even companionable. These horses, however, were relatives. And he who was accustomed to the very best-mannered relatives and comrades, he who had been reared in an atmosphere of luxury and noble refinement, suffered because of the hatred, the coarseness and the low attitude of his present companions. They were all hard-worked, badly nourished, constantly irritated by torments of the most horrendous kind. They gave their utmost without thanks or recognition. They were in a state of embitterment brought on by misery and envy. They who had never been shown pity, constantly held Florian's noble past up to him, cursed his lineage, mocked him because he was as low as they. Florian had no answer for them and remained aloof and unresponsive. His unhappy suffering silence was interpreted as conceit. With every movement of their heads and their ears, with all the pawing of their hooves and the mute vulgarity of their language, they hurled abuse at him.

On the way home Florian always breathed more freely. He was rid of his persecutors and defamers, and soon forgot the unearned taunts and offenses. He was no longer nauseated by the hundredfold noisome smells of the market. When the road led up-hill through the woods, he was permitted to walk, and then he imbibed the scent of the meadows, of the foliage, and a zephyr of hope always blew refreshingly through his soul.

The rest of the day and all night long he stood with

the cows. He suffocated from their smell, and hated to inhale the steam that rose from their dung. He accustomed himself only slowly to the green fodder, to the sour hay that was put before him.

There was a big, black, hairy dog of indeterminate breed on the farm. His name was Nero. During the day he lay on his chain. During the night he roamed around the house and kept watch.

Florian made a bid for his friendship. He thought of Bosco, and the poignant memory conjured up a picture of Anton. But Nero took no interest in horses, and kept his distance.

In his loneliness, Florian never ceased to ruminate over the past. Where had Bosco gone? And why had Anton disappeared? What had become of his staunch comrades, of the magnificent stables, of the luxurious existence he had once known? How had he got here among cows? What had he done to have to lead such an ugly dreary existence? These thoughts did not etch themselves clearly in his mind. They floated like clouds, like vaporous pictures, foggily by.

A long time passed.

One day Wessely asked his wife: "Now that we've got the truck, what are we to do with Florian?"

Mali replied dryly: "He'll go to the butcher, or to the flayer."

Wessely voiced his dismay. "To the butcher! But he's still quite all right. Why, Mali! A horse that has belonged to the Emperor. . . ." He looked at her helplessly.

"I don't care," Mali decided. "Keep him. He doesn't cost much. What he eats does not mean much."

Wessely laughed. "You're right. That little food doesn't matter at all."

Chapter Thirty-Seven

A LATE SUMMER EVENING. FROM the mountaintop through the green wood comes a man. He reaches the road at the foot of the ascent, the road that stretches down toward Sievering and thence on to the capital.

Here on the road between the trees there still lingers a trace of the dying day.

The man walks erect. His slenderness is somewhat gnarled, shriveled. He has grown old too soon, though he is no longer young. But if his appearance is that of an old man his carriage and his firm gait disaffirm it. He wears clothes of faded elegance; they are visibly worn and betray the attentive care that people grown poor devote to their wearing apparel.

Wessely stands before the latticed door of his farm, his eyes fixed on the solitary wanderer. As the man comes close, Wessely cries out:

"Oh, Herr General! My compliments!"

The man stops in his tracks. "You know me?" he asks sternly.

"Why, of course!" Wessely is glad-faced and full of excitement. "Oh, of course, I know General von Neustift."

"From war days?" Neustift asks.

"From war days, too," says Wessely stiffening to attention. "And from long before. At that time you were Major, and adjutant to his Majesty."

Neustift's stern face relaxes. The expression, "his Majesty," has placated him. "And now you have a job here?" he inquires.

"A job?" Wessely laughs happily. "I am the owner."

"Really?" Neustift is disinterested. "Well, good evening," and starts to go on.

Wessely steps into his path. "May I take the liberty . . . Excuse me, your Excellency, I would like to have the honor to have the General as my guest. . . ."

"Thank you," Neustift declines. "I've got to get home."

But Wessely detects the indecision in his answer. "Herr General," he pleads, "a coincidence like this . . . after these many years. . . . I am so happy. . . . You would do that to me—just walk by?"

"It's almost night," the older man protests.

"Not by a long shot," Wessely insists, his voice overflowing with veneration. He is anxious to show his home. "Back of the house I have a nice little spot, really very nice . . . on the grass. . . . If the General would do me the honor . . ." The words tumble over one another. "The General will surely like it . . . and it will do him good . . . to rest . . . and a glass of fresh milk. . . ."

Neustift admits to himself that he is tempted to rest a while and quaff a refreshing drink.

Before long he is actually seated on the rustic bench before a rough table, has his milk, and even a mouthful of bread. Wessely and old Mali soon notice that he wants to be alone, and they slip away.

Around him is the pulsating quiescence of the dusk. Crickets chirp shrilly. Bats wing noiselessly under the wide sky which has gradually turned gray.

Neustift closes his eyes. He is tired. Tired of the journey, tired of worries, and tired of his unsoftened bitterness. His head nods.

Suddenly he straightens up, for a warm breath has blown upon his neck. By him stands a white horse.

Neustift is startled. He hasn't heard the horse approach and hasn't had a glimpse of the animal till now. Yet there the white horse stands, close by him, stretches his neck and sniffs at Neustift's face and hands, confidently, sweetly.

"What is it you want?" Neustift murmurs. "Oh, the bread. . . . Yes, yes. . . . That you shall have. Gladly."

He breaks off a piece and holds it out on his palm. As the white horse takes the proffered bread with, careful lips, a phrase rushes through Neustift's mind: "Just like a kiss."

He holds out another piece of bread, and as the soft velvety lips again kiss his palms, he suddenly says: "Florian."

The ears of the white horse come forward, small, delicate ears.

"Florian," Neustift repeats, "Florian."

Florian raises his head.

Neustift stares into the mirror-clear eyes which suddenly become dewy.

Neustift rises. "Dear Florian," he whispers, "old friend . . ."

Florian snorts and his lips quiver with his escaping breath. And then Neustift realizes that Florian's lower lip is not closed, that it has become limp and sags a little.

"Poor fellow," he says, "you've grown old, too."

He strokes the forehead, the neck, the back.

"I was there, in Lipizza, when you were born." He caresses him tenderly. "That was a different world, an entirely different world. And yet it seems to me as if it weren't so long ago, after all ... as if it had been the day before yesterday, or two or three weeks ago. ..."

He smiles. "What have I gone through since then ... and you, old Florian." He continues to smile, "Old Florian ... how strange! Yes, my dear Florian, what we men call time has something strange about it." He pats Florian's shoulder. "Something droll and cruel."

Florian enjoys the patting hand, holds his head bent. His ears play, drinking in what is being said to him. But it is the consolation they really drink in, the sympathy. For as he sniffs at Neustift he remembers, not clearly, yet unerringly, that this is a man from the strangely vanished past for which he is forever longing. In misty pictures the past rises before him. Neustift embraces Florian, takes his lowered head in his encircling arms. Florian nestles contentedly against his breast.

"We two," Neustift says in his ear, "what have we been? Once upon a time. Once! Now we are through, we two. Nobody needs us any longer. And we mean nothing. We are through, you and I. ..."

How he would have loved to hear a word, one single word from Florian. He is so close to him, feels so bound to him through their like fate. The bond between him and Florian he has known with no other creature for years. But the secret door which divides man and beast never opens, no matter how longingly they beat against it.

Neustift's hand glides softly over the sensitive nostrils while he says: "Only the last thing is still waiting for us, the very last . . . for you and for me. . . ."

Florian, however, is incapable of sentimentalities. Gently he disengages himself from the man's embrace and stands for another few moments beside him, as if in deep thought.

Then he slowly moves away. Slowly he strides across the meadow, is distant, and is a pale luminous shadow in the falling mantle of the night.